REMEMBERANCE
IN MEMORIAM
BOOK I

EVELYN GRIMALD STONE

Tarney Brae Creative Endeavours

 Formatted with Vellum

For those who want, desperately
Yet refuse to compromise your values.
Look to the stars;
They're waiting for you

CONTENTS

Chapter 1 . . . 11

Chapter 2 . . . 25

Chapter 3 . . . 41

Chapter 4 . . . 57

Chapter 5 . . . 73

Chapter 6 . . . 89

Chapter 7 . . . 105

Chapter 8 . . . 121

Chapter 9 . . . 139

Chapter 10 . . . 157

Chapter 11 . . . 171

Chapter 12 . . . 187

Chapter 13 . . . 203

Chapter 14 . . . 217

Chapter 15 . . . 233

Chapter 16 . . . 249

Chapter 17 . . . 265

Chapter 18 . . . 281

Chapter 19 . . . 295

Chapter 20 . . . 309

Chapter 21 . . . 325

Chapter 22 . . . 343

Chapter 23 . . . 359

Chapter 24 . . . 373

Chapter 25 . . . 389

Chapter 26 . . . 405

Author's Note 421
Acknowledgments 423
About the Author 425
Also by Evelyn Grimald Stone 427

AdHor

AdHor
Ynysfawr
Kinbreck
Altier
Baldarskiel
Craigsmuir
Great Ashmur
Lynn Rhosalwyd
Melkirk
Amontys
Mellaig
Dunnaig
Colkadi
Balmahvie
Ynyswen
Corkesi

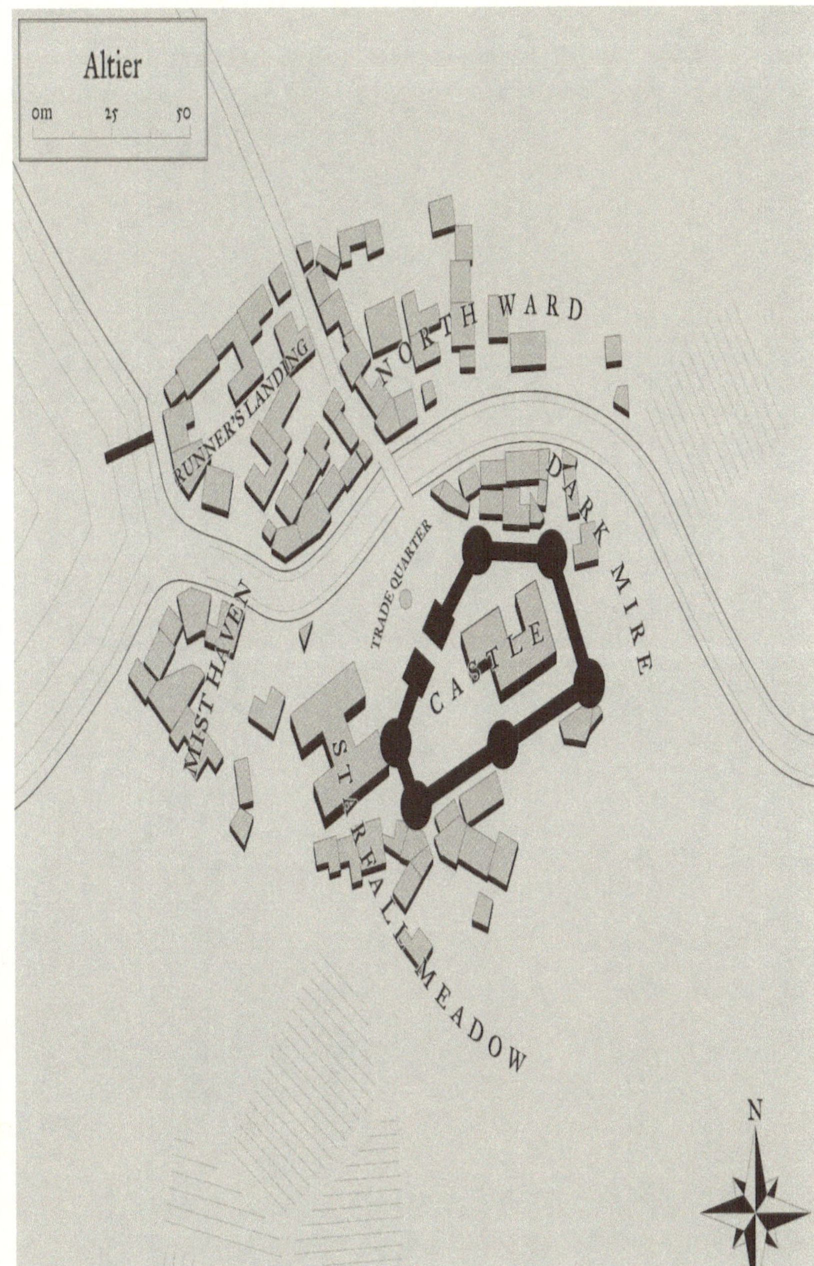

Altier
0m   25   50
RUNNER'S LANDING
NORTH WARD
DARK MIRE
MISTHAVEN
TRADE QUARTER
CASTLE
STARFALL MEADOW
N

CHAPTER 1

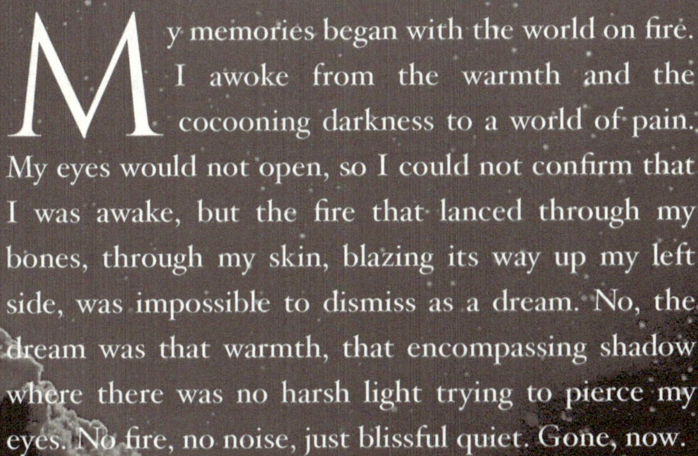

My memories began with the world on fire. I awoke from the warmth and the cocooning darkness to a world of pain. My eyes would not open, so I could not confirm that I was awake, but the fire that lanced through my bones, through my skin, blazing its way up my left side, was impossible to dismiss as a dream. No, the dream was that warmth, that encompassing shadow where there was no harsh light trying to pierce my eyes. No fire, no noise, just blissful quiet. Gone, now.

I wrenched my eyes open and cried out, hardly able to catch my breath. There were lights above me —arcane things of horrible brightness—people rushing around, speaking too quietly for me to hear over the roaring in my head.

Then, "She's awake! Healer, she's awake!"

The voice was vaguely familiar. Deep, masculine, perhaps with a touch of panic to it, and something else I couldn't identify. Something sad.

Someone appeared in my line of sight, an aged woman dressed in black robes, a black circlet at her brow keeping her curly greyish-blonde hair back. She stared down at me with a solemn expression. Her hand reached for my own, the touch a single spot of gentleness in this fire.

"Calm yourself, Chosen One," the healer said, her voice as soothing as her touch. Immediately she spoke the words, that fire eased, as if the need to burn and to destroy was erased from my body. I relaxed, not realising that I had been arching my back above the bed, muscles locked together.

"It hurts," I said, my voice a whimper.

Another face appeared in my line of sight and I somehow knew that it belonged to the first voice, the sad and panicked one. He was young, though there were lines of worry about his mouth and eyes, with short dark hair, a few strands falling into his eyes, deep and solid as the earth. He had tan skin marred with dirt and scratches, and his clothes, finer than the healer's and in a deep grey, were torn and stained with blood.

Was it mine?

"Calm yourself, Astraea. Breathe deep. Do you know where you are?" The healer's voice was swimming, just as my vision was moving once more to that delicious, comforting darkness.

"Astraea," I murmured. "Who is Astraea?"

Then, I slipped away.

✦

When I awoke again, the fire of before was little more than a persistent throb starting in my left hand and going all the way up my arm, across my shoulder, and rising into my face. I tried to move a finger and hissed as that throb turned into a sharp burn. I squeezed my eyes shut until the pain passed, then opened them, ready to grab onto any detail to spare me from thinking about why I hurt so much.

The room I was in was harshly lit by arcane lights, unshielded and vibrant, casting stark shadows where they hit objects. There was my bed as well as two others, plus a myriad of potions and tinctures on shelves and strewn across wooden tables, holding down papers and drawings. The room smelt of chemicals, with a hint of lavender. I turned my head as best I could manage, wincing again with the pain, and found a small vase with a sprig of the plant on the side table.

"You are awake." It was the healer from before, the sleeves of her black robes rolled up, her hands smudged with various substances. She studied me for a moment, clicking her tongue. Then she shook her head. "Do you remember what happened?"

I swallowed, my tongue thick and heavy in my mouth. "I remember fire. I woke here, and you were there, and someone else. And you called me Astraea. Am I...am I Astraea?"

Talking hurt, but it was a tangible thing, something physical to grab onto that I could anchor in reality. I didn't understand entirely what was happening, but the pain, at least, was real.

The healer's mouth tightened and something dark flashed in her eyes. She went to a basin set under a water pump and began washing her hands, slowly, methodically. Only when they were dry did she answer me.

"What do you remember from before the fire? From before waking up here?"

I closed my eyes and cast my thoughts back. There was fire. Bright tongues, tinged with green as well as oranges and blues and yellows, licking at everything in their path. Had there been someone else there with me? Where was there? What had burned? And why had I been there? I pushed past the fire, the memory of its touch a phantom compared to the agony of before. My thoughts went dark, full of shadow and silence.

"There is nothing before the fire," I croaked. "Only darkness."

The healer shuddered, leaning against the basin. She straightened her shoulders, nodded once, then turned back to me with a sympathetic smile that surely could not be sincere. "You have extensive injuries, besides the burns. We did all we could to repair your broken bones and lacerations, even getting the palace physician in for arcane spells to mend. But there is only so much that magic can do on the human body, and yours was quite damaged."

"How badly?" I asked, though I could already feel the injuries. My left arm, shoulder, face. All of it screamed whenever I moved. But there were other hurts, too. My feet felt sore, my muscles ached. My head felt like it had been torn open and emptied.

"The burns are perhaps half healed. The rest is up to you. The lacerations on your feet and ankles were deep, but they were an easier task. Your ribs were a simple mend. Your head…We closed the wound and repaired the damage to your skull, but there is nothing arcane magic can do for wounds of the brain."

"Is that why I do not remember anything? Why I do not know who I am, or where I am, or any of it?" I asked. My throat was dry, and not just from thirst. The healer closed her eyes and nodded.

"You are Astraea, the Chosen One. You are the reborn of a fallen star, sent to save us all from the void that encroaches farther every day." The voice was new, yet familiar, and it made me jump. I sucked back a hiss of pain as I turned to see this intruder into what felt like a private conversation. I realised I recognised him as the voice from before, the man who had sounded worried and sad as I had awoken into fire.

Instead of grimy and exhausted, he looked clean and put together. His dark hair, a shade of brown like walnut wood, was combed back from his face, revealing the aquiline features and clear, tan skin. His eyes were intelligent and just a touch calculating, instead of sad as they had been. He wore clothes of a fine cloth, the trousers a hunter's green that hugged the legs, covered by a tunic of matching green embroidered with gold and bound by a leather belt with a sword and dagger and pouch of velvet hanging from it. His fingers bore rings of gold and emerald and he had a ring in the shell of each ear, also of gold.

I don't know why the finery surprised me. He wore it like a second skin, unlike the dirt and grime of before. But something about the presentation was discomfiting. More so, even, than the mystery of my life.

Then, the full meaning of his words struck me and it became impossible to breathe.

"Astraea!" The healer rushed towards me. She

plucked a phial of some dark blue liquid from a table and uncorked it, holding it to my lips. A single drop of the liquid fell into my mouth and I began coughing, my lungs suddenly clear, the air rich. I screamed as I sat up, my head swimming, coughing until breathing became natural again.

"Don't strain yourself," the man said, suddenly at my side, his hand hovering at my shoulder as if to guide me back down. I shrugged him off.

"Who are you?" I demanded. "What do you mean I'm the Chosen One? Where am I? What happened to me?"

The man took a step back and exchanged a glance with the healer that spoke so much more than words. I understood none of it except pity. The man sat on the bed beside mine and folded his hands neatly in his lap, twisting the ring on his thumb: a signet ring with what looked like a comet engraved into it.

"Do you remember anything about the void?" he asked, like I was a child. It was infuriating, yet how could I protest when I couldn't even remember who I was?

I closed my eyes and licked my lips, wincing as my tongue touched the edges of a burn. "The void...it came for the star after she fell to Adhor at Ynysfwar, to be with her lover?"

The words meant almost nothing to me—I had no idea where Ynysfwar was, or why a falling star would matter—but I knew them to be as true as anything else in this new reality of mine. I opened my eyes to find the man nodding his head encouragingly, still with that patronising look.

"The legend goes that a star fell in love with a mortal man and fell to Adhor at Ynysfwar to be with him, defying the gods and her fellow stars. The void which surrounds the stars in the heavens grew jealous and came to Adhor to bring her home. The void then grew desirous of all the pleasures that could be found on Adhor and tried to devour it. The star and her lover gathered an army to fight the void. Eventually, she and the void were the only ones left. She used her power to expel the void, burning herself up in the process. But the void was not defeated, only banished, and would return. So the star gave her last drop of immortal life to send her power into the people of Adhor, ensuring that when the void returned, the star's power would appear in a chosen vessel to fight it, until such time as the star became reborn and would defeat the void forever."

I couldn't tell if the man believed the story or not, so casual was his recitation. But again I felt that ring of truth, as if at least parts of the tale were real.

"I am one of those chosen vessels?" I asked.

"You are," the healer said. She lifted my chin with a finger, mindful of the burns, and tilted my face towards her so she could look at it. "The burns are only half-healed. Your face is the least damaged, but there will still be scarring. Your arm and hand, though, will likely have permanent nerve damage. You will have to go through extensive therapy to regain at least a moderate amount of movement."

I pulled back, laying on the bed again, cradling my wounded hand against my chest. Nerve damage. Therapy. What did that mean for being the Chosen One? What did being the Chosen One even entail?

"Who are you?" I asked the man again.

"I am His Royal Highness, Lord of the Sundered Land and Keeper of the Sacred Flame, First Son and Heir Apparent to the throne of Baldarskiel, Devereux Alastair Theobold Icarius Thorquan the third." He smirked, as if it were all a joke. The Sundered Land, the Sacred Flame, none of that meant anything to me, and I could not tell if he was being sincere. "I don't usually bother with all the royal titles and nonsense unless the occasion calls for it. You, my dear Astraea, may call me Devereux."

Royalty. That explained the finery. I wondered if I were meant to be impressed by him, or just feel friendly. I felt none of those, only more discomfort.

I looked at the healer. "And you?" I asked.

"High Healer Eugenie," the woman said.

"How did I come to be here?" My mind was heavy with all of this new information, swirling around my thoughts with nowhere solid to land. Everything felt like mist and fog, and trying to hold on to tangible details was impossible. The need to know, though, was overwhelming.

Devereux winced. "Perhaps we should talk about that another time."

Eugenie nodded. "Indeed. You have expended far more energy than I would recommend for your first day awake. I have to clean your burns anyways and put some ointment on them before bandaging them. It's not a process you want to be awake for. I recommend a small sleeping agent and—"

"Tell me." My words were a command, the force of it instinctual, like I'd given commands before and expected to be obeyed. I frowned, unsure.

"You arrived at the palace in Altier—the capital city of Baldarskiel, the land where the star first fell, and since separated by the void from the rest of Adhor, if you must know—some six months ago. Your blood shone with the power of the star, proclaiming you to be exactly what you are: the Chosen One. We celebrated your arrival," Devereux said with a sardonic smile. "The void has been expanding dramatically over the last few years, and our void runners are barely able to get through to the rest of Adhor for trade and diplomacy. We almost despaired that a Chosen One would arrive in time to help. Then there you were."

His eyes grew distant and the smile slipped away.

"But what happened?" My arrival at the palace was information, and any information was better than none, but I wanted the whole story. Immediately.

"We trained you. For six months, you studied sword craft, hand to hand combat, strategy, arcane magic, everything. We even found a wild magic tutor to help you use your star-given power. The mission was meant to be a test, nothing more. A tiny void pool had been found at the edge of Starfall Meadow, just outside Altier. You and seven Void Runners were to go and close it."

Devereux's mouth twisted distastefully. He looked at Eugenie again, one of those knowing looks that told me absolutely nothing. Then he continued. "It went badly. The void pool exploded and you tried to contain it, only everything began to burn under the heat of your star's power. The Void Runners died killing the monsters that the void pool spit out and you nearly died trying to contain the pool."

Fire. Darkness. The void pool. A tiny speck of grasping darkness and shadow, pulling me in with a hypnotic song. I didn't remember anyone else being there. I only remembered the fire and the pain and the darkness. Always that darkness, just out of reach, whispering to me.

If that was only a pool, a tiny drop of void, then perhaps I had come to the palace too late. It would take months of further training and therapy just to be able to move somewhat normally again, let alone use what magic I possessed. I couldn't even feel any magic beneath my skin. It was like there was nothing at all. Emptiness. Or, and here I swallowed back a gasp that threatened to break apart my fragile stability like glass, some of the void that I had tried to fight now lived inside of me.

It was impossible, surely. I didn't even know how the void worked, let alone the magic that I supposedly possessed. But the fear of it being true, of failing in my destiny before I had even remembered what that destiny was, kept me silent.

Devereux took my right hand, squeezing the unblemished fingers hard enough that I felt the ridges of his rings digging into my skin. He smiled at me, like there was something more to the story, like there was something more there unspoken between us, too. "Don't worry, Lady Astraea. You need only focus on healing. Your time to face the void will come, and you will succeed. Of that, I have no doubt."

Without a second's hesitation, he stood, bowed his head a fraction, and swept from the room in a storm of glittering green. Instead of absence, the loss of his presence felt like a relief, like I was taking a full breath since the first time he'd appeared.

"He can be a bit overwhelming," Eugenie

murmured. She shook her head. "The prince is so full of hope that he often forgets what it is to fear the void. A pity his parents never let him train as a Void Runner. He would have been one of the best."

She turned to me, holding a cloth and basin of water. She set both down on the table beside me and picked up a phial of bright purple liquid speckled with light. "Drink this, it will help you sleep through the treatment."

I drank, the liquid slimy and tasting of overripe fruit. I grimaced and wished for clear water. Eugenie smiled down at me and picked up the cloth. A brush of her fingers pushed back my hair, and a thought struck me.

"What do I look like?" I asked, already feeling exhausted, my eyelids drooping, my words heavy on my tongue.

Eugenie froze, her eyes wide. She licked her lips and looked away. "Worry about your looks later, my Lady Star," she murmured. "We can cover up the scars when they're healed."

That hadn't been what I was asking. I wanted to tell her that, but the words fell away and my thoughts grew heavy. I closed my eyes, unable to keep them open another moment. Then, just before I fell into the beckoning darkness, I felt a brush of the damp cloth against my skin and the fire of pain once again consumed me, following me into the deep.

The last thought I had was that surely none of this could be real. I could not be the Chosen One. I hurt too much for that burden, and I did not wish to let anyone else down like I apparently had done with the Void Runners who had died at my hand. Surely, I would wake again and all of this would be a dream. The only real thing was the darkness, cool and soothing and comforting. I welcomed its embrace with gladness.

CHAPTER 2

The next days were a blur, nothing more than a series of wakings and cleaning of my wounds, a few conversations over how much I remembered—no more than before—then I was fed, drugged, or I fell asleep from exhaustion until the next time. It was a cycle that left me dazed and empty, a vessel with no memories waiting to be filled, and knowing that only sleep was of any relief. I was alone, staring up at a world of healers murmuring around me, never at me. All the while, the thought that I was the Chosen One was forefront in my mind. How could I be such a thing when I had failed so profoundly?

Finally, nearly a week after first waking, I was able to sit up in bed without my muscles seizing from pain. I could stay awake for several hours at a time, and I no longer felt like agony was the only thing grounding me to this reality. I began to feel like a person, albeit one with something fundamental missing.

A novitiate healer brought me a mirror after much begging and I was finally able to learn what I looked like. A piece of the puzzle as to who I was.

"They're not so bad, really, Lady Star, just a bit like ripples over your skin. Not that you can't hide them with powders or creams like other ladies use, of course. And maybe there's an arcane spell that could be performed to make them less visible. Though they're really not so bad." The poor boy was babbling, hardly more than a youth, all knobs and knees, his face bright red with embarrassment. I pretended I did not hear him, to spare us both, and studied my reflection. It wasn't my scars I was looking at, though, it was *me*.

I was not golden tan like Devereux, my skin earthier and browner, sun-touched, spattered with freckles from time out of doors. My hair was a deep brown, almost black, but with an undertone of red, like wine. I had regular features, made gaunt by my injuries and my poor eating. And my eyes... I don't know what I expected from someone they kept calling Lady Star, but the sharp, guarded green that was dark enough to be almost night was not it. I looked wary. The wariness was expounded by the scars the poor noviciate was still babbling over.

As he said, they were like ripples over my skin, starting at a point just under my left eye and spreading outward in a vicious slash down my jaw, to my neck and shoulder and crawling along my arm and hand. The ones on my face looked much like the ones on my arm, though the ripples were smaller, more delicate. They were more healed than I had expected, given how much they hurt, but they were still angry and red, with only the very peaks of those waves becoming startlingly pale scar tissue.

I turned my head in the mirror, wincing as the burns stretched with the movement. I don't know what I had been before, if I were considered beautiful. Judging by the whole half of my face, I would say that I was little more than average, the sort of person you walked by in the street without a second glance if they were not dressed well or surrounded by something of interest. Not ugly, but not striking enough to draw attention. With the scars, though, I looked not only striking but fierce. A star indeed, burned by her power and willing to do whatever it took against the void.

It was an illusion.

I pushed the mirror aside with startling vehemence. The healer boy spluttered his speech to a halt and quickly snatched the looking glass away from me.

He practically bowed, his face now drawn and pale. "I will go ask Healer Eugenie immediately about something for the scars—"

"No," I murmured. It still hurt to talk, but the pain was more in the stretching of my skin over my jaw than the sharp burn it had been before. "Leave the scars."

"L-leave the scars?!" He seemed horrified, his eyes darting to them and then away, as if he were embarrassed to be staring and yet could not help himself.

"Leave the scars," I repeated. "It is all I have left of whatever came before. I will keep them."

That, and Eugenie had told me more than once she did not think there was anything they could do besides applying layers of face powders. Already she had done various tests on my nerve function in my left hand and found it wanting. The masters of the arcane magic had come and said there was nothing more they could do. The rest of the healing was up to me. This young boy didn't know that, though. And far be it from me to disillusion him, when he was obviously so horrified by the fact that they existed at all. Better to let him think it was my choice.

Perhaps it was. How could I mourn the loss of what I had been when I did not know who that was? The scars, at least, were a reminder that I had once been something else. Someone else. Now, they were the only mark on my life that I could identify beyond the boundaries of these four walls.

The healer spluttered apologies and assurances of my beauty before practically sprinting from the room. He took the mirror with him.

"What did you say to that poor boy that had him so scared?" Devereux's smooth voice drew my attention, and he sauntered into the room, once again wearing finery that glistened and gleamed, this time in various shades of blue. He walked with the sort of confidence that was sure of people moving out of his way when he approached. I wondered if he practised the movement as a facade, if the scared, sad man I saw through fog upon my first waking was the truth. Or perhaps that was the fiction, and the saunter was reality.

I didn't bother answering Devereux. I had learned that he liked to use words as swords, and his teasing was often exhausting. He would keep talking regardless, so I just let him talk.

"I've been informed by Head Healer Eugenie that you are well enough to start your physical therapy, so long as you go very, very slowly." Devereux cast himself onto the bed beside mine, still empty, and grinned at me. "We're going to get you out of this room."

"Thank the gods," I blurted out before I could stop myself. I'd been going a bit stir crazy.

Devereux's grin turned wicked. "I thought you might say that. I'm all for taking you on a full tour of the palace. I get to show you all the things that you've never seen before. Well, actually you have, but as you don't remember, it will be like new. And this time, I won't leave the tour up to servants who drone on and on. I'll show you everything myself."

"You will not." This new voice cut through the air with ease, the tones deep enough to feel endless, yet soothing. I immediately turned away from Devereux to the door and found a man, no more than a decade older than me, standing there, imposing and yet contained. He was paler than me by a fair bit, looking nearly wan in comparison to Devereux, but the edges of him seemed blurred and darkened, like he had been smudged in ink. Indeed, his fingers were fully black, the colour travelling up his hand through his veins and over his skin. His eyes were bright, like ice, yet too were tinged with shadow. His hair, tied up at the nape of his neck, was pure darkness, with only the very roots showing nearly white.

Something in me recoiled at his presence just as surely as it was drawn to him. I hadn't yet felt a hint of whatever star magic made me the Chosen One, their Lady Star, but I instinctively knew that some sort of power in me called to some sort of power in him. It was impossible, out of reach, yet sure as the burns on my skin.

Devereux broke through the moment with a dismissive wave of his hand and a long-suffering sigh. "Naturally you would disagree."

The man raised a single white brow and frowned. "As I have been tasked with overseeing Lady Astraea's recovery, so that she is *prepared* to fight the void when the time comes, rather than leaping before she is ready, as before, then yes, I disagree. This process will not happen quickly, and it will not be easy. You will hurt, and while I am sorry for it, it cannot be helped."

This last was directed at me, and while I felt the words were true, something in his tone made me question his sincerity. I would have frowned, but I'd learned that the motion pulled on my burns far more than was comfortable. Instead, I kept my features carefully blank.

"Who are you?" I asked.

The man blinked and recoiled, as if I'd struck him. He searched my face for a moment, his eyes only glancing over my scars, as if they were incidental. He must have seen something there that he did not like, because he rounded on Devereux and growled, "Explain, Your Highness."

Devereux winced. "Ah, yes. Did I forget to mention that? We are trying to keep the details quiet so the people do not panic. No one wants a Chosen One who doesn't even remember her name, let alone what she's meant to do."

I swallowed at that, because he was right. I remembered the fire and the darkness, but the reality of being this Chosen One, this starborn or whatever I was, felt more like a dream, words whispered to me over and over while I slept, enough that they were meaningless. If I had magic, then it was sleeping. Or vanished entirely.

"Don't remember..." the stranger said, slowly, carefully. He looked at me. "Is this true?"

I nodded.

The man's jaw clenched, and he turned back to Devereux, looking for all the world like he wanted to strangle the prince. "You should have said. When you told me she was injured, you should have said."

Devereux just shrugged. "Perhaps. Anyways, it's done now. You know."

The man still looked furious, but he swallowed it down. Then he turned to me and bowed at the waist. "Lady Astraea, I am Casimir Rivale, Ambassador of Cortaesi, Void Runner of the First Order, and your personal guard and trainer."

Cortaesi. That must be a place, though I wasn't sure I could picture it on a map. Some information came to me in fragments, like trying to remember words from a book read many years ago. It was usually general knowledge, things that I would have known as a matter of course, like the names of places, of the seasons and flowers. But it was things that required more specific knowledge that often tripped me up.

"A pleasure, Ambassador," I said, inclining my head as much as my burns would allow.

"Casimir, please," he said. "Cortaesi is a long way from here, and you of all people have no need to stand on ceremony."

Me, of all people. I took a breath before panic could crush my chest and changed the topic. "What... what is a Void Runner?"

Both men gaped at me.

I lifted my right shoulder, my left too sore for a casual shrug. "I've heard the term several times, but I don't actually...I think I once knew what it was, but it's just shadows and mist."

The people who had died had been Void Runners, I'd been told, and the fact that it meant nothing to me hurt. I wanted it to mean something. I didn't want their loss to be forgotten.

Casimir cleared his throat. "You—that is, do you know of the void?"

"Yes. The emptiness. Devereux explained the legend to me." As imprecise as that legend was, at least it was some explanation of what people expected of me.

Casimir, though, flinched. "It is a great deal more complicated than that, my lady. The void is more than simply emptiness. It calls to the living and draws them in, feeding off of life and energy and power. It won't kill you immediately; people have been known to survive for up to a month without arcane spells to protect them, though they're often mad when they emerge. The void...corrupts. It twists the original intent of things and makes them something new. Animals caught in the original expansion, for example, have become monstrous, ravenous, more than feral. They, and their descendents prey on everything they can. Some can even emerge from the void or void pools across Adhor on moonless nights."

Devereux shuddered. "The last voidling to make it as far as Altier nearly massacred all of the Dark Mire district."

Casimir did not elaborate, and I did not ask him to. He rubbed his ink-stained fingers together, a tic, then stopped as he noticed me watching. His expression hardened. "A remnant from the void, if you must know."

I felt my right cheek warm, though my left was in a constant state of numb heat. I was blushing.

Casimir's expression softened the slightest bit. "Void Runners are those of us who have trained in specialised techniques for breaking through the void, to facilitate trade and diplomacy, and to help protect the lands. We are, in essence, blockade runners, though our target is the void surrounding Baldarskiel, not a blockade of ships. People from all over Adhor send their children to be trained as Runners, so that they might have protection from the void pools that spring up."

Devereux snorted and fiddled with his signet ring. "More like they do it for prestige."

The look Casimir gave was icy, but the prince either did not notice or did not care. Devereux shrugged. "Everyone knows that Void Runners are second only to royalty, especially here. Runner's Landing is the nicest district in the city except for the Castle District. They're well compensated, well treated, and respected everywhere they go. They're responsible for our wealth, our prestige, for keeping Baldarskiel in touch with the world instead of locked away behind a shroud and forgotten. Only the Chosen One is received better."

He winked at me, and I again had to suppress the urge to frown. Was that meant to make me feel better? It did not.

"Anyways, Lady Astraea," Casimir said, his jaw tight again. "We are trained enough in the arcane magic to protect ourselves as well as small shipments. We guide merchant caravans, pass messages, fight voidlings, and do our best to prevent the spread of the void, be it with fire or spells. And, in this instance, train you."

I looked away, my eyes touching on his fingers again. "I will do my utmost," I murmured.

Casimir said nothing for a moment. Then he sighed and nodded. "Very well. Your Highness, if you would leave us?"

"I'll stay," Devereux said with a casual wave of his hand. "Someone has to keep the Lady Star entertained."

"Please," I said. "I would prefer to do this alone. I...this will be difficult enough, I think, without an additional audience."

That sharp sadness flickered in Devereux's eyes for a moment before he leaped off the bed with a charming smile. He gave a flourish and a bow and reached for my right hand to kiss it. "As my star commands."

Then, as always with his departures, he simply left. In his wake was that same sense of loss and being able to breathe normally again. I clenched my good hand into a fist and closed my eyes a moment. When I opened them, Casimir was watching me, his expression inscrutable.

"I think he means well," I said by way of breaking through the silence. "He just...not everyone reacts well when they see me like this."

"You will recover," Casimir said with impossible certainty. He stepped over to the side of the bed and held out his hands. "Now, the first thing we need to do is help you stand."

I'd done this a few times over the past week, with

a great deal of assistance, to use the necessary and for the healers to change my bedding. My legs then, and now, felt like water, quivering and without strength of any kind. I lifted my hands, both of them, and placed them in Casimir's. My left hand burned with the agony of being touched; I shoved the sensation aside. Then I swung my legs over the side of the bed and winced as the sudden movement sent under worked muscles twinging in my back.

"Carefully," Casimir cautioned. "Do this too quickly and you will cause more harm than good."

I nodded, because that was all I could do besides pant for breath. I inched my legs to the floor, planting my feet and feeling the coolness of the stone beneath my toes. My feet still ached from whatever injury had been dealt them before the healing, but they were whole and bore what little weight I put on them.

"Good. Now, when I tell you, put your weight on both feet at once. Try to stand." Casimir waited a beat while I took in a couple of deep breaths, then nodded to me. I pushed down onto my feet, my legs wavering even as I demanded more out of them. I knew, in that moment, as I hovered between sitting and standing, that I was going to fall. I looked at Casimir to tell him so and froze. Those eyes, bright and blue and piercing, had more shadows in them than before. It wasn't the pupils blowing wide, but like a wave of darkness was over-taking his eyes.

I stood and took a step away without once thinking about what I was doing. My panic at the sight was more than enough to override whatever signals of desperation my muscles were telling me. It lasted only a moment, though, before I wavered and nearly fell. Casimir's hands tightened around mine, squeezing the burns. I yelped and took another step back, wrenching my hand away from his.

"No! I'm—I'm sorry, Lady Astraea," he said, pulling back as he realised what he'd done. "I did not mean to hurt you. I was merely trying to steady you. I did not mean...my apologies."

I nodded, trying to catch my breath so that my vision stopped swimming. A moment later and I sat back on the bed. "Perhaps," I panted, "we should see if the healers have a balm for the pain before we proceed any further."

Casimir nodded. "Yes. Indeed. I will go inquire."

Then, he too was gone, leaving me in that room, my breath shallow as I fought through the pain. But I knew that it wasn't entirely the pain that had stolen my breath. It was that shadow over Casimir's eyes.

A Void Runner, he'd said, travelled through the void, protected with arcane spells and incantations. Only, he himself had admitted to being void touched, his skin decorated with those beautiful, dark stains of ink. What if these Runners weren't as protected as they thought? What if the people meant to protect against the void carried it with them?

Suddenly, being the Chosen One, needing to fight the void, wasn't quite as much a dream. It was real, and these people claimed that I was the one meant to push back the void. Meant to save them. In the midst of a vast empty place where my memories should have been, I had only that knowledge. I was the Chosen One. I would save them. The only question was whether I could figure out *how* before things got worse. Worse than seven Void Runners dead at my hand.

I shuddered. If I were the Chosen One in truth, then I was a poor one. I needed to figure out how to use my magic. More, though, I needed to learn everything I could about the void.

Over the next week, I worked several times a day with Casimir to stand, take a few turns around the room, and eventually go on a stroll through the palace. He did his best to touch me as little as possible, avoiding my burns entirely. And I couldn't quite bring myself to look him in the eye in case I saw that shadow again. It was awkward, tense, and painfully polite between the two of us.

The only relief was when Devereux would visit, interrupting our stilted conversation with invitations to go walking with him—these I always refused on the grounds that I had barely made it to the end of the hall without needing a rest—or plates of food. Several times, he'd handed me a pastry or tidbit which he assured me I loved. I usually didn't.

On this particular day, Casimir was walking backwards before me, hands ready to catch me should I fall. His expression was solemn, eyes studying my legs for any sign of weakness. There were no shadows there, only blue, and trying to figure out what that meant was hardly enough to distract me from my struggles. I felt like my muscles were too tight to move, and each step was just shy of agony, but I also did not want him to see me falter. I'd had enough of that.

We made it to the end of the hallway. I leaned on the stone wall to catch my breath. There were tapestries on most of the walls, massive and some of them quite ancient. It gave a little warmth to what was otherwise a very cold, impersonal building. I'd discovered that the entire palace was made of the same dark stone as the healer's quarters, and that the windows were infrequent and small in the walls, a holdover from many centuries ago when this place had been a true fortress instead of a palace. As such, the halls were dimly lit by torches and arcane lights, both of which cast stark shadows over everything.

"Good," Casimir said, frowning. "You've done very well."

"Please do not lie to me," I said, still trying to catch my breath. The burns on my face and arms felt tight, stretched taut, and each breath pulled on it more. "You fully expected me to do considerably better by now. I can see it in your expression."

Casimir's eyes widened, and he looked away for an instant. Then, he sighed, rubbing his jaw with his shadowed hands. "As you wish, Lady Astraea. Yes, I had expected you to be farther along in your recovery by now. The arcane magician who healed you informed me that your injuries were mostly healed, except for the burns. But you are still quite weak, which tells me otherwise."

My face warmed, and I looked to the tapestry across the hall, a piece of greens and warm ivories in which a handsome young man offered a hand to a maiden guarded by a unicorn. A pretty piece, if an empty one.

"I will do better," I murmured.

"It's not your fault that the healing is—"

"I will do better," I repeated. I looked at him and he managed only an abrupt nod. "I *need* to do better. If I cannot even walk down a hall, how am I expected to be able to fight the void?"

Casimir took a step forwards, though he still did not touch me or get closer than a few feet. "If I may, you would be able to fight the void even in a wheeled chair. It is not a matter of mere physical ability, though that does help against voidlings."

"Ah, yes. My magic." I scoffed. The moment I met Casimir had been the only time where I'd felt like I actually *had* magic. I hadn't felt a glimmer of anything since. No, all I felt was cooped up, weak, and exhausted. Useless, in short. "I cannot even summon a spark."

"We will work with your magic later. It is difficult for magic to be performed when the body is so injured." Despite contradicting what he'd just told me, his words sounded so reasonable. I wanted to rage at him for that. Everything with him was reason-able, or even, or solemn. I needed someone to tell me the truth, not coddle me.

I pushed myself off the wall and started farther down the hallway, farther than I'd been before. I saw a window at the end of the hall, an aperture slightly wider than an arrow-slit, but a window nonetheless. I walked towards it, putting every ounce of anger and spite into my steps to propel me onwards.

"Lady Astraea," Casimir said, sounding alarmed. He quickly got out of my way, though he still walked beside me. Poised to catch me. "There is no point in pushing yourself too hard. It will take time."

I kept walking. The pain was growing, as was the weakness. My ribs began to ache where they had been broken and my feet felt like sharp knives had buried themselves into the bones. My burns, ironically, only hurt because I was clenching my jaw.

"Please, there is nothing to prove," Casimir said. He started walking in front of me going backwards, as before, but this time his hands were actively reaching for me, his expression concerned. He grabbed my elbows—gently, but with intent.

"To you, I have nothing at all to prove," I agreed. I lifted my chin. "To myself, I have everything to prove."

He studied me, then closed his eyes and nodded. He released my arms and started walking backwards again. "You always were stubborn."

I faltered, throwing my hand out to steady myself on the wall. "You...you knew me before?"

He winced. His entire body went tense. "You and I were only formally introduced a few weeks before the...incident. But I had seen you around, working with the other Runners, training. It, ah, was well known that you were quite stubborn."

I frowned. That made sense. I hated that it made sense. I'd been hoping that he could provide me more insight on myself, who I had been before and if I were different now, but if we only knew each other's names, then there was little point in asking. I started walking again, my steps getting closer together and slower. I cast about for a topic of conversation, anything that would distract me from the pain. From the disappointment.

"What about the Void Runners who died?" I asked. I kept one hand on the wall for support and studiously avoided looking Casimir in the eye.

His voice was tense. "What about them?"

I fixed my gaze on the window and tried to breathe past the lump in my throat. "Did you know them?"

"I knew them."

"Will you..." I paused, leaning against the wall. "Will you tell me about them? Healer Eugenie won't let anyone talk to me about them, because she doesn't want to distress me and make my recovery worse. And when I ask Devereux, he changes the subject."

Casimir let out a soft, mocking laugh. "He would. Devereux is not especially fond of Void Runners, because we uphold a great deal of the international economy and because we are the few people in Baldarskiel that can question the monarchy without repercussions. They need us. All of Baldarskiel—all of Adhor needs us. His family has been at odds with the Runners for years."

That didn't sit quite right in my stomach. Devereux seemed to like Casimir; certainly he respected him. And everything he'd told me about Runners—and what little he'd said about the ones who had died on my behalf—was good, even a bit awestruck. I hadn't met the king and queen, as they were making a trip to some of the nearby Baronies, but everything Devereux had said was positive. It was the first thing Casimir said that hadn't made sense, I realised. I wondered what it meant.

Maybe Cortaesi was at odds with Baldarskiel. That would make sense, given that Casimir was an Ambassador. But he was also a Void Runner, and he would know of any tensions between them and Devereux's family. I decided to hold my tongue instead of asking questions; I would learn more that way. Things people didn't want me to know, perhaps.

I pushed onwards, making my way to the window, which was now only a few feet away. Casimir stepped aside and let me reach it on my own, without his hands hovering to keep me steady. I lay my head against the window and breathed deeply. The air outside was crisp, not quite cold, and full of life, unlike the stale healer's room. If I strained my ears, I could even hear the bustle of the city beyond the palace walls. All I could see, though, was the protective wall that ringed the palace and a slice of green on the ground below.

"All but one of the Runners who accompanied you to Starfall Meadow had graduated from training the year before. They were...eager to prove themselves, and I think the Void Runner in command made a mistake in placing you with them for training." Casimir did not sound critical, only sad. I turned away from the window and met his gaze. He turned away.

"There were three women and four men. Analise, Maria, Valerie, Gregori, Timo, Rikard, and Nathan. Analise was cunning, a master of strategy. Maria, a dancer, who moved like the wind. Valerie was solid, strong, and could withstand just about anything. Gregori loved music of any sort. Timo could eat his weight in sweetmeats and still be hungry. Rikard was serious, even dour, but loyal to a fault. And Nathan was...well, he was young and so very determined to prove himself."

I put my face to the window again. This time, the sick feeling in my stomach had nothing to do with confusion and everything to do with the fact that seven people were dead at my hand. Perhaps I hadn't been the one to strike them down. Perhaps they had been killed by the void and the fire and whatever had actually transpired at Starfall Meadow, but it was my fault they were there. My fault that I wasn't good enough to take on even a small portion of the void. It was all my doing, and now I would never even get the chance to remember them properly, because I didn't know who they were. I had spent six months training with them, laughing and struggling with them, and I'd needed someone else to tell me their names.

"I'm ready to go back to the room now," I breathed. Not a moment later, Casimir was threading his left arm through my right and leading me back to the healer's room. My prison. He let me lean on him, my muscles so weak and my bones so painful that I could barely take two more steps without support. I revelled silently in the warmth of another human being touching me rather than shying away. I reminded myself that it was only support to get back to the room, that he hadn't touched me for days and that this was nothing more than the result of me pushing too hard.

My throat tightened more.

"They would not have wanted you to blame yourself," Casimir murmured as we stepped into that den of potions and balms. "They were strong, proud people, and they knew precisely what they were getting into at Starfall Meadow. Void Runners are not afraid of death, Astraea. Only afraid of doing nothing in the face of darkness."

That did not make me feel any better.

He helped me back to bed, where I sank into the mattress with a smothered groan. Immediately, Eugenie was there, looking me over with a critical eye, a jar of balm for my burns in her hand. She sniffed at Casimir and stepped between him and me.

"I almost forgot," Casimir said, his tone oddly formal after the words he'd just shared. "Her Supreme Majesty, Queen Raya, and His Royal Majesty, King Consort Istir have extended an invitation for tomorrow evening. A dinner. They have returned from their trip to the outer Baronies and learned of what transpired here. They wish to celebrate that you are well."

I blinked. It hadn't really occurred to me that the queen and king would care a great deal about me. Yes, Devereux visited nearly every day, but I thought that was just because he was bored. Now I wondered if it was some vested interest in my well being. A celebration in my honour, after everything that had happened, felt like ash on my tongue.

"I do not see why they would be so concerned with me," I murmured. Eugenie slathered a thick layer of the balm over my arm and I hissed as it first stung, then numbed my burns.

"Don't you?" the healer asked, voice sharp. "You are the Chosen One. The fate of all of Adhor rests in your hands. *Everyone* is concerned with you."

I looked at Casimir in alarm. He merely folded his hands behind his back. "I will be here tomorrow evening at seven to escort you to dinner. The queen has arranged for a tailor to come and see to your clothes, so there will be no exercises tomorrow."

I could see this pained him. I wasn't thrilled either. Yes, I would be pleased to get out of the collection of white, shapeless shifts that the healers kept me in, but I did not much enjoy people preening over me. The healers were bad enough. Tailors, servants, then a whole dinner with the royal family? The thought of that many people scrutinising me had my muscles tightening, which stretched my burns and had me hissing, despite Eugenie's balm. I wanted to move forwards with my exercises, wanted to push my therapy as far as I could so that I could get on my feet sooner and work to actually be worthy of the people's interest.

Worthy of the Void Runners whose deaths I had caused.

"Thank you," I said. Casimir nodded, gave a quick, sharp bow, and left.

✦

The nightmares started that night. I was surrounded by fire, the heat as terrible as I remembered. Beyond the flames, there was only darkness, impossibly illuminated in stark relief, endless and grasping.

Astraea, a voice whispered, ancient. Malicious. Hungry.

"Who are you?" I demanded, clawing at the flames as they leaped for me. A force inside me yearned to combat the fire, but I knew that if I let it out, the destruction would be impossible to contain. So I held it in check, and I burned because of it.

The fallen star. The voice laughed from behind me. I whirled. A shape in the darkness flared with light before vanishing. *Come to dance with me again?*

I backed away, stepping straight into the waiting flames. I screamed, my flesh melting away even as I held back that answering fire in my very bones, to keep from exploding outwards. The ground shook as if mirroring my pain, cracks running through the earth and opening wide. The voice cackled and that same shape leaped over the flames for me. It was lupine and ursine, with a tail that lashed at the air. Claws made of pure shadow cut through the fire like it wasn't even there. Its maw dripped with darkness. And its eyes, bright as stars, watched as I tried uselessly to flee.

I ducked, burying my head in my arms and hoping the climbing flames would be enough to save me. They weren't. They never would be.

I woke, gasping for breath. I sat upright and leaned over my knees, trying to get enough oxygen into my lungs to fight back the dizziness that rose up and threatened to overwhelm me. Around me, the stone walls and floor seemed to tremble as I trembled. I wrapped my arms around myself and took several deep breaths. Eventually, the panic subsided and everything felt more stable, more real.

The door to the healer's room burst open and several people rushed in all at once. One was Eugenie, wearing a tattered dressing gown over her shift. Beside her, two apprentices in shirts and dressing gowns looked around in alarm, automatically reaching for potions and bottles. Eugenie took a look around, then looked at me.

"You are well?" she asked, though it wasn't much of a question. I nodded.

"Astraea!" Devereux skidded around the door and into the room. His hair stuck up at odd angles and he had tucked a shirt into the blue and silver trousers he'd worn the day before. His shoes did not match. "Are you alright? What happened?"

"Just a nightmare," I said. Why was everyone here? I was certain I hadn't cried out in my sleep, and even if I had, the stone walls of this room were thick enough to drown out even the most ardent screams. I would know; I'd yelled my throat raw during the more painful of Eugenie's treatments.

"A nightmare?" Devereux asked incredulously. "The entire palace shook. We thought that voidlings had got in and were using their magic to anchor this place into a void pool. We thought they were coming for you."

I froze. The palace shook? The ground had shaken in my nightmare, and when I woke the palace had seemed to be trembling. "I didn't see anything," I said. "I just woke up, and the ground was shaking."

Casimir entered the room then, far more put together than any of the others. He wore ivory armour over black, the loping dog insignia of the Void Runners nearly blinding in the dark of the night.

I looked around. Why were the arcane lights not working? They usually flickered to life when someone moved within the healer's room, as I'd learned during several midnight trips to the necessary.

In fact, everything seemed eerily quiet, like the darkness was smothering any noise outside of this room. No light, no movement, nothing. A stillness that was loud after the trembling of the palace.

"Everyone is well?" Casimir asked, his hand resting on the hilt of a sword I'd never noticed before. It matched his ivory coloured armour and seemed strange in the midst of the healers. For the first time, I realised that he was dangerous despite his gentle touches and deferential treatment of me.

"Was it a voidling?" Devereux demanded. This was the first time I'd seen him acting regal, acting like he was in command. It was in the sharpness of his voice, the firmness of his jaw. I could feel concern radiating off of him in waves. Concern, or fear. "Did one get into the palace, past the palace walls?"

Casimir shook his head, a strand of white hair mixed with black falling into his eyes, the only sign of dishevelment I saw in him. "No. There's been no void activity at all near the city. No sentries have ridden in, and the beacon fires burn brightly along the coast. None have gone out."

That meant the void hadn't spread. That was good. Right?

"So what happened?" Eugenie asked softly. Her hands were resting on a table near the wall, but her eyes were fixed on Casimir. She was scared, I realised. A voidling was perhaps a matter of course, but this unknown? It frightened her.

"Just an earthquake," Casimir said with all the calm true authority gave. "I'll ask the temple tomorrow, but I recall stories in their archives about times of various Chosen Ones in the past being surrounded by earthquakes and storms."

Temple? What temple?

"This is normal?" Devereux demanded in that same, sharp, commanding voice.

Casimir locked eyes with me, and I could have sworn I saw the shadows flickering there again. I froze, unable to move, unable to breathe. Something deep inside me called to him and I instinctively pushed it down.

"Perfectly normal," Casimir said, watching me.

I couldn't bring myself to look away.

I knew, though I didn't know how, that he was lying.

CHAPTER 4

I felt like I was girding for battle. I tried to tell myself that going into actual battle had to be much worse, but though I'd been told I had done so—ending with my arrival in the healer's quarters—I couldn't remember. Therefore, the constant parade of baths and scrubbings, the dressings and the powderings, the arranging of my hair, the discussions over whether to garb me in jewels when there was the matter of my mostly healed burns on my neck and shoulder to contend with, all of it felt like I was planning to go to war. My skin felt raw, stretched; my muscles were watery, my bones weak. War indeed.

Perhaps this was a war, if of a different sort, I mused as I stood before a large silver mirror flecked with black. Beside me, two women in veils and white dresses and a tall, gangly man preened over me. The women were fingers deep in my hair, tying it up in various twists then taking it down before trying something new. The man was adjusting the lacings on my gown, a deep blue trimmed in silver, studded with clear crystalline gems that sparkled when they caught the light. The dress was meant to mimic the night sky and her stars, I imagined, but it just looked gaudy. Heavy. The fabric was tight around my torso and loose around my legs, with sleeves that were long enough to hide my hands entirely should I choose. The neckline was high, but there was nothing that any of these well-meaning dressers could do about the scars on my face and neck.

I lifted my head high and stared myself down in the mirror. This was who I was. This was who I had been for as long as my memory went back. The scars were merely a representation of what had happened, nothing more. The winces and flinches of everyone as they looked at me, studied me, were as baffling as they were infuriating. They all looked at me as though I were damaged.

I may have been weak, struggling to regain mobility, to regain the full use of my left arm, but I was not damaged. Everyone else seemed to think so, though.

Except Casimir. And Devereux, though he still stared at the scars on my face. At least he did not flinch. I appreciated his humour as he tried to make an awkward situation less so.

"I think this is the best we can do," the man muttered to the women. I'm sure I wasn't meant to hear, wasn't meant to be listening to the conversations of the people dressing me, but they stood right there. How could I not notice their comments when they couldn't stop staring at my burns?

"Lady Star," one of the women said, finally meeting my gaze in the mirror. "You look..." She faltered.

"Fierce," the man supplied, resting his hands on my shoulder. He smiled at me, the action not quite reaching his eyes. "You look fierce."

I nodded. There wasn't anything else to say. I looked like I'd walked through fire. No amount of fine fabric or jewels threaded through my hair would change that. I thought that I looked fine. It was far better than the loose, shapeless shift the healers had me wear, and I was confident enough to admit that I liked the way my hair was piled on my head, making me seem taller, stronger, when I lifted my chin and let the jewels catch the light. Yes, the dress was gaudy. Yes, decking me in jewels was a bit ridiculous, especially when I'd done nothing to earn them, but I was pleased with the end result, nonetheless.

"Thank you," I murmured to the dressers. They bowed as one and shuffled to the door, only the man hesitating a moment before he vanished. I was alone only long enough to wish for a chair, then someone knocked and the door swung open to reveal Casimir.

Sombre, without a trace of a smile, he gave a half-bow. He wore that same ivory armour over black, though the black clothing caught the light in a subtle shine that told me the fabric was formal dress wear of a fine fabric. His hair had been pulled back and secured with a jewelled stick that matched the ones shining in my hair, and the hilt of his sword now bore that same jewel. It was clear, with just a hint of shadow at the centre, bright enough to catch the light and reflect it. When lit, it shone like a star.

"They're called Fallen Stars," he said, startling me.

"That sounds...ominous." I frowned. Casimir replied with a half-smile.

"They're bits of meteorite that melted and crys-tallised in the crater at Ynysfawr. Legend has it that's where the first star fell, and it still burns today with the strength of her power. Gems harvested from there are for the exclusive use of the royal family and those they deem their friends. They are relatively rare, given that Ynysfawr is now surrounded by a veil of void, making the island all but inaccessible. It is considered a great honour to wear the jewels," Casimir said. He reached out and brushed a finger over one of the ones threaded into my hair. "They suit you."

"Thank you," I said. "Though, I doubt my

dressers would agree. They were baffled at how to make me look the most gaudy—star-like, if you will—while also paying heed to my burns."

Casimir pulled his hand back, a flicker of some dark emotion crossing his features. He held out his arm. "Scars are merely visible marks of the story our lives have woven. Those who fear them, disdain them, are fools."

I flicked my gaze to the mirror again, and this time I found I was smiling ever so slightly. I slipped my arm through Casimir's and he led me out of the chamber and towards the dinner. I hadn't had much time to think on it during the day, with all the activity around preparing me as I'm sure the cooks were preparing the meal, but now I had a long, slow—and painful—walk to think on just how disappointed the queen and king consort would be when they saw me, saw the person who was responsible for the death of their Void Runners.

"Are you tired?" Casimir asked.

"No." I shook my head. I bit my lip and looked up at him. He paused, brows raised. As if he would whisk me back to the healers as soon as I complained of pain or weakness. I hated that he felt it necessary, and I was grateful that he cared. It was less overt than Devereux's constant questions and offerings, but seemed the more sincere. "I'm...nervous."

"Ah." He nodded, and we started walking again.

He fixed his gaze straight ahead. "The queen and king consort are…well, they can be intense in everything. They are responsible for the country that keeps the void at bay from the rest of Adhor. It's a heavy burden, and they do reasonably well. Despite its isolation, though, Baldarskiel is one of the most influential countries in Adhor. That alone is a temptation, as well as a danger. But they are also not immune to the games of politics that go on between the royal court and its accompanying advisors, and the Temple. The people, too, get drawn into the politics, as do all those sent here to train as Void Runners. Everything is about power, about holding onto it and manipulating events so it works in their favour. They're not malevolent, just…"

He fell silent. I tightened my grip on his arm a bit and he slowed his steps. Casimir flashed me an apologetic glance and another one of those half smiles.

"Devereux would be upset if he knew I was telling you this," he said. "He may seem bright and bold, but he is a very capable prince, all temptations included."

"I'm surprised to hear you say that." Devereux himself appeared around a corner, once again wearing glittering finery. I realised a moment later that the tunic and trousers matched my dress, and that he wore a heavy collar of Fallen Stars set in silver. The prince grinned at Casimir, who sighed, and bowed his head. "It's almost a compliment coming from you. My dear Lady Star, Lord Casimir may claim to eschew politics, but he is far more capable than I will ever be. He can have a room dancing to his tune faster than anyone I've ever met, including my sister."

Casimir still didn't say anything, just bowed his head again. Devereux waved him off.

"I've come to escort the beautiful Lady Star Astraea to dinner." Devereux made a flourish and bowed at the waist to me. I was still too weak to curtsey and not fall over, so I simply nodded and slid my arm through his. I could feel Casimir's eyes boring into my back as I took the prince's arm. I barely suppressed a shiver.

The dining chamber of the queen and king was only a few doors away, it would seem, as our little procession stopped at a finely carved wooden door flanked by two guards in steel armour. They bowed to the prince and opened the door.

"His Highness, Crown Prince Devereux, the Lady Star Astraea, and the Ambassador to Cortaesi, Lord Casimir," one of the guards announced. Without further preamble, Devereux pulled me forwards and into battle.

Before I could take a breath, or examine the room and its occupants, a figure wrapped in diaphanous white material prostrated on the floor before me. "Lady Star!" a woman's voice cried, muffled slightly by the fabric. "You honour us with your presence, and we express our gratitude for the day you came to fight the void and protect us all. By all the stars in the sky—"

"Dear sister," Devereux said, his voice full of scorn, "can we not even attend a dinner without you spouting your religious proselytising?"

The woman sat up, resting her hands on her knees. She had the same features as Devereux, though her eyes were a sharp shade of green. Her hair was braided and fell over one shoulder with Fallen Star gems woven into the strands. She wore a silver circlet over a white veil, had several shining silver rings and bracelets on both hands, and, I realised, had silver beads sewn into her gown to shine like stars. The effect was even more dazzling than my ensemble, and intimidating in its full splendour. She glared at Devereux with thinly disguised annoyance.

"Lady Star," she said again, this time in a purr. Her hands snaked out and snatched at my right hand, then she kissed it almost reverently. My skin crawled at her touch. "We have not met before, but I am High Priestess Beatrice of the Temple of the Fallen Star, and I am truly honoured to be here with you."

I pulled my hand back and nodded my head. "A pleasure," I murmured, though I wanted to do little more than run. Even if I were strong enough for that, Devereux still had my arm wrapped through his and he was already steering me towards the wide table in the middle of the room.

The table was set with dozens of plates, some bearing fruit, others cheeses and breads, cuts of cold meat and vegetables. At one end of the table, a woman in a deep grey dress with fine embellishment fiddled with a napkin, looking bored. To her right sat a man in a similar shade of grey, his embellishments not nearly as overt. Both wore crowns studded with those Fallen Star gems. The queen and king consort, then.

"My dear Lady Star," the queen said, reaching out a hand to me. I went to her and did my best to curtsey, though I wobbled slightly. I would have fallen had not Casimir rested a firm hand on my back, hidden by his own bow. "I am Raya, Queen of Baldarskiel, and this is my husband, Istir. I wish we had met before your accident, but we were on progress across Baldarskiel to our vassals. Still, I am pleased to meet you, now. There is so much to discuss!"

I murmured an, "Indeed," and sank gratefully into the chair held out by Casimir. Devereux sat across from me, and his sister sat beside him, her eyes watching me hungrily. The king clapped, and servants glided into the room, bringing with them steaming platers of food, completely disregarding the items that were already present. Before I could say otherwise, my plate was piled with some sort of meat drowned in a cream sauce, steaming vegetables seasoned in something orange, a pile of rice studded with what looked like raisins, and more that I couldn't name. Despite my hunger, I was suddenly certain I would be sick.

"Eat slowly. Very slowly. No one will care how much you eat, as long as you take consistent bites throughout the evening," Casimir advised under his breath, taking care to spread a napkin neatly in his lap. I did the same, nodding my gratitude.

"So, tell me Lady Star," Beatrice said, stabbing her fork viciously into her meat. "What do you think of the Temple? We'll have to arrange another visit for you."

"The Temple?" I asked. Was this the Temple she belonged to?

"The Temple of the Fallen Star, of course!" Beatrice smiled widely. "I know you haven't been able to go due to your accident, and all your training to get better, but surely you've been once, at least."

I glanced at Devereux with desperation. He coughed.

"Ah, yes. About the accident." He took a sip of some wine and looked at me with the same sort of desperation I'd just given him.

He hadn't told them? His parents? His sister? He hadn't told them I'd lost my memory and that it was unlikely to ever return?

"The Lady Astraea suffered a severe injury to the head at Starfall Meadow, as well as her other injuries," Casimir said, interjecting smoothly, as if he were just reporting on the weather. "Her memory has been impaired as a result."

The queen flinched. "Impaired?" she asked, voice cold.

"Gone," I said. "I woke in the healer's rooms with no memory at all."

Silence reigned over the room, no one daring to move. I thought about taking a long sip of the wine from the goblet before me, but decided against it. I needed my judgement, not the temporary relief that the wine would bring. Devereux studied his plate. Beatrice stared openly at me, her green eyes nearly predatory. The king seemed generally disinterested, except in his wife's reaction. Queen Raya flicked her gaze between Devereux and myself, mouth in a tight line.

"I am sorry to hear that," she said at last, and the room seemed to let out a collective exhale. "Lord Casimir tells me that you have been progressing well in your other recovery efforts."

"Yes, Your Majesty," I said.

"If you remember nothing, then I will have to bring you to a service at the Temple for the upcoming equinox," Beatrice said, smiling widely again. "It will be the most beautiful, as that's when the Temple is decorated for the celebration, and the people all wear their finest."

"Temple?" I finally asked again. If I was going to be involved, invited places, at the centre of everyone's attention—no matter how much I wished only to retreat back to the healer's rooms and sleep—then I needed to know what I was getting involved with. This was my role, after all.

"The Temple of the Fallen Star," Devereux said, rolling his eyes. Beatrice smacked his arm, and he winced. It seemed like such a normal interaction, one that siblings might share with ease. A sudden pang ached in my chest, though I didn't know why.

"Children," the king said on a sigh. Both the prince and princess straightened, suddenly the perfect picture of well-behaved royalty.

"The Temple of the Fallen Star was started after the first star disappeared, all those centuries ago," Queen Raya said. "It was begun as a means to help people follow the tenets that the star set out to guide our society, and to help her have a place to return to when she finally appeared again in this world. The temple also assists her Chosen Ones, providing them funds, guidance, knowledge, and the use of any magical acolytes in their order at the time. The Temple in Baldarskiel is, of course, considered to be the guiding light for the rest of Adhor, as we are those who helped the star when she fell. And it is to us that she entrusted her guiding words."

Beatrice nodded eagerly. "We teach people how to live a life appealing to the light of the stars, one detrimental to the greed and hunger of the void. More importantly, we watch the stars and wait for the right moments to act against the void. It wouldn't do to act during a time when the stars' power is at its weakest, now would it?"

I thought of that strange feeling that lived inside of me and reacted at the sight of the shadows in Casimir's eyes. If that was the power I possessed as Chosen One and not something more visceral or imaginary, then I doubt it had anything to do with the stars above. I think it was more interested in the shadow. The void.

"You will be fully healed by the equinox, will you not? Lord Casimir? What do you think?" Beatrice asked, waving her fork at him. He stiffened, then inclined his head.

"I think that the Lady Astraea is fully strong enough to do whatever she sets her mind to." He nodded at me, one of those quiet, mysterious glances. I tried to smile in return, but my mouth went dry. The equinox was a moon's cycle away, and I thought that maybe I could be fully mobile by then. But I would need many, many more months before I could be considered fighting ready. Ready enough to present to the people and give them a hope, no matter how distant, that I could help them against the void. Save them.

I reached for the goblet and downed half the wine, no longer caring about my judgement and remaining clear headed. It would be better to endure this conversation with a bit of distance.

"Yes, the equinox," the queen said. "It will also be the perfect time to publicly announce the betrothal."

I spluttered into my goblet. "Betrothal?"

"The marriage of the star's Chosen One to my son and heir, of course," the queen said. She smiled at me, more than a hint of cunning behind that look. "It will be magnificent, your union, and it will mean the strength of Baldarskiel for many generations to come."

I had barely eaten five mouthfuls of food, taking Casimir's advice, and yet in that moment, I knew it wouldn't matter. I was going to be ill. Before I could express my discomfort, Devereux stood. He rounded the table and bowed deeply, taking my hands in his. The unblemished right hand felt tingly, sweaty in his grasp. The burned left hand felt nothing at all.

"It would be my greatest honour, Lady Star, to ask for your hand in marriage, so that we may spend a life together, learning to love one another to the depths of our hearts. Together, we will lead Baldarskiel into a bright and glorious future, where the void is beaten back until the day the fallen star returns. Will you accept my proposal?" Devereux asked. His words were soft, smooth, and I felt a hitch in my throat that was dangerously close to illness. He did not meet my gaze, his eyes focused firmly on the band of jewels around my throat.

Being the Chosen One was one thing. I had been given that task by this star, bearing her power or whatever it was that marked me so that I might fight back the void. I was *destined* to fight the void, to save the people in its path. That was what I existed for.

Marrying Devereux was another thing entirely. I was meant to push back the void, not be the future queen of a country I couldn't even remember. I knew nothing beyond the walls of the healer's rooms and the halls I had taken to get here. I did not know a thing about politics, about the geography, about the people, about any of it. And Devereux! He was kind, yes. He did not seem to treat me any the different for my scars or my status, but I did not love him. I did not even know him!

I glanced at the queen, who watched with that same predatory gleam in her eye that Beatrice bore. The king looked on with mild interest, his wine goblet held casually in one hand. Casimir alone seemed calm, cold even. He looked away as our eyes met, and I felt the tightness in my throat even more.

Finally, I smiled, though the gesture was weak.

"Thank you, Your Highness. I am...extremely grati-fied at your proposal, and would be happy to accept."

What else could I have done?

The queen inclined her head in a subtle nod. Beatrice clapped. Even Devereux looked ridiculously happy.

I tried to swallow down the bile in my throat with another mouthful of wine. It didn't help. I couldn't eat another bite of food, and spent the rest of the dinner in a daze.

<h1 style="text-align:center">CHAPTER 5</h1>

"Hold the line!" The voice was firm, but there was an undercurrent of fear, like she knew that the order wouldn't be obeyed. I didn't know where I was; everything was shadow. There were only brief flashes of light, and the shouting.

"They're coming!" A new voice, male this time. He was panicked, holding none of the assurance of the woman.

"Torches at the ready!" The female was screaming now. In an instant, seven flashes of light filled the air, resolving into torches. The shadows parted around the warriors, all clad in black with white armour. The shadows growled, and I realised they were not shadows at all, but creatures. Terrible creatures, bastardisations of things that had once been natural. Long legs tipped with massive claws, articulated tails, some with horns, others with fangs or tusks. One that looked like a boar with unnatural spikes rising from its spine. Another that might have been a deer, its antlers razor sharp and its maw full of fangs. They were chattering at one another, their eyes glowing white and fevered, their energy frenetic.

Voidlings. A massive herd, and only seven Void Runners to stand against them.

And me. Why couldn't I move?

"Torches up!" the woman shouted. She was dark skinned with youth highlighting her every feature. Untried, untested, only the strength of her resolve and her pride keeping her people in line. The Void Runners raised their torches. The Voidlings screeched and skittered. One of the monsters darted forwards and tossed its head, catching the leftmost Runner with a horn. He screamed, then he died.

"Annalise—" one of the other women said, her voice high.

"Hold. The. Line." Annalise grit her teeth and glared. "We do as the star bade us. Keep the Voidlings at bay while she gathers her power."

Was that what I was meant to be doing? I tried to lift my hands and failed. I tried looking around and could not turn my head. I was frozen, a statue in the midst of the fray. The Voidlings moved around me as if I weren't even there, and the trees at my back seemed to hold me in place. I did not know how I had come to be there, only that I was.

"Any moment, now, Chosen One!" a man shouted, looking over his shoulder. But he wasn't looking at me. No, he looked at a figure shrouded in white, her features blurred *and uncertain. She raised her hands, palms glowing with unearthly power.*

Then, chaos. Another Voidling charged, its legs long and wolflike, its maw sporting terrible tusks. It broke through the line of Void Runners as easily as if it hadn't been there. None of their swords seemed fast enough to catch it, none of their defences strong enough to stop it. The Voidling latched its jaws around Annalise's arm, and the torch flew from her hands. It landed on the grass beside the Chosen One.

Fire burst forth. I felt a surge of power inside me at the sight, and then the flames roared. The Voidlings screamed in terror at the fire's approach, fleeing back to the Void Pool that had birthed them. The Void Runners were either dead or injured, unable to escape the fire. And the Chosen One?

She burned.

I felt the flames sear my face, my neck, my arm, as I held out a hand to stop them. The pain was blinding, but more than that was the knowledge that I had failed.

✦

I sat up, gasping for breath. The room around me was cool with night air that flowed in through the window. The skin on my face tingled, turning into numb emptiness where the burns were. I was sweating, shivering, yet I couldn't seem to move.

A nightmare. A memory. Both.

I had a face that I could place with a name.

Annalise, the brave woman who had tried to hold everything together while I failed. Who had died in agony.

I threw back the bedclothes and swung my legs over the edge of the bed, bracing myself as I stood. I'd been granted my own quarters a week ago, now that my body was healed enough I could walk without assistance. I was still weak, but every day I could do more and more on my own.

My burns were also declared as healed as they would get. Eugenie hadn't met my eyes when she informed me of that. The tightness in my skin was constant, and even though I could move my left arm and hand, the movements were often imprecise. I felt little pain in the markings on my skin. They were swirls and ripples forever melted into my skin. The scars would never be beautiful, but they were hardly something to be ashamed of.

Perhaps they were, I thought, if I had got them while being unable to do anything while the Void Runners died.

The room I now occupied had a window that was big enough for me to rest in, the cool night air a balm to my mind. Out there, the air was clear and fresh and open, instead of in the room where it seemed like I was only going to have my thoughts for company.

I shivered and pulled a dressing gown on, going to the door and slipping out before I could reconsider. I had taken to wandering the halls late at night, when I couldn't sleep. None of the guards or servants stopped me or did more than glance at me. I wondered if they even knew who I was, or if they had orders to ignore me, to not get in my way. I had got better at avoiding them entirely.

I made my way to the library, a place where I was sure to find a bit of warmth without being disturbed. But as I walked, I heard voices. Heated. Angry, even.

I stopped at the edge of a door, the wood left open just enough for me to see that the room was wide and open and empty but for two figures, swords clashing. One, I recognised: Devereux. He wore training clothes, but they were no less fine than anything else he owned. The other figure had their back to me, but a turn and a flash of hair suggested that it was his sister.

"Wise choice, accepting the Chosen One in marriage," she crooned, swiping her sword through the air with a practised aura of casualness. Devereux blocked with just as much ease, though he gritted his teeth.

"Did I have much of a choice? You announced the betrothal in the middle of dinner without consulting me first. I knew what was expected of me. Obviously you and Mother have been conspiring again," Devereux snapped. He thrust his blade forwards and nicked the edge of Beatrice's tunic. She laughed.

"Hardly conspiring!" A flurry of movement, and the two moved behind the door so that I couldn't see. I stayed still, listening.

"Of course you were conspiring," Devereux said. "Word got out about the Chosen One being here. We had very little time to waste after the accident, and only a couple of weeks afforded us for her to heal. Then, what, were the Council of Nobles demanding her presence? Their meetings begin again in three days, after all. Having her irrevocably bound to me in marriage would give them little influence over her, no matter what she or I think of the matter."

"My, my, after a life of tutoring, you finally begin to grasp the political schedule." There was a bout of metal striking metal. Neither sibling appeared to be holding back.

Beatrice continued. "Very well, dear brother, I will admit to conspiring for the betterment of Baldarskiel. You know as well as I that the void is spreading. Having the Chosen One here means a great deal for our country. Not to mention as a rallying point for the religion of our people. A living religious artefact, here? Altier will be a point of pilgrimage for generations. Consider the influence we will have!"

"But marriage?" Devereux sounded...disappointed. I swallowed down my nerves and continued listening. "She already lives in the palace. Surely—"

"Surely what? The Void Runners could easily have got hold of her, swayed her loyalty to them. Lord Casimir already has much of her time, as her new training master. The Ambassador to Cortaesi, can you imagine? Such a backwater country. And the other Void Runners are no better. The sons and daughters of nobles and wealthy merchants from across Adhor. As opposed to us, the true rulers, the royal family of the country that has stood between the void and the rest of the continent for time immemorial. Marrying her into the family will mean that all of your descendents will be starblooded, icons for the entirety of Adhor, even behind the veil of the void." Beatrice spoke with the fervour of someone who believed what she was saying without hesitation or reservation. It was that same tone she had used the other night when talking to me. Was it religious fervour or just a quest for power?

"Brother mine, the Temple can only do so much. We can influence people into living better lives, more appealing lives, but religious influence only goes so far when dealing with those outside the common horde. As heir to the throne, you are the most appealing prospect for our dear Chosen One. We have to claim her before she realises just how much power and influence she has. How much the people will do for her."

Devereux was quiet for a moment. "I am well

aware of the duty I hold to Baldarskiel. I would have preferred forewarning, though. That way I could at least..."

"At least what?" Beatrice laughed, then there was more metal clanging on metal. "Charm her? Woo her? My goodness, Dev, she's a broken, scarred shell of a person. Her magic isn't even fully restored. She should be *honoured* to be considered for such a match before she's even pushed back the void."

A hand dropped onto my shoulder, another going across my mouth and stifling any sound I might have made. I whirled and found Casimir standing before me. He wasn't wearing the armour of the Runners, so he must have been off duty. His hair was out of place, though, like he'd been running. His eyes were wary.

"You shouldn't be listening at doors," he murmured. "You might hear something unpleasant."

I pulled back, wrapping my arms around my waist. Casimir gestured to a hallway, and I nodded, following. Only when we had gone far enough away from the training room did I take a full breath. I wanted to wipe at my cheeks, brush away tears, but I wasn't crying. In fact, I wasn't feeling much of anything except disappointment.

"What are you doing wandering around at this hour?" Casimir demanded, folding his arms and glaring at me.

"It seems everyone is awake in the middle of the

night," I retorted. "You, Beatrice, Devereux. What, were you going to join in their conspiracy to control me?"

"I don't think I could control you if I tried, Astraea," Casimir breathed. He sighed and pinched the bridge of his nose. "It's not safe for you to be wandering around without an escort."

"Why not?" I demanded. "Because I might hear something about how people are manipulating me? Or because I'm such a valuable commodity, and you don't want me stubbing a toe in the dark?"

"Because the number of Voidlings wandering around has tripled in the last week."

I deflated. "Oh." The nightmarish memory of those terrible monsters filled my mind, and I hugged myself tighter. "Have they..."

"The palace walls remain intact, and Altier is so far unharmed, but some of the outlying villages have been attacked. The Void Runners are spread thin, especially with so many out of Baldarskiel, seeing to the void pools in other countries." Casimir leaned against a wall, and I realised that he looked weary. The dark rings under his eyes weren't due to the shadows that inked their way onto his skin or lived in his eyes; they were from exhaustion.

"Is there anything I can do?" I asked, my voice small. I was meant to be the Chosen One. I was meant to be helping these people fight against the void and its terrible creations. If my nightmare was any indication, I was doing a terrible job.

"I had hoped to give you more time before starting your training, in both combat and magic, but I fear that we have no time to spare."

I nodded. A part of me was relieved that the training would begin, and this terrible waiting would end. I would finally start to prove my use. And as more than just a political pawn. Casimir studied me, his mouth flat.

"Why did you accept Devereux's proposal?" he asked. I jerked, taking a step back.

"Why would you ask such a thing?" I snapped.

"You cannot love him. You barely know him."

I turned my head away. "I might not know him, *now*, but perhaps I did? We worked together for months before...and just because I don't remember doesn't mean we weren't friends. I'd rather marry a friend than..."

"You don't have to marry at all!" Casimir snarled, towering over me. "It's not a game, Astraea, marriage. It's a commitment, for life. Through better and worse, good and bad, right and wrong, you are stuck together."

"I know that!" Why would he think I didn't? Was I that flighty, that unstable? "I would never renege on my commitments."

Casimir snorted. "No, of course not."

I was suddenly exhausted, ready to fall back into my bed and pretend that this whole night hadn't happened. I shivered. Immediately, Casimir was there, wrapping his arms around me as though we'd done this a hundred times, as though we fit together perfectly. And we did, my head fitting neatly beneath his chin, his arms strong around my shoulders.

"I don't love him," I admitted. "I agreed because... because it was so sudden, and because how could I refuse? After all I've done, it was the only way I could prove that I was committed to this cause, to the future. Without Devereux and the royal family, I would be out on the streets without a coin to my name, weak and without magic and completely useless. This way, I can be useful. Even if I am little more than a pawn."

Casimir stiffened and pulled back, brushing a strand of hair away from my face. "After all you've done? Astraea—"

I shook my head. "Seven people are dead because of me! And I can't even remember them, except in my nightmares. I...How can I be a true Chosen One if that is the result of my efforts?"

He studied me, expression solemn, and a bit bemused. He didn't contradict me, nor try to make me feel better, and I was immediately grateful for that. I was so tired of people trying to make me feel better, about my injuries, about my accident, about all of it. They glossed over the pain like it wasn't there, wasn't relevant, and expected me to move forwards. Casimir just let it be.

"I'm going to bed," I murmured, brushing past him. His hand snagged my wrist.

"Astraea, wait," he said. I froze, every muscle tense. That spark of magic or acknowledgement flared where he touched me. After a moment, he released his hold. He did not look me in the eye. "We're...friends, aren't we?"

"Of course we are," I assured him. "You and Devereux are probably the only people I can be myself with. Whoever that may be."

I winced as soon as the words left my mouth. After hearing what Devereux and Beatrice had been saying about me, about their plans for me, and the only value being my usefulness as the Chosen One, I wasn't entirely sure I trusted Devereux any more. Then, what did I really know about any of these people, Casimir included? I had woken up from a nightmare into a world I didn't know, didn't understand, and couldn't remember, no matter how hard I tried.

"We are friends," I said, though I sounded more subdued. I wasn't sure I believed it.

Casimir nodded. "I'm glad."

There was a moment of silence and hesitation between us as we each waited for the other to speak, to fill the emptiness with something meaningful. Instead, I wrapped my arms around myself again and started back towards my bedchambers.

"Goodnight, Lady Astraea," he breathed behind me.

"Goodnight, Lord Casimir," I returned. I did not look back.

I tried to wander back to my chambers, but I must have taken a wrong turn on my search for the library earlier, because I found myself in a part of the palace I hadn't seen before. The halls were narrow and empty, like they hadn't been used in quite some time. The stone felt older, stronger, meant for defence rather than beauty. And, at the end of the corridor, there was a set of stairs, winding downwards at a steep angle, the steps so narrow that I could reach the wall on either side just by lifting my hands.

I paused. I should go back to bed, not explore, and certainly not if there were Voidlings about, as Casimir claimed. Then, he'd also said that none of them had breached the palace walls, and I wasn't really eager to return to the land of nightmares.

A tantalising scent rose from the stairwell, along with the slightest brush of coldness. I hesitated no longer, instead bracing myself against the wall as I forced my weak legs to carry me downwards. I was trembling by the time I reached the ground, my breath a little ragged. I'd pushed too hard, too soon.

No. I shook my head. I'd pushed just enough.

There was an old door at the bottom of the stairs, made of worn wood that was so ancient it had become practically as hard as the stone surrounding it. The hinges were iron and the handle little more than a latch. I lifted it, expecting the door to be locked. Instead, it swung open with only the slightest squeak. This door was used. Often.

I was struck first by the overwhelming scent of fresh air. Unlike the breeze that flowed through my windows, this was bigger, wider, somehow full of life. This door led to the outside. I hadn't been outside since before my memory vanished. I hadn't realised until then just how much I longed for the outside.

I took a single step into the yard, my eyes barely able to make out any shapes in the darkness. I could see the faint pinpricks of torchlight and arcane sconces on the wall some distance away, but the yard was nearly full dark. I took another step.

My toes sank into the ground, reminding me that I hadn't worn slippers. And thank the stars for it, because as soon as I touched the earth, an impossible sense of awareness flooded me. I knew I was standing on a bed of clover, that it stretched the entire span of the yard, except where other plants grew. Roses were in one corner, climbing over a trellis. A collection of herbs—yarrow, chamomile, mugwort, mint—grew along one wall, twisting and dominating the little yard. And near the roses were bushes of honeysuckle, the flowers already dropped, so late in the summer.

I knew the name of each plant that bloomed there. I knew where they were and how far apart they stood. I could hear them singing to me, just as I knew the paths that the earthworms had taken beneath my feet, just as I knew that the roots to an ancient and mighty oak tree that grew on the other side of a stone barrier by the roses were pushing their way into this yard. I knew that water pooled in a dip in the ground by the mint, and that a frog had taken up residence there.

I could feel everything.

I staggered backwards, my feet hitting the stone floor of the stairway landing. Immediately the awareness vanished, and I was left with nothing more than my own mind, my own thoughts, erratic as they were.

"Could it be...?" I whispered, a desperate hope taking root in my belly.

I put a tentative foot on the clover again, and my senses sprang to life once more. I heard the earth singing to me, every plant, every stone, every root. And it was magnificent.

We have been waiting for you, the roses seemed to say. I turned my head towards them and they reached for me, tendrils of their thorny stalks stretching into the air, blooms opening before my eyes.

You are here at last, was what I heard from the

herbs, all twisting and growing, leaves wide and twined amongst one another.

Now, things may begin, said the ancient oak as it leaned over the low yard wall. A single branch reached out and brushed some hair back from my face. I leaned into the embrace.

Magic.

I had magic.

After all this time, searching, wanting, waiting, *hoping* for a chance to be useful, more than the broken Chosen One, I finally found my magic.

CHAPTER 6

"Earth magic?" Casimir frowned. He had come to get me the next morning before the sun had even risen over the palace walls, so that I might begin my training. I had wrestled with how much to reveal to him on the walk to the training hall, a building off the east wing, across a courtyard. In the end, my magic decided for me; I could not cross the yard without getting grass tangled about my feet, without trees reaching for me and flowers blooming in my wake. It was subtle, so much so that no one seemed to notice until a gardener who had been plucking some thistles let out a startled yelp when their thorny blooms began to grow.

I'd quickly explained my midnight revelation to Casimir. He did not seem pleased by the situation.

"Is having earth magic not...not a good thing?" I asked.

Casimir considered while he wrapped his hands for combat training, the movements practised and fluid. I, on the other hand, was at a complete loss as to what to do with the wrappings that had been thrust at me by an assistant training master. The girl, perhaps twelve, studied me solemnly before reaching out and doing up the wrappings herself.

"Thank you, Eloise, you may go," he said once the girl had finished. "I will continue from here."

"Yes, Lord Casimir," the girl said, giving a bow and running off.

We were alone, and I could feel the emotions rolling off of Casimir in waves, though I didn't know if it was disapproval or confusion. I waited, fingering my simple linen skirt. If I concentrated, I could almost feel the whisper of the trees outside the heavy wooden doors.

Casimir finally spoke, making me jump. "It is well known that the Chosen One has wild magic rather than any sort of arcane talent. Wild magic being instinctive, intuitive, elemental, rather than the spells and framework of arcane potions and rituals."

I nodded. This had been explained to me when Eugenie had told me how neither wild nor arcane magic could heal me any further. She had been furious. I had been weary.

"So this is good," I prompted. "My earth magic. Right?"

Casimir winced. "I...do not know. The Chosen One is usually described as having magic over light and darkness, even fire and wind. All magic associated with the sky, rather than the earth. I...have never seen *you* use earth magic before."

I frowned. "How would you? You told me yourself that you never trained with me before, and none of the Runners who did are here to say otherwise."

And it was my fault.

Casimir stepped over to a bench and sat, his arms resting on his legs, showing off the strong lines of his back and shoulders, but also the fact that there were inky lines climbing up his spine, showing through the thin material of his shirt. My breath hitched, and something in my belly tightened, that same spark that responded to his shadows flaring.

"Astraea," he murmured, looking up at me. I wavered, something in his voice calling to me in a way that I didn't fully understand. When I didn't move, Casimir just sighed and started undoing his boots. "It's not impossible...I was hoping to train you in physical combat—or any physical activity, given the weakness of your muscles—before attempting to test your magic, since a stronger body can often help with magical control. But if your earth magic is responding so strongly just by you being outside, then we need to do the testing today."

I twined a strand of hair around my fingers. "Wha-what does magical testing entail?"

"I'll set up some obstacles bound by affinity spells. My arcane magic is reasonable, but I don't know how well this will work." Casimir rose and studied me for a moment. There was something deeper, there, as with all his looks. Like they held a weight I couldn't possibly fathom, but that he expected me to grasp. I felt again and again the frustration of having no memories. Maybe if I could remember, this testing wouldn't be necessary.

"I have earth magic, isn't that enough?" I asked.

"I just don't know the full extent of your power," was his response. Before I could ask more, he was across the open training space and calling for Eloise. She appeared, and after a few exchanged words, dashed off again. A few moments later, she returned with a bowl of water, then again with a candle, a pot of earth, and what looked like a ribbon on the end of a stick. The last was a simple clear stone, which she held with reverence. All of these items went into a circle. Casimir began to walk around the circle, murmuring under his breath. At each item, he paused and leaned down to brush his hand against the floor.

When he completed the circle, it flared into life, shining with a deep green mixed with a blue so dark

it was almost black. I could feel the power thrumming off the circle and instinctively took a step
backwards.

"Step into the centre of the circle, if you please,"
Eloise said. I hesitated, then closed my eyes and did
as she asked. Sparks flashed against my skin, making
my hair stand on end and sending shivers down my
spine. My left arm, though, was as numb as always,
even as I clenched my fingers into as much of a fist as
I could. I looked at Casimir and Eloise. The girl
nodded, looking eager. Casimir only watched.

"What do I do, now?" I asked.

"Turn towards the water," Eloise said. I did so.
"Now, reach out your hand."

I lifted my right arm at the same moment that
Casimir stomped his foot down on the spell before
the bowl of water. The liquid inside rose into the air
and rushed towards me, splashing over me before I
could draw a breath or make any move to turn away.

I spluttered. "What was that?!"

"No water magic," Eloise said, biting back a laugh.
I was half tempted to stick my tongue out at her, but
held back, the necessity of finding my magic weighing
down my good humour. The water had been *cold*. The
girl pointed towards the earth.

I turned towards it, lifting my arm again as
Casimir stomped once more, activating the spell. The
pot of earth exploded towards me, but this time, it

swirled around in a net of intricate patterns. Flowers, trees, leaves, the earth floated through the air, changing shapes and designs with ease. I knew that I was controlling it, but the magic felt effortless, as though I wasn't even thinking about it. I twitched my fingers, and the earth coalesced, coming together into a sphere that was so perfect it gleamed. A squeeze of my fist had the sphere compressing more until it fell to the ground as a stone.

Casimir stared at the stone, a muscle in his jaw twitching. He did not look at me, his attention fixed on the marble-sized ball of hardened earth.

"We already knew about the earth magic," Eloise said, "but your control is very good."

That was encouraging, especially given Casimir's lack of response. At least the apprentice to the training master thought I was capable. I straightened my shoulders.

"What's next?"

"Air," Casimir said, walking to the ribbon and streamer. He raised his foot and stomped, the spell crackling to life again. I raised my hand, but nothing happened except a wall of wind buffeted me, tangling my skirt around me and whipping strands of hair into my eyes and mouth. I brushed them back.

"No air, then," Eloise said, hiding a snicker.

It was fine, I told myself. I didn't need air magic, not when I had the earth whispering to me, singing me songs. I turned next to the unlit torch, and suddenly my palms grew sweaty. Cold tingles ran up my spine and I took an involuntary step backwards.

"I'm not sure I can do this one," I murmured, clenching my left hand close to my chest. Casimir blinked, and his expression softened for the first time that morning.

"It will not hurt you, I swear it," he said. "Upon everything that I am and stand for, it will not hurt you."

The vow settled like a weight on my shoulders, providing comfort.

I closed my eyes and nodded. He was right. This was just a test, a controlled situation where all the elements were at Casimir's command, bound by the arcane spell and its constraints. This wasn't the terrible landscape of my nightmares, nor the memory of pain that accompanied my first waking into this world.

I opened my eyes just at the moment that Casimir's foot met the ground. The torch flared to life in a burst of white and orange and red and blue. The flames leaped eagerly into the air, burning through the wood and pitch of the torch faster than they should have. Then, in a riot of twisting tongues, they turned to me.

Casimir let out a wordless cry, the flames surging

higher and faster. They lunged, almost with intelligent intent, towards me.

I screamed, my ruined left hand swinging upwards to cover my face even as I fell to my knees. I squeezed my eyes closed, whimpering, preparing to relive that impossible pain once more.

"Astraea," Casimir said, his voice awed. "Open your eyes."

I did so.

That part of me which feared turned to ice. The flames were dancing around me, taking the shape of a hound, then a bird, then a cat, leaping and gambolling with joyous abandon around my hands. I took a shaking breath, and the flames drew closer. On the exhale, they swirled away.

"You have fire magic," Eloise said, words quiet. "That shouldn't be possible. Fire and earth are opposing magics. You really are the Chosen One."

Immediately, the flames snuffed out, as if the air had suddenly vanished. I lowered my hand and swallowed down that icy fear. I had fire magic. That shouldn't be possible. If it were, then why...I brushed a hand along the burns along my neck and face. I had fire magic, so why had I burned?

I had the sudden, stifling urge to flee, to run far, far away and get lost in the forests and fields. A strange creaking sounded from outside, and the windows darkened slightly, revealing that the trees had stretched their branches over the openings. I wrapped my arms around myself and quietly pleaded with the trees to retreat.

"I'm okay, I'm not hurt, everything is alright," I murmured over and over. "Everything is fine."

"Astraea," Casimir said. I looked up at him, desperate. Instead of a helping hand, or a comforting look, all I saw was his finger pointing at the last test, the clear rock. "One more."

"I can't," I breathed. "I *can't*."

"You can, and you will." He said it with such certainty, like he'd seen me do so much more than this. Like he had faith in me. With trembling limbs, I pushed myself to my feet. Took a breath. Turned towards the stone.

Casimir raised his foot one last time and brought it to the ground with a defiant *crack*. I threw both hands into the air.

Light flared from the rock, a beam so bright that it was blinding. I shielded my eyes and willed the light to dim, to quiet the hum that surrounded it. The light merely laughed at me.

You think you can control us, it crooned, dancing through the air like it was a solid thing, a living thing. I grit my teeth. None of the other tests had felt like this.

Obey, I commanded silently. The light laughed again, cruel and vibrant.

Why should we obey one such as you? It asked. Its motes danced closer, swirling around me much as the fire had done, but without my control.

Because, I am the Chosen One. I clapped my hands together and the light let out a quiet shriek, suddenly pushed back to the stone that was its source, even as shadows appeared over my shoulders, driving the light away.

Sweat began to drip down my forehead, stinging my eyes. I let the tears fall as I gritted my teeth and demanded that the light, and its shadowy counterparts, obeyed me. They did. Both of them.

The light became a woman, no bigger than my thumb, dancing with abandon. The shadows coalesced into a man of the same size who danced with her. They twirled and twined, leaping, turning, their movements becoming more and more frantic until finally, they collided.

My vision filled with blinding bright light followed by impossible blackness. I collapsed to the floor, my knees taking the brunt of the impact. Then, with the sound of the light still laughing in my ears, I succumbed to the silence of darkness.

When I woke, my head was splitting in a headache. I groaned and pressed a hand to my forehead. Without even opening my eyes, I knew I was lying on a hard surface and that someone's hands were dabbing my face and neck with a damp cloth.

I opened my eyes and found Eloise leaning over me, grinning. "You're awake," she said. "She's awake!"

A moment later, someone was helping me to sit up far too quickly. I pushed away, the room spinning. "Slowly," I murmured.

"Stars above, Lady Astraea, you scared us to death." Devereux. What was he doing here?

"Where am I?" I murmured.

"Still in the training hall," Casimir responded, his voice alone an island of calm. "You were only unconscious for a few minutes."

A few minutes. That was good. Right? I looked around now that the room had stopped spinning. Devereux was kneeling before the bench where I sat, looking concerned and flustered. Eloise rocked on her heels behind him, smiling with that cunning look only children have. Casimir sat by my feet, just watching me.

"That...stuff with the light, and the shadows," I started, licking my dry lips. "What was that?"

"Proof," Casimir said in a flat tone. For a moment,

I could have sworn that anger coloured his words, but that didn't make any sense. Why would he be angry?

"Proof indeed!" Devereux said, reaching out and taking my hand. He pressed his lips to it, eyes shining with interest. I had to remind myself that he was my betrothed, that I didn't need to recoil at the look in his eye. "You are truly the Chosen One, not that there was any doubt. But such a display of magic has never before been seen—well, not since the last Chosen One, I'm sure. That was generations ago, and no one could have imagined how strong you would be!"

Strong? Yes, I supposed control over two elements and the light and dark that was demanded of a star reincarnated would be considered strength. And yet, it wasn't enough to save those seven Void Runners who had come with me on our first mission. Where was my strength then? It didn't make sense, and gripped my heart like a vise.

Devereux grinned up at me. "We'll plan a ball immediately to celebrate. Your magic and our betrothal. It will be magnificent!"

"A ball?" I frowned. "Shouldn't I be training so I can fight against the void? Doesn't that take precedence over our, ah, betrothal?"

I remembered the words he had spoken to his sister when he thought I wasn't around, wasn't listening. I was nothing more than a pawn to him, and I accepted that. But wouldn't a pawn be more useful after completing its task? Would I not be more revered, and therefore more valuable, after I had pushed back the void? Surely I had time before the wolves of politics and religion and power came for me.

"That will take a great deal of time," Casimir said, once again with that hint of some dark emotion in his voice. Yet his expression was perfectly calm. "Surely one ball will not derail your training, especially as you are still weak from your injuries. You will take time to recover your full strength. A ball will distract you from the... slowness."

I didn't want to be distracted. I wanted to avenge the Void Runners who had leapt into danger for me. I wanted to prove that I wasn't a danger. A burden.

Instead, they wanted to parade me about like a pretty bauble, when I could be doing so much more. I didn't understand, and I didn't like it.

"Beatrice and I will plan the entire thing. We'll do it on the equinox, after the ceremony at the Temple. It will be magnificent. A harvest festival and betrothal ball on the same day." Devereux looked up at me like I was the world, like he actually loved me. When I didn't say anything, I saw a flicker of doubt and frustration in his eyes. It vanished a moment later as he bowed his head to kiss my hand again.

"You need not worry about a thing except your train-ing, my Star."

I nodded. What else could I do? Devereux squeezed my hand, then rose and strode off without a backwards glance. Presumably to go tell his family about my magic and this new ball.

"Be careful, Astraea," Casimir murmured. He shot a look at Eloise, who squeaked and ran off, ever obedient to this Void Runner, this master of his craft. I felt her absence keenly in the realisation that I was alone with Casimir and that something had closed off between us during my testing. I didn't know what. Or why.

"If you mean Devereux, then I am fully aware of what I'm getting into," I snapped. "I know what betrothal to him means."

"I wasn't referring to the prince," was his heated response. Casimir rose and loomed over me, his eyes flickering again with those shadows. They called to the ones that I controlled, I realised, as well as the light that was its opposite. I could feel the magic rising in me like it had during the test. I immediately tamped down on it, crushing the urge to let it loose and see what happened.

"Then what do you mean?" I asked. "I am doing everything that is asked of me, am I not?"

"Oh, indeed you are, Chosen One." The words were spoken with bite, not quite derision but close.

Casimir leaned close, his lips brushing my ear, sending waves of heat through me. "I don't know what game you're playing, Astraea, but you had best be careful. I won't let people get hurt, not again, not like last time."

Then, faster than I could catch my breath, he was gone. I sank onto the bench, my legs no longer stable beneath me.

Last time.

He had been there when I went out with those seven Void Runners, despite saying otherwise. He knew what really happened. He had confirmed that it was truly my fault.

And he wasn't going to let me put people at risk again, even if it meant defying me. All his talk of being friends, was that just so he could get close to me and keep me from making another, terrible mistake?

I wrapped my arms around myself and trembled, now aware—too aware—of the magic living inside me and begging to be released.

CHAPTER 7

"Lift your arms up." This was approximately the seven-hundredth time that Eloise had scolded me, but the young girl was as patient as ever with my fumbling. She had her black hair tied up in a neat braid, and wore a dress much like mine, so that she could show me how to move in it while fighting. Presumably, I would also be given training clothes and armour at some point, but as Beatrice had reminded me the other day, no one knew when I would be expected to fight, and I needed to be able to do so competently in both official fighting garb and a gown encrusted with gems. Just as I was relegated to a practise sword, lighter of metal and blunted, as opposed to any real weapon.

By the look in her eye, I fully believed that Beatrice never expected me to fight at all, just to use my magic against the void. And even that could be delayed until after I'd proven my use to the royal family and the Temple. I was grateful to them for taking me in, for putting up with the reality of my failures, but I did not deny that there was a seed of bitterness in my stomach at their manipulation of me.

Thankfully, aside from one lunch with him and Beatrice, Devereux hadn't been around this past week, too busy planning his ball and telling everyone about my magic. He didn't have to bear the brunt of my temper. No, that was reserved for myself. And the hurt silence I directed at Casimir.

"Higher!" Eloise snapped. I complied, lifting my arms higher and thereby raising the point of the practise sword up into the air. My right arm was weak, but my left was practically useless in carrying and lifting. The muscles were not only atrophied and unstable, but the burns deadened so much sensation in the arm that it took active concentration to make it comply.

Eloise paced before me, nodding. "Good. Good. Your stance is decent, and for all that you don't even know if you've held a sword, your grip is reasonable. I can work with this, if we ever get strength back into your arms. Lower your sword."

I did so, gasping. Such a simple thing. I'd been raising and lowering the sword for an hour, now, and I was trembling, drenched with sweat, and wavering where I stood. "Please tell me we're done," I practically begged the girl.

"Lord Casimir had to go do patrols, and he put me in charge of your training for the day," Eloise reminded me. She lifted her chin. "I take that task seriously, even if you do not."

I closed my eyes and took a deep breath so I wouldn't snap at the young apprentice Runner. The magic that I'd awakened at the testing roiled within me, responding to the slightest of my emotions. It was mostly the earth and the fire, the former which responded in attracting all the plants in the immediate vicinity to me, and the latter which I dared not explore. The light and shadow were thankfully silent.

"I *am* taking this seriously," I assured Eloise once I had got the magic under control. "But I am also about to collapse."

The girl hesitated, then sighed. "Alright. A quick break. But then we're going to practise the basic fighting forms."

I staggered over to the bench and sat, my legs trembling. My arms tingled, and I was certain that they would never function again, at least not until Eloise thrust a ladle of water into my line of sight. I drank eagerly, dipping it back into the bucket twice more before I was satisfied. Then, I leaned back against the wall and groaned.

"You're not what I expected," Eloise said. I raised

my brows. "You're the Chosen One. I mean, yeah, you have some impressive magic, but you're so...so..."

"Weak?" I asked, the bitterness in my voice sharp. The girl flinched.

"It's true that you can't fight at all," she said, "but that's fixable. No, you're so closed off. It's like you don't want people to see the real you, like you don't want to be at the centre of attention at all. Like you're afraid of people, when it's the void that's the problem. You're like a frightened rabbit."

Eloise's words were frank, honest, perhaps because she was young and her training master hadn't yet taught her otherwise, or perhaps because it was just her nature. Either way, I didn't deny what she said. I just shrugged, earning a twinge of protest from my muscles.

"Ever since I woke up with no memory of anything, I've had a difficult time discerning what is true. About me, about other people, all of it. Everything I know has been told to me. I've experienced none of it. I guess I just want to know what everyone's motivations are, what part they expect me to play. I don't know what I think about all of this," I waved my hand at the training room, though I meant the palace beyond as well. "I just don't remember any of it, so how can I trust that it's true? How can I know that *I* am true?"

"Lord Casimir wouldn't lie to you," Eloise said

immediately. I smiled, but it was barely there. "It's true! Master Linwood says that Lord Casimir is the best Void Runner we have because he's a good man, not just a good Runner."

"That is quite the compliment," I murmured. The trouble was, I doubted his word most of all. The Queen and King were easy to read; they wanted to control me for my influence as the Chosen One, as someone people would rally around and behind. As long as they could control me, they were happy, because I could bring unity and power to Baldarskiel. Beatrice was an easy read, as well. She cared about appearances, and would never say anything controversial to my face, but when I was turned away, she touted me as only a pawn, an object. To her, I was a thing to be used for the sake of the Temple. At least her parents saw me as a person.

Devereux, too, I understood. He was doing his duty as best he could, while also trying to make the most of a situation that was not his doing. I did not think he loved me, as he claimed, nor did I think that he cared to spend the rest of his life with me. But it was his duty, and he would do it for the sake of his people. He was trying to make the most out of a difficult situation, and I was glad to be his friend.

Casimir, though...

He of the shadowed eyes and the words that cut straight to the heart of the matter without revealing more than a sliver of information. He still had not confronted me about the dead Runners, about what he knew, about how he had seen me fail so spectacularly. Sometimes, when we were alone, I could feel him watching me with a weighty interest. And yet, he was perfectly polite, friendly even. I felt comfortable around him. That was why I kept my guard up, because that sort of comfort would surely prove dangerous.

"I don't even know how old I am," I admitted to the girl. She screwed up her face and looked at me. I felt my skin flush; what was I doing, telling things like this to a child?

"I think you're about as old as High Priestess Beatrice, and she's two years younger than Prince Devereux," Eloise said. Oddly enough, it made me feel better. It was a reference point, a place to start. I didn't know where I came from, if it was Altier or some other town in Baldarskiel, or if it was beyond the void, or anything. I didn't know if I had parents or siblings or if I was alone in the world. I knew nothing, and therefore anything I might have had—family, friends, a home—didn't really exist. Except now, I had a general idea of how old I was.

I smiled at the girl. "Thank you. Now, if you're going to try and beat me into submission, we may as well begin. My muscles are going to freeze up completely if I continue to sit here."

Eloise beamed at me and leaped to her feet. Over the next few hours, she drilled me through the basic fighting stances and I did my best to follow without collapsing. She deemed I wasn't a complete failure, but I needed a great deal of training. I thought that was a generous statement.

By the time I was done with maiming my body for the day, Eloise had worked me until my body felt like water. The stairs to my room felt daunting, and I stood at the bottom, wondering if I could just sleep there.

"Lady Star." Devereux stood at the top of the stairs, his finery, for once, subdued. He wore black with no embellishments, no jewels, nothing. Just black, and one ring on his left hand. He looked, frankly, like he was up to something. "Are you well?"

"I've been training all day," I said. "The stairs were an obstacle I had forgotten."

A cheeky smile broke out on his face, and Devereux easily jogged down the stairs to stand beside me. "Then let me offer my assistance. I am at your service, though if you need me to carry you, I will be considerably slower. Alas, I am built more for good looks than physical feats."

I scoffed. "I think I can manage." Maybe.

He held out his arm, and I leaned on it more than I would like while climbing the stairs. Halfway up, I was so exhausted that I cast about for anything to distract me. "Are you planning on sneaking out?"

Devereux froze, causing me to stumble. I managed to catch myself on the wall, but he just stood there. His face had gone pale. "H-how did you...?" he breathed.

"Your clothes. They're nothing like what you normally wear. I assumed it was so you wouldn't be recognised. That, and I was told you would be in the library all evening, and we weren't required to dine together. The library is in the other direction from the training hall, so you coming down these stairs seemed unlikely." I pulled myself up several more stairs, and only then did Devereux follow after me. He licked his lips and smiled, the look hardly convincing.

"You won't tell anyone, will you?" he asked in a hushed voice.

"What good would that do me?" I asked. My words came out colder than I expected. Devereux either didn't notice, or didn't care. He just squeezed my hand tightly.

"Thank you. Really, thank you."

I stared at his hand in mine until he let me go. Then, I looked up at him. He was nervous. Afraid, even. That I would tell? Or of where he was going?

"What are you going to do?" I asked. He closed his eyes and shook his head.

"I'd rather not say."

"Devereux," I chided. "We are not lovers, despite our betrothal. I know full well that I am nothing more than a pawn to your parents and your sister. That does not mean we cannot be friends."

Devereux flinched. He leaned back against the wall. His entire body slumped, his shoulders falling and his eyes staring at the floor. He licked his lips again. "I...I am going to Runner's Landing. There's a, ah, warehouse there where the Runners keep stores apportioned from each trade journey across the void for times of emergency."

I studied him for a moment and realised that he wasn't going there to check on the stores. No, he was going to steal them. "Why? Surely as the Crown Prince you could—"

He shook his head. "I cannot. The Runners won't allow the royal family access to the stores. And even if I tried, my mother would strip me of all my authority. I barely have any as it is. I'm allowed to participate in the Council of Nobles, but my vote doesn't count towards the royal family, only the lands I inherited from my grandfather. And that's little more than a barony. Beyond that, I preen and I prance in front of crowds to spout some agenda that my mother has deemed appropriate. Or I do good works at the Temple of the Fallen Star, under the watchful eyes of my sister."

He lifted his eyes to mine, pleading. "There are people *starving*, Lady Astraea, because of these new voidling attacks. The void perimeter is shrinking and there are void pools opening up closer and closer to settlements. The voidlings are growing more bold. Twenty families have been injured, or killed. Farms have been ransacked, livestock slaughtered. People are fleeing for Altier, but we just aren't prepared for such a rise in population. My mother refuses to dip into the royal stores, saying we might need them before..."

I knew exactly what he was saying, hinting. That I'd supposedly had six months before now to train and practise with my magic, and that ended in ruin. Now I had to start over, and I had to be better, do better. The next time I faced the void might be the last time. It would be awhile before I was even remotely prepared to face the void, and if the people were already being pushed from their farms, then food might be a considerable concern. To deny it to starving people now, though, seemed harsh.

"Surely, the Runners would distribute the food if they were asked," I suggested. Casimir, at least, seemed to be inclined to listen, and he was a Runner of the First Order. I was unfamiliar with their rankings, but surely that was significant.

Devereux scoffed. "The Runners will break out the stores at exactly the right moment to make them look the heros and sway public interest in their favour. They want to wait. But there are people starving *now*!"

I shuffled, my legs protesting the movement. "Perhaps you could ask Lord Casimir about—"

Devereux fixed me with a cold look, one that was almost disappointed. "Casimir is a good man, Lady Astraea, but he is still loyal to the Void Runners. They have made their position about the royal family clear; we are not to interfere in their business. If there were another way, surely I would have done it? Perhaps you should keep to matters of your understanding and stay out of political games that are beyond your ken."

Temper flared in me, my magic rushing to respond. I shoved the eager flames and patient earth back down, before they could escape and wreak havoc. I didn't know the political games because I had no memories, not because I was incapable of understanding. If people bothered to explain things to me, I was certain I could help. No. I shook my head. That was not my role. I was the Chosen One. My enemy was the void. That was all.

"I'm sure your efforts will be appreciated," I murmured, taking a step back. "I will not report you. Not for trying to help your people while I...prepare to fight the void."

While I dithered and delayed after my last failure, for that seemed like all I was doing.

"Not even to Casimir?" Devereux pressed. I frowned. "I know you two are friends. He's training you, after all. And he's a decent sort, but he is a Void Runner, and they're not always out for the good of the people."

What could I say to that? Every side was accusing the other of trying to use me, trying to manipulate the situation so that they came out on top. Eloise said Casimir was a good man. Devereux said he was just as selfish as the royal family. Casimir did not seem keen on revealing anything of himself or what he knew of me and my failings. Perhaps he was waiting to see if I made things worse. I didn't know who to believe any more. At least Devereux was honest. Mostly.

"Go, Devereux," I murmured. "I'll say nothing."

He smiled—genuinely, this time—and ran back down the stairs, disappearing around a corner before I could call out and ask if he wanted my help. It was a foolish thought, anyways. I was weak and exhausted. My magic was unpredictable. And I owed a debt to the people to work against the void and end this predicament before it got worse. Gallivanting about at night, releasing stores and subverting the queen and the Runners, that would hardly help against the void. No, that required training. Constant training.

Maybe, I thought, I could work with the palace gardeners to grow more food. That way I'd be practising my magic, and Devereux could distribute the excess. If, of course, the queen allowed it. It seemed at least a tangible way to help the people of Altier, which seemed more useful than being hidden away until I pushed the void back.

Thoughts of the outside world swirled in my head as I made my way back to my chambers. I had barely been allowed in the gardens, especially with my unstable earth magic calling for every plant in the vicinity. My entire life consisted of the stones beneath my feet and the walls of the palace. I knew the training hall, the palace, and nothing else.

What did the rest of the world even look like?

"Just another thing that my actions stole from me," I snarled to myself.

"What do you mean, my dear?"

I whirled, having barely reached my chamber door. Queen Raya was walking down the hall, resplendent in a dress of green silk studded in gold. Her hair was wrapped in a pearl net and it looked like she had Fallen Star gems on every finger. I quickly cobbled together a curtsey, my legs weak and unstable.

"Your Majesty," I murmured.

"Rise, Lady Star," she said, stepping up to me and tapping me under my chin. "I've come to dine with you. My servants informed me that you were training all today, so I thought I would come to you instead of having you come to me. After all, we are to be family once you marry my son."

I nodded, swallowing back my discomfort at the sharpness of her smile. "Of course, Majesty. Please, come in."

Queen Raya swept into my rooms with a small sniff, taking in the simple decor with a haughty glance. She settled at the table near the window, and servants began swarming immediately. They cleared the table of my candlesticks and few books —poetry, mostly—spread a tablecloth down, and set out plates and cutlery before I could do more than walk into the room. Trays with food were heaped down, then the servants bowed as one and departed.

"Sit, sit! No need to wait," Raya said, already serving herself a cut of meat. I sat and prepared my plate, knowing I needed to eat to keep up my strength over the days to come. My appetite, though, was gone.

"Now," the queen said, smiling serenely at me, "what were you saying about something being stolen from you?"

I nearly choked on a cooked plum. "Oh, only that, um, my memory. Since I've been awake, I haven't been outside the palace, and I don't remember what the outside world is like. Altier. Baldarskiel. It's a mystery."

I tried to sound cheerful, but the truth felt like ash in my mouth. The queen studied me intently for a moment, her eyes lingering on my burns, then she nodded.

"Yes, I can see how that would be distressing. And it should be remedied immediately!" She skewered a piece of squash with her fork. "I had thought you and Devereux would go on a grand tour after the equinox, as a celebration of your announcement to some of the outlying provinces. But with the ball, everyone will be coming here, so there's really no need. However, I agree that you should get out, see Altier, meet the people. Perhaps a parade? No, too gaudy."

"If I may, Your Majesty," I said, trying not to hunch my shoulders. "Why not just a day out? Shopping, perhaps. Or a tour of the city, so I can see the historical monuments and the places of import."

Raya's eyes lit up, her smile turning eager. "Yes, indeed! A tour! You can visit the various quarters of the city, spend some coins at the best merchants, spread goodwill throughout the populace. It will do them good to see you as Chosen One, even before they know you to be their future princess. My son told me you were clever. I see now that he was absolutely right."

I smiled and murmured my thanks. Somehow,

though, this victory didn't feel like a good thing. The thought of going out into a mysterious world, full of people I'd never seen or known, had my stomach churning anxiously. I was eager, yes, but also afraid. I didn't know why. We ate in silence for a bit longer, then the queen asked about my training.

"I've had several little birdies tell me how impressive your magic is," she said. "As you may know, the Council of Nobles is now in session until the end of the harvest, and I thought you might like to meet them. Perhaps arrange a demonstration of your magic, too, so they can be assured of your status. After all, we want very much to prove that the void is truly no threat don't we?"

"As you say." I pushed my food around on the plate. I needed to eat, but I couldn't bring myself to chew, to swallow, not with the queen looking at me like that. Like I'd just given her everything she wanted and more.

"Perfect. Tomorrow, a tour of the town, and the day after, a meeting of the Council. You'll do fine, Lady Star. I know it."

With the alternative being another catastrophic failure, I didn't have much of a choice.

CHAPTER 8

"That seems like a lot of people," I said, coming to a halt just outside the front steps of the palace. Amidst the cultivated gardens that still sang to me and reached for me, despite my tamping down the magic, there was a carriage surrounded by guards, some wearing the silver armour of the royal family, others wearing the Void Runner ivory over black. I counted ten in total, not including Casimir, who was standing closer to the steps. To me.

"Mother is being cautious," Devereux said, taking my arm in his as he led me down the steps. "She doesn't want us getting hurt, what with all the voidling attacks."

Neither one of us had mentioned his activities of the night before, and it hung between us like a scythe. He seemed better able to handle the tension, with relaxed posture and self-assured expression. My shoulders, though, were tight and the back of my neck prickled.

"Surely the voidlings only attack at night." Even I knew they were repelled by light and wouldn't emerge in the daylight.

Devereux cast me a glance and looked away, a muscle in his jaw tightening.

"Oh," I said. "She wants to protect her commodity."

"I wish you wouldn't talk of yourself that way," Devereux sighed. "It's hardly fair."

"It is how your mother, father, and sister see me. You, too, on occasion." I nodded politely to Casimir as he joined our party, his expression set in solemnity and caution. Devereux winced. He handed me up into the carriage, where I was joined by the two men.

"You really don't mince your words, do you?" Devereux asked. Casimir raised his brows at this, but said nothing, only looking between the two of us, mouth in a thin line.

"What point would that serve?" I retorted, my temper having me speak before common sense could curb my tongue. "You wanted to be friends. Would you rather I hide my thoughts behind polite masks?"

The prince sighed again and slumped into the carriage seat, running his hand over the green velvet cushions. "No. You're right. I don't *mean* to see you that way, and I will try to do better."

I nodded, my throat tight. Looked out the window as the carriage started to lurch forwards. Then, "If it makes you feel better, I occasionally see you as a means to an end."

Devereux winced again, the motion barely visible out of the corner of my eye. "It really doesn't."

I flushed. "Oh. Sorry."

Casimir chuckled quietly, and I would have drawn him into the conversation, just to save myself some of the awkwardness, when the carriage passed beyond the gates of the palace walls. We were moving slowly, the horses keeping a measured pace so that the guards could keep up. It gave me plenty of time to see the world around me, and I was entranced.

The palace was finely sculpted, even if it was a monument better suited for defence than beauty. There were intricate details in the stonework, seen in the gargoyles above stairwells, or the ivy carvings in the lintels above doors. There were tapestries artfully arranged to provide both warmth and decoration. Rugs, paintings, statues, sculptures were all present, designed to make a fortress into a palace. All of this was encircled by gardens of lush greenery and cultivated splendour, caged by a wall of stone that had withstood ages, and would withstand countless more.

The city of Altier, on the other hand, was stunningly chaotic. The roads were the only thing about the place that seemed planned. Everything else was cobbled together from stones or mudbrick or wood and thatch. There were buildings leaning up against one another to hold themselves up. Clotheslines stretched across streets and narrow alleys, strewn with washing. There were patches of greenery between houses, springing up into overgrown vegetable gardens and herb patches, some with chickens, others with pigs, some with nothing more than natural beauty. Houses were thrown together next to what were obviously shops, delineated by a single sign out front. There were pop-up carts of twisted wood on several corners, selling pasties and roasted nuts. There was no order, no logic, no reason. Only colour and chaos. It was *magnificent*.

I stared openly at the people walking by, wearing their dyed wools and linens. The women wore layers of skirts, some tucked up while they did washing by a well, others neatly pleated that swayed as they walked. The men wore tunics and hose, or loose breeches and shirts, some had doublets, others jackets. All, whether young or old, neat or unkempt, rich or slovenly, had colour. Everywhere.

And the people themselves! Those in the palace were of such a kind. The guards, whether men or women, were physically intimidating and fit. The servants were lean and slunk through the halls in an attempt to be invisible. The royalty all had their shoulders straight, their chins high, their steps paced with purpose. Here in Altier, though, I saw every sort of person I could imagine. Dark skin, brown skin, light skin, everything in between. Postures that were so straight they belonged in a tree; others were so bent the person could barely toddle forwards. There were large people, small, crooked, those with missing limbs or who had obviously suffered a pox at some point in their life. It was myriad, and I was enthralled.

"What do you think?" Casimir startled me enough that I jumped, pulling my head back from the window.

"It's so…"

"Loud?" Devereux offered.

"That, but it's so full of life," I replied, unable to keep my gaze away from the city. "Everything in the palace is structured, from the way I dress, to where I spend my time, to the people who walk the halls. Here, it's just so…free."

There was silence following my words, and I tore my gaze from the window to see both Casimir and Devereux staring at me. Casimir with a quiet sort of disappointment, Devereux with anger.

"Lady Astraea—" Casimir started.

"Don't you see the poverty?" Devereux snapped. "The beggars in the streets? The people who fight over the coins tossed into a sacred fountain, just so they can afford a scrap of meat this month? Do you not see the whole families who are living in tents and shanties, who have no proper home? Or do you just see people, happy as can be, *proud* to live at the foot of the royal palace, where the Chosen One resides."

I recoiled, backing into the corner of the carriage. A glance out the window told me that none of the guards had heard, or if they had, they didn't care. Devereux just glared at me, fuming.

"How do you not see?" he demanded.

I didn't know. I didn't have an excuse. Upon closer inspection, I saw exactly what he was talking about. I saw how thin some of the people were, their cheekbones jutting out and their bodies shivering despite the relatively warm day. I saw how dirt lingered in the roads, despite their proximity to clean greenery and gardens. I saw how wary people were, walking with knives at their belts and eyeing their fellow Altians with unease.

I hadn't known that this wasn't normal for the city. It was all new to me, a place I had never been and could never have imagined, because all the memories I had were dust.

"I've never seen a city before," I murmured, a defence only to myself.

"How could you have *not* seen a—" Devereux sucked in a breath, then he was suddenly there on the bench beside me, reaching for my hands. I stiffened. "Stars above, Lady Star, I'm so sorry. I didn't realise that...that this was all new to you. You didn't know."

I nodded, a tacit acceptance of his apology. The shine of the city had worn off, though, and looking out the window only brought me distress. I had wanted to see Altier to know the world in which I lived. I had wanted to know something more than the walls of the palace. Well, it seemed I knew it, now, and I wasn't even allowed to see the good in it. Instead, it just made me sad.

The carriage halted after a few more streets, and the door was opened by an older woman in the Void Runner armour. She had dark skin and lines around her eyes, which were deep and wary. Her white hair was pinned back in a tight braid; her hands were scarred when they reached up to help me out of the carriage.

"Thank you," I said. The woman, to my chagrin, bowed.

"My pleasure, Lady Star." She took a step back, falling into formation once more. My stomach clenched.

"Welcome to Altier," Casimir said in a formal tone. "This is the Trade Quarter, where you will find most of the merchants, though it is said that some in Mist Haven, to the north west of here, are the better craftsman. Across the river is Runner's Landing, where the headquarters to the Void Runners are located, as well as most of our training halls and our academy for young Runners candidates. To the north east on this side of the river is the Dark Mire, and across the river from that, you have North Ward, where most of the people make their homes."

He pointed in each direction as he spoke, indicating buildings off in the distance that I could barely see. The river was nothing more than a sliver of brightness amongst the houses, and I wondered how big Altier was. Then, I wondered something else.

"Where is Starfall Meadow?" I asked.

Devereux paled. Casimir's hand fell to his side. "To the south, wrapping behind the palace walls."

The place where I had failed so catastrophically was so close. I was struck by a sudden desire to see it. To see if the scorch marks from the lost battle remained.

Devereux took my arm a moment later with a sort of desperation that told me he wanted nothing to do with my unvoiced plans. "Come. We should visit some of the merchants here. Perhaps you can have a dress made up for the equinox ball."

There was nothing to do but be swept up in his plans. I was taken from store to store, surrounded by guards and Runners. People gave us a wide berth, but they stared. They stared and gathered, congregating in small groups and watching our movements with intensity. No one got close enough to hold a conversation, but I could still feel their need burning into my shoulder blades almost as strongly as the fire that had scarred me. The shopkeepers all fumbled over their words and didn't look Devereux or myself in the eye, though that was partly because of Casimir staring them down.

I wasn't even sure if these people knew who I was, what I was meant to be to them. Had news of my stay at the palace spread? Did they know that their Chosen One was scarred with the evidence of her failure? Or were they just staring at the guards, the finery, the prince and Ambassador of Cortaesi who payed deference to a burned woman who could not even muster the courage to voice a greeting to the people? A woman, pregnant, rested her hand on her belly and smiled at me as though I held every answer. They knew who I was, then. I shuddered.

"Come," Devereux said after our third stop. "This is the best silk merchant in the city. You'll like it."

I was dragged into another shop. This one looked very similar to the other two I'd just visited: square in structure, filled to the brim with merchandise, in this case, bolts of fabric. There were, as Devereux claimed, bright bolts of silk, but there were also wools and linens, all in more subdued colours.

A woman of ancient years sat on a stool behind a counter, a sewing project in her hand. She had thick glass spectacles and skin so wrinkled that it was hard to tell her expressions. Her eyes, though, were a bright, piercing, clear blue.

"You've finally come, Starblood."

Casimir stumbled over something on the floor and mumbled an apology. Devereux eyed the woman, frowning.

"I beg your pardon?" he asked, full of royal haughtiness.

"Starblood," the woman said, pointing a thimbled finger at me. "Bringer of stars, with fire in her veins. The only thing that the void and all its monsters truly fear. Even burned, I can see your power. Time will tell if it shines brightly or if it burns long."

"Please excuse my grandmother!" A young woman, about my age, bustled, out, slipping neatly through the bolts of fabric until she slid to a halt before the old woman. She had brown hair and skin two shades darker, with the same blue eyes as her grandmother. Her frame was lithe, and she wore a knife at her belt, though it was small and subtle. Someone used to danger, perhaps. She gave a deep curtsey before Devereux and myself, her deep blue skirts rustling with the movement.

Before I could study this woman more, she was babbling on again. "My grandmother is old, likes to tell stories. She meant no offence, I swear it."

"I do not understand," I murmured to Casimir. His mouth tightened.

"Starblood is an old title for what is now called the Chosen One. It is said that the Starblooded are descended of the first Star, and that the power to fight the void lies in their blood. Many of them were sacrificed at the edge of the void to keep it back. We now know that the power of the star is, more or less, random and has nothing to do with blood. We also know that bleeding people out on the border of the void does nothing but feed its thirst for life."

He said the words dispassionately, but I sensed deep anger there. When he glanced at me, more emotion flickered in his gaze, tangling with the shadows, before vanishing into a calm veneer. Why would calling me Starblood make him so angry?

"Please," the woman said, hands clasped before her. "She meant nothing by it."

"Think nothing of it," I replied before Devereux or Casimir could take further offense on my behalf. "I am Astraea. What is your name?"

"Tali," the woman said, sagging a little. There was a sharpness in her gaze when she looked at me that had me tugging at my sleeves and wishing for a higher neckline on my dress. "Have you come for silks? We have a fine batch, only recently imported from Mellaig. It was brought in by Runners just two weeks ago. With things the way they are, it may be the last shipment we get."

I frowned, looking at Casimir. He did not meet my gaze, the set of his jaw speaking of anger. "The incursions of the voidlings, as well as the spread of independent void pools, has made it difficult for us to spare the appropriate numbers for void crossings. Trade has become...strained."

Devereux ran his fingers over a purple silk, as if he were little more than a vain man in search of the latest fashion. I thought perhaps he was not as good at feigning disinterest as he hoped. Not after what I'd seen the night before; his tells were in the flush of his cheek and the shine in his eyes. "I've heard rumours that Runners stationed across the continent are all kept busy as well, with void pools growing in number even away from the void in Baldarskiel."

Tali's breath hitched, and she looked at Devereux with wide interest. Her attention flickered between Casimir and finally myself. I was saved from having to explain things I didn't know by the Void Runner at my side. "There have always been fewer of us stationed across Adhor than here in Baldarskiel, but we do our best to keep everyone safe, and have managed reasonably well for quite some time. I would think that a delay in shipment of silks and other goods would be a worthy price."

Devereux flinched, nostrils flaring. He lowered his

hand from the bolt of fabric. Tali, sensing the tension, stepped up to me, threading her arm in mine and pulling me along to a different collection of fabrics, these all embroidered with metallic thread.

"Baldarskiel has the most diverse markets in all of Adhor. You won't find any better. Altier will not disappoint! I can assure you! There is great honour in being host to the place where the Star first fell." Tali was smiling, but I felt the hollowness of her words.

The Void Runners moved merchandise, trade, across the border of the void. At least, they had, when things were quiet enough that they could do so. When the voidlings weren't attacking in greater numbers than ever before. When the void pools weren't spreading and people were fleeing their homes as they waited, *desperate*, for the Chosen One to push back the void for another two generations or more.

Waited for me.

"I think I need some air," I murmured, and bolted for the door. The guards pushed out of my way, and I hit the street with the magic in my veins humming uncontrollably. Around me, the gardens that people had cultivated started growing, reaching for me. The earth beneath my feet, pounded flat into roads, began to tremble, the dirt shifting as I stepped.

People cried out in alarm, and the guards and

Runners around me settled into defensive stances. Sweat beaded down my back. I shivered.

"Not now, not now," I begged the earth, trying to get a grip on the magic that sang through my blood. It surged up, replying to my distress with more animosity against the perceived threat. I couldn't quite convey that the threat was my own magic, my own reactions to the reality in which I'd been thrust without knowledge or choice.

A root as thick as my arm burst through the road before me, waving off the guards. They struck at it with swords and axes, but the root was too thick, likely from one of the many trees around in the yards, ancient and enduring.

"The Lady Star is under attack!" This came not from the guards, but from a man across the street, his clothes grimy from labour, wearing a purple hat to cover his hair. He pointed at me, at the root, at the guards, and I realised that he thought the guards were attacking, that the root—my magic—was defending me.

"No!" I cried, but the damage was done. The people of Altier, who had been watching me with such unveiled interest since I stepped out of the carriage, who had not cared for the burns on my skin, only for the hope I represented, came to my defence.

The guards turned away from the tree root to the people who were brandishing shovels and wooden staves. They fell on each other like rabid dogs, shouting out old grievances as well as the desire to protect me. This was an animosity that ran deep, and I'd provided the spark that set it off.

I pushed back where I could, directing the roots that sprang from the earth to hobble the people at a safe distance. I wrapped oncoming people's arms and legs in pumpkin vines and ivy. The street, which had once been relatively orderly, soon looked like an overgrown forest thicket. The skirmish, which was once again all my fault, ceased.

The people hacked at the vines, the guards doing the same to the roots which bound them. I ran between the two factions. "Stop, please," I begged. "I am not under attack, I am fine. Just fine."

I held out my arms and spun in a circle so all could see that I was unharmed. The Altians stopped shouting, their makeshift weapons lowering. The man who had initially called out the attack looked at me wide-eyed, bound on his knees by ivy, a deep cut across his cheek.

"You go with them willingly, Lady Star?" he breathed.

I knelt before him and wished I had the power to heal. My hand hovered over the cut on his face, then I lowered it. "I do, Goodman. I thank you, though, for your kindness in looking out for my safety and wellbeing."

"You are our last hope, Lady Star," the man whispered. He was crying, now. "There is so much more than the void to fight, but we can do nothing with darkness at our doorstep."

"I know," I said under my breath. And I did. How could I not, when Devereux pointed out to me the strain that these people were under? When these people were looking at me with haunted eyes? There were so many more things than I could fix in the world. The poverty, the lack of food to go around to all the new refugees to Altier. The suffering that was surely to come.

And there I was, out shopping for the day as a means to distract myself, to see the city when I should have been training, not mourning lost memories. These people had lept to my defence when they thought I was in danger, and what had I done to deserve that? Killed seven people and not pushed the void back at all.

I stood and turned to the guards. "You will not harm them."

The one closest to me spluttered. "They attacked us!"

I turned on him and lifted my chin. "They were defending me. There may have been no need, but these people did not know that. Would you fault them for defending their Chosen One, when you were trying to do the same?"

The man flushed, his skin turning bright scarlet. He lowered his gaze. "No, Lady Star."

I nodded. "All who participated in this incident, know that I find you no fault. I will give this Goodman—"

"Thomas Key, Lady Star," the man said, bowing his head.

"Goodman Thomas Key will take possession of this ring, which should be enough to cover the cost of any healing that is required. I apologise for putting you all in this situation, and I will do my utmost to be sure that it never happens again. I do not fear you, my dear people, and the guards now know that you may approach me whenever you wish." I pulled the ring from my finger, a gift of emerald from my royal benefactors among the many jewels that they showered on me, and gave it to Thomas. He bowed his head.

Then, I closed my eyes and called to the magic that was so desperate, so eager, inside me. I pulled back the plants, vines, and roots, releasing the people and guards with as much care as I could. The gardens would still be overgrown, and though I called for the earth to harden back into a road, it was more uneven than before. When I was done, my body ached and my muscles trembled.

Casimir caught me before I could fall to the

ground. "What are you doing, Astraea?" he murmured in my ear.

"I truly do not know," I admitted. "And that terrifies me."

He studied me for a moment, his arms wrapped around me, his gaze unwavering. Then, he smiled. A true smile. "We will figure this out. It won't be like before."

I thought of the dead faces that haunted my nightmares. I thought of how easy it was for my mere presence and apparent upset to cause a near riot in the streets. Failures, both of them mine. I shook my head. "No, it won't be like before."

CHAPTER 9

"What were you *thinking?!*" The queen rounded on me, her face twisted in a mask of fury, eyes shining. She wore a dress of resplendent silk in an ivory grey, the colour subdued for someone with so much fire. We were in the throne room, alone for a few minutes before the Council of Nobles was to begin. Alone, that is, but for Devereux, Casimir, and Beatrice. The king was off seeing to some fortifications on the palace and the wall, for which I was grateful. I didn't need more people to see this humiliation.

It was exactly what I expected, yet my skin still flushed and my fingers twisted in the skirts of my own dress, tugging at the material until I was sure I would tear it. I told myself this was necessary. That Raya needed to see me for who I was, not as some object to be moved about a gameboard. I was the Chosen One, and I was here to fight the void, not get enmeshed in a political scheme. My actions the day before were justified, and I did not regret them. I regretted losing control of my magic, and the panic that came with it. I regretted letting my failures put people in danger. But the aftermath? What I had done to keep everyone from harm, Altians and guards alike? I stood by that choice, even if it had put the royal family in an awkward position, forced to support my demands, to hear the cries of their people regardless of political manoeuvrings. Surely at least Devereux would be pleased with the outcome of the previous day?

I buried my left hand in the folds of my skirt and clenched my fingers into a fist so tightly that I could feel it, even through the nerve-deadening burns. Then, I lifted my head. I forced a serene expression to my features, hoping that my ploy would work. Inside, I trembled.

"I apologise if I caused any distress, Majesty," I said, tone soft. "I was doing what I thought you would want. When my magic, ah, reacted to my panic at being around so many people in such a short amount of time, I did my best to quell the unrest. I know you wished for my tour of the city to be more subdued, but under the circumstances..."

My hands spread in supplication, the marks of my

fingernails in my left palm surely invisible between my scars. Casimir, standing to one side of the throne in an official guard capacity, was staring at the appendage. He swallowed, throat bobbing, and shook his head at me the tiniest amount.

I glanced at my palm and saw that I was bleeding from two points where my nails had dug in too deeply. I hadn't even felt the skin break. My chest felt tight and my skin clammy.

Raya saw the blood and smirked. It was a quiet sort of smirk, the one someone might wear if they were concerned with image and control above all else. She sank onto her throne and curled her hands over the edge of arms. "My dear Lady Star, are you feeling quite well?" she asked, a hint of concern in her voice. "It would seem that you have hurt yourself. Was this done in yesterday's altercation?"

I flinched. My show of false confidence had failed. I lowered my hands. "Just a scratch, Majesty, when putting in my hairpins this morning. The burns make it difficult to feel when I accidentally push in the wrong direction. I do hope I haven't ruined the dress; the blue silk is so lovely."

The queen's nostrils flared as she studied me. Then, the tension slipped out of her as if it had never been there. "It is merely a cast off of Beatrice's. Think nothing of it."

Beatrice, standing off to the side with her broth,

sported a brittle smile. She stared at her mother, never once turning to look at me. Devereux stood with his hands folded neatly in front of him. He, too, did not look at me.

Was what I had done truly so terrible? Whatever the answer was, it churned my stomach.

"As you say, Majesty," I murmured on a curtsey, careful not to touch my injured hand to the skirt. Raya appraised me, chin raised.

"Though I do not agree with your actions, especially in giving a valuable ring to people to cover expenses that could easily have been paid with a few pieces of copper, not to mention defying the guards, I must say that the result has been quite favourable. I've received reports that the people of Altier are all but rejoicing at your name." She leaned forwards. "Do not think that these reckless actions of yours come without consequences, however. We will have to abide by your promise to let the people talk with you. Devereux is already setting aside one day a week where you will go out to hear their pleas. But, *think*, Lady Star! What you did is dangerous. Not only to you, but to the people around you. You are the *Chosen One*! If anything were to happen to you, then this entire country would be lost to the void. We would spend the next fifty or more years until the next Chosen One came in darkness, fighting for our lives each night and scrounging for scraps during the day. We cannot lose you. Do you understand?"

Her concern for me had very little to do with losing the Chosen One. I was never in any danger from the Altians; they'd been rallying to me, not against me. Though, I knew her concerns were not without merit. Losing me, before I'd had a chance to fight the void, would be devastating.

"I will be more careful," I said, bowing my head. And I meant it. I would keep my head down, training as much as I could so that I could face the void as soon as possible. Only then would Adhor be safe. All of Adhor, not just these people before me, so determined to make me into an object of their games.

Raya nodded, her smile beneficent. "I knew you would, Lady Star," she said. She lifted her hand and gestured to a servant lingering in the back of the chamber. "Please let the Council know we can begin, now."

Almost immediately, the doors at the back of the chamber swung open. A stream of people swanned in, wearing elegant, well-tailored clothing in a myriad of colours. Following them were what looked to be scholars of some sort, their robes uniform and indicating the house which they served by the colour of the cords at the shoulders. They carried books, papers, scrolls and quills, setting them on the long table in the centre of the room.

Raya descended from the throne and greeted several of the newcomers. "Lord Ashcroft, how good to see you this morning. I hear your daughter is doing well at school; have you heard any more about her progress? Oh, Sir Eglamore, you look well today. No more gout problems? It is sometimes good to get away from rich food for an evening, though I myself do enjoy a good lemon tart. Lady Rhybern, you must tell me what you use for your skin. You look like you're positively glowing, and to be so fair after taking all that sun with the gardener!"

These greetings went on until each member of the Council of Nobles was seated at the table, their attending scholars behind them. I didn't realise until moments later that there was no place for me to sit, though I was meant to be a guest at the meeting. All their attention was taken up with each other and the queen, their words rife with hidden barbs, their looks secreting and venomous, yet hidden behind polite veneers.

"Come, sit over here," Casimir murmured in my ear, causing me to jump. "There are formalities they must endure before you will be introduced."

I dutifully followed him to a couple of seats in the corner, obviously meant for waiting guests, like myself. I sat and started tracing the scars on my left hand.

"You did well," Casimir said, voice still quiet. He

stood at my side, his attention still on the queen and her nobles. "Defending yourself against the queen. She will try to turn you to her cause, Astraea. You must be wary."

"I have no idea what I'm doing," I admitted. "I only know of the suffering of these people because you and Devereux pointed it out to me. I have no concept of what should be, what is right, what is wrong in this society. I only know that I have to fight the void, or things will get worse. Without that, my mind is a blank slate, erased when my memory was taken."

"I think you know more than nothing." Casimir's mouth twitched in a silent smile. "You have an innate instinct of right and wrong. If you didn't, you would not have given that ring to the Altian."

"I didn't have any money," I said. "I needed to fix what was another mistake of mine, and the ring was the only way I could do that. I'm not a healer. I have no arcane spells at my disposal, like you do. Just wild magic that's barely under control, even now."

"Another mistake?" Casimir asked. "Astraea—"

"I need to learn," I said, cutting him off. "If I'm to make the difference you and Devereux seem to think I can make. I need to learn everything I can about the void, about the voidlings, about how to stop it and defend against it. If that's my purpose, my only way to make this world a better place, then I will do everything I can to fulfil that bargain!"

"And you think, what, book learning will teach you what you need to know to step into the shadows and burn away the injustices of the world? This began long ago, Astraea, and you know it. The void makes us unequal, and those in power have abused that divide until it is inherent, permanent. There are many, many years of wrong to undo, and reading books or fighting with swords will help with very little."

It wasn't the first time I'd heard Casimir be critical of me, but it still stung. Who was I but one person, even if I was regarded as important. Significant. What a joke. I was meant to fight the *void*, a thing, a mindless opponent. I wouldn't even be able to win, only push it back for a while until the next Chosen One came, and the next, and the next, until finally the Star herself returned. This world was so much more complicated than just the void, with its politics and many peoples, with lands I couldn't even comprehend. I understood none of it, and I could do nothing about it, except fight the void.

I didn't deserve to be influential. I didn't deserve to be so highly valued as a pawn or a tool or an object of power. I was already a proven failure, unable to even keep control of the vast power that ran through my veins and lived in my bones. I couldn't even call up the light and shadow I held upon command; they had to be invoked by whatever shadows shone in Casimir's eyes.

Power was seductive. Influence was a temptation. It was like the fire in my veins, that even now yearned to be let free. It was the one thing I couldn't let myself use, because it would grow out of my control so quickly. It already had, and my abuse of power had led to the deaths of seven people. Never again.

Just as my resolve was at its strongest, Queen Raya stood and gestured to me. The entire Council of Nobles turned to stare.

"And here she is, our very own Chosen One, the Lady Star, Astraea," she said with a flourish of her hand. I rose and gave a brief curtsey. Whispers broke out immediately amongst the members, most unable to take their eyes away from me. Raya gestured, smiling. "Come closer, my dear."

I did as she asked, and the closer I got, the more the people stared. The whispers died down a touch, just so I couldn't hear the words being said about me, but that didn't stop their eyes from tracking my face. No, not my face: the burns scrawled across my cheek and neck and arm.

"The Lady Astraea has been practising with her magic," Raya said. "She can command earth, fire, light, and shadow."

One of the members snorted, her chin lifting. "Surely not fire," she muttered.

My skin warmed. I clenched my hands in my skirts, being at least a little careful not to reopen the wounds on my left palm. Casimir came to my rescue.

"It is possible that her fire magic had not awakened when she received the burns, Lady Indira," Casimir said. "Unfortunately, there is no way of knowing. What is important is that she commands fire *now*."

Not that I'd tested that particular skill after the testing. It roared in my nightmares and I wanted nothing to do with it during the day. I even had servants tending the fires and candles for me, instead of doing it myself. Just the thought of getting near a flame was enough to send shivers down my spine.

"Indeed," Lady Indira sniffed, looking down her nose at me.

"We all heard how impressive her earth magic was yesterday," an older gentleman with a shock of white hair said. "Surely you cannot dispute her power."

"I dispute nothing, Sir Castan," Lady Indira said, though the frown at her mouth told me otherwise. I said nothing, did nothing. What defence could I offer?

Devereux sat at the opposite end of the table from where I stood and didn't look up at me. He had said that he sat on the Council, though his vote counted for little. He had not said he would keep silent in my defence. Beatrice, too, sat at the table, though she did not have a scholar at her shoulder or papers strewn before her. Her hands were neatly folded together, her smile serene.

"It is truly astonishing to believe that a Chosen One has come, given how bleak it is outside these walls," Beatrice murmured, her voice taking everybody's attention without effort. "To believe in hope during such desperate times is a monumental task. And yet, history has shown us that the Chosen One always emerges when the void expands. Always."

She smiled in my direction and nodded her head so that the circlet atop her white veil shone in the weak sunlight that penetrated into the room. "The Lady Astraea is, truly, the Chosen One. But, sometimes even hope needs to be proven to be believed. So we arranged a demonstration for today."

I stiffened. I looked at Devereux, who continued to study the table, looking drawn. Raya was radiant, smiling with that victorious smile that told me she expected the Council to be eating out of her hand at the end of this. Casimir, beside me, was expressionless.

"Douse the lights," Beatrice called. Almost immediately, servants stationed around the room doused the arcane lights and what few candles there were. The room became shadowed, barely lit with that weak daylight which shone through the thin slits that were the windows of a fortress. It was dark enough to be twilight in that throne room. My eyes took a moment to adjust, and I heard the disgruntled murmurs of the Council members. What exactly did Beatrice have planned?

Then, that magic which called to the shadows in Casimir's eyes, that magic which taunted me with its silence and will, stirred. I felt both the shadows and the light inside me come to attention, turning their focus on a guard who entered the room. In his arms, which were armoured and gloved, was a large box shrouded in black cloth. He set it down in the open part of the room, on the other side of the table from me. The light and shadow inside me coiled up as if they were holding their breath.

I was, too.

"Release it," Beatrice ordered with a wave of her hand.

"What is going on?" I breathed to Casimir. I couldn't take my eyes from the box.

"I do not know," he answered, equally quiet. That answer, and the uncertainty in his tone, worried me. I took a breath just as the guard leaned down and removed the cloth.

The entire room gasped, excepting Beatrice and the queen. Beneath the cloth was a cage of metal—iron, perhaps—small enough for the creature inside to only turn in a tight, panicked circle. It was unmistakable, though. Through the bars, caged and panicked, was a voidling.

The guard leaned in and pulled a metal pin from the top of the cage, releasing the door. He leapt back, hand on a sword, while the voidling cowered down on the cage floor. I walked around the table as if my legs were moving on their own. That magic of light and dark crooned gently to the creature, hardly threatening.

The voidling was about the size of a cat, with sleek fur made of shadows, striated in darker shades where stripes might be. It had eyes that glowed the colour of molten gold, which were currently wide and staring at me. As it moved, it appeared that shadows dripped off of it in misty waves, vanishing before they touched the ground. A creature of darkness, of beauty, summoned from insubstantial shadows. It crouched down on the bottom of the cage, ears pinned back, tail tucked in tightly. Afraid.

"You bring a voidling, *here*?!" I recognised Lady Indira's voice, but I couldn't bring myself to turn away from the creature. I didn't know if it was the magic inside me that held me in fascination, or if it was coming face to face with one of the things from my nightmares, against which I'd failed so dramatically.

"Do relax," Raya said casually, completely calm. "It is only an infant. One of the shadow tiger variety, captured by Void Runners only yesterday. We thought to study it, but I imagined a demonstration of our Chosen One's powers would be more useful. Wouldn't you agree?"

The Council members murmured agreement. Then, silence fell. They were waiting for me to do something. Watching. I could feel their stares on the back of my neck. Yet, I could do nothing more than sink to my knees and hold out a hand to the creature.

This thing was so entirely different from the slavering monsters that had attacked in my dreams. It wasn't twisted and terrible, for one, brought to madness by its own deformity. No, it was perfectly formed, and there was intelligence in its eyes. I knew that I needed to kill it. I needed to destroy this creature, so I could prove to these people, and *myself*, that I was perfectly capable of fighting the void and all it held.

But my magic, the light and the dark, the earth and the fire, it was quiet. Interested. Unafraid.

I reached out a hand, just the tiniest tingle of light flowing into my fingers, nudged along by sheer determination. I grit my teeth as the magic bucked against my will, trying to pull back. I reached towards the voidling.

"*Astraea*," Casimir whispered. I heard his voice as if he were directly beside me, and I hesitated.

Immediately, my hesitation shattered my will. The light magic vanished from my fingertips, leaving the darkness in its wake. At this change, the voidling let out a startled yowl, cowering down further into the cage. Its eyes stared up at me as if it knew I was meant to be its doom.

"Lady Astraea, we will find you plenty of voidlings to study, if that is your wish," Raya said, the humour in her voice edged with sharpness. "But I would prefer this demonstration not go on all day. We do have business to attend."

There were light chuckles around her from the various council members. My throat tightened. This was my purpose, my *entire* purpose. I existed to fight the void, to push it back and destroy the monsters that inhabited it.

And yet...

The tiny voidling before me was obviously terrified. It was not mindless, nor desperate for my life, my blood, any of it. It was frightened and alone. And the shadows in my veins were singing to the creature a song of belonging.

My fingers began to darken, much as Casimir's had, the tips turning black as night. A single drop of shadow coalesced at the tip of one finger, then lifted from my skin and floated through the air to the voidling. It froze, eyes staring at the drop, then at me, and at the drop again. After an impossible moment, it stuck its head out and flicked a grey tongue towards the drop, drinking it in from the air.

Emotions flashed through my mind, overwhelming my thoughts. Fear, pain, acceptance of death, longing for freedom, for the family that had been lost, curiosity at me, then the knowledge that it was safe. That *he* was safe. Here. With me.

"I can't do it," I said, even as the voidling crawled from the cage and into my lap, burying his head into my arms, mewling in fright at the world around it, bright and cruel. "I can't kill him."

"What?" Raya croaked. "What do you—"

"The Lady Astraea has tamed the shadow tiger cub," Casimir cut in, his voice filling the room so there would be no doubt of people not hearing his words. "She has tamed it, and made it her companion, her familiar. A true master of the void! She will have victory, because she understands it. Because she can *tame* it."

Stunned silence followed his declaration. I couldn't bring myself to turn and face the Council, face Devereux, Beatrice, any of them. Casimir was covering up my latest mistake, my inability to act when faced with what was meant to be my enemy. All

I knew, as my stomach sank, was that I had failed yet again. The voidling curled tighter in my arms and I threaded my fingers through its fur, soft as midnight.

I was never going to be able to fight the void, not if I could not kill a single voidling. I had, single handedly, doomed the entirety of Adhor to the shadows.

CHAPTER 10

"Obviously, she's insane."

I ignored the note of hysteria in the queen's voice and waited for the response. I was standing in the corridor just beyond the entrance to the Queen's wing, away from the view of the guards. The doors were open, though, and I could hear everything that was being said.

The rest of the Council meeting had gone on without me. Casimir had taken me and the voidling— who would not leave my side—away from the increasingly panicked and amazed shouts of the nobles on the Council. He'd left me in my rooms without a second glance, and I'd been on my own ever since. Now, it was late in the evening, and I'd deemed the palace quiet enough to venture forth. The voidling remained at my heels, a loyal companion despite the fear that I knew it still felt at every light, every flame. I found comfort in its presence, perhaps the only indication that I had done the right thing.

I thought to find Devereux, to see what he thought of the events of the day, but instead found myself listening to the shouts of the queen.

"She is not insane, Mother." Ah, there was Devereux. Trying to explain away my failure. "Didn't you hear Lord Casimir? She *tamed* a voidling. She can tame the void."

"She is not meant to *tame* the void! She is meant to fight it!" Raya was nearly screaming, now. I leaned against the stone wall, fingers running carefully through the inky fur of my new companion. I was still stunned by all of this, and couldn't quite get a grasp on reality. The world was still spinning, time still marched on, yet there I stood, numb.

"This could be a good thing," Beatrice chimed in, her voice much more controlled, calm even. "As far back as the Temple records go, no Chosen One has even been able to get close to the void without the voidlings going insane and attacking. They've all pushed back the void with sheer brute strength of magic. It's violent and the Void Runners are always diminished afterwards. But if the void could be tamed? Calmed? Pushed back with minimal loss of life? Then the Chosen One would be even more beloved."

"No one will trust a woman who has a voidling, and a shadow tiger at that, at her side," Raya insisted. I looked down at the scrap of fur by my side, scooping him into my arms. He looked up at me and yawned, showing off a mouthful of gleaming grey teeth and a tiny, pinkish-grey tongue. For an instant, I smiled, then it slipped away.

"Why not?" Devereux asked. "When they see how controlled it is, how it obeys her every command, surely they will trust her completely. After all, it is something not even the Void Runners have managed, no matter how they've tried."

"The people will fear her," Beatrice purred. "And they will love her in equal measure. And, dear brother, once she formally connects herself to this family, to you, then that adulation will spread onto us."

"You may have a point, Daughter," Raya said, though she still sounded incredibly angry, "And I would agree with you, but I was *there*. I heard her say that she couldn't kill the voidling. I heard her admit to failure. If I heard it, others did, too. They won't take Lord Casimir's announcement lying down, as I did not. How do we even know she commands the tiger? All it did was crawl to her, likely drawn by her dark magic."

I snorted softly. She was probably right. Though the little voidling hadn't left me since, and seemed content to sleep in my arms, I doubted very much I could command it to do anything at all. What I did had nothing to do with taming the creature, and everything to do with an inability to kill it. Perhaps it was the dark magic in me, perhaps not. Either way, I was hardly going to push the void back by asking it, which made me nearly useless as a Chosen One.

"The Void Runners will want to train her even more seriously, now," Beatrice said. "A Chosen One with control over a voidling, no matter how tenuous, is valuable to them. She could teach them, and then who knows, we might have a dangerous force on our hands, especially if they manage to tame their own creatures. Mother, it doesn't matter what the nobles heard, only what she does now. We must train her, control her, and get her wed to Devereux as soon as possible. Or we may lose control over the Chosen One entirely."

Suddenly, a figure was before me. This time, he didn't cover my mouth, only folded his arms and quirked a brow. Casimir looked haggard, his features drawn, but he was still wearing his armour. He was likely going to meet the queen and discuss my future along with the others. I smirked up at him.

He jerked his head, indicating a turn in the corridor. I shrugged and followed, the tiger of ink still asleep in my arms. When we were far enough away from the queen's wing, I stopped.

"You should learn not to listen at doors," Casimir grumbled.

"How else am I to learn about the deciding factors in my life?" I asked. "Have you come to add your opinion to the queen's, and the high priestess', and the prince's about how my life should be planned out?"

"I could plan until the moon fell from the sky, but I doubt you would do anything I suggested." Casimir studied me, his gaze lingering on the tiger. "You're going to keep it, then?" He sounded surprised.

I hugged the little voidling closer. It made no sense, not to me and not to the world, but I couldn't just abandon him, now. The others of his kind still haunted my thoughts, and holding him in my arms was proof of my failure as a Chosen One. Yet, I think I loved him, foolish as it was.

"I cannot leave him to die, now," I said, brushing a finger along his tail. Casimir frowned, looking bemused.

"You surprise me, Astraea," he said. "I would have thought you'd send it back to the void, now it's served its purpose in setting you apart from the previous 'Chosen Ones'. Or are you going to use the creature for something else?"

"Served its purpose?" I felt a slinking, dark feeling

in the pit of my stomach. "Do you think this is a game to me? That I'm manipulating my image to, what, make my impact on Adhor all that more astonishing when I push back the void? Do you think all of this is an act?"

Casimir said nothing, remaining absolutely still. Then, "Isn't it always?"

I hissed and turned away, inadvertently waking my charge as I did so. He mewled and wriggled, so I set him down before whirling to face Casimir. My eyes burned with tears and the skin on my face felt tight, especially around the scars. I jabbed Casimir in the chest, my finger bouncing off the breastplate and sending stings back up my arm.

"How dare you?" I seethed. "How dare you accuse me of that? Of manipulating things so that I look better, so that I seem more of a hero when I finally perform my task. My gods, what must I have been before to be so terrible to you? Do you think that I am so low that I would value the *lives* of the people around me less than what they think of me?"

He remained silent. Still. Watching and waiting, his expression guarded and impossible.

"You do," I realised. "You do think that of me. Stars above, I knew you hated me, but I didn't realise that you thought so little of me. I know you witnessed whatever went on at Starfall Meadow, that it went so badly that you think you have to stop me from ever doing it again, but—"

"You think I *hate* you?" Casimir rasped. His eyes widened, the shadows that seemed to live there flashing at me. His skin was pale, the inky spots on his fingers and neck almost pulsing in time with his heartbeat. If it were real, not an illusion, then his heart was racing. As was mine.

"Why else would you think such things of me?" I snapped. "I would give *anything* to bring back those seven Runners. To undo the fact that those six months of training were nothing but a waste. To make sure that *no one* dies at my expense ever again. I have failed over and over and over again, but not because I value the lives around me so little. It's because I'm useless at all this...this...nonsense! I'm the Chosen One, and yet I cannot even kill a voidling when it sits before me! I cannot keep people alive when they're right in front of me. I can't even remember what it was that made me so damn special that I have people falling over themselves to prostrate at my feet when I cannot even grasp my magic without it spinning out of control. Despite all of that, the failure and the emptiness in my mind, it does not mean I won't try, you utter bastard."

Casimir was suddenly moving, crossing the distance of the hallway and pushing me back until I was pressed against a wall. One hand lifted to cup my face, brushing against the whorls of my burn, the sensation feather-light. I shivered. Despite the fire in my veins, the beating of my heart so loud that I could all but hear it, I shivered.

"I don't *hate* you, Astraea," he breathed, pressing his forehead to mine. Sparks danced between our skin where it brushed, and the magic in me that was both light and dark rose up, shining and dancing, creating shapes along the wall and brushing patterns on our skin. Casimir licked his lips, and those tanta-lising shadows filled his eyes. "I have never hated you."

Then, he kissed me.

It was soft at first, just a brush against my lips. But when I did not hesitate or retreat, he swept in and devoured me, hungry and desperate. There was such power in his movements, the way he held me, kissed me. It was heady, enough to make me dizzy. Then, he let up until he was gentle, his touch so deferential that I was dizzy for an entirely different reason.

I didn't know if I'd ever been kissed before losing my memories, but if I had it surely could never measure up to this. My skin was aflame, my magic was singing, the shadows and the light dancing around me so that we were in a world of our own. The stone palace did not exist. The political games between the queen and her Council, between the

Void Runners and the royal family, between Beatrice and Devereux, none of it existed. In that web of light and dark, of a touch that ignited, there was only us.

Finally, he pulled back. He put his palms against the wall and laughed quietly. "Empty night, Astraea."

"I'm inclined to agree," I breathed, the words falling from my tongue before I could think about them and what they meant. I let my eyes flutter closed, and I leaned my head back, basking in my emotions.

Casimir brushed a hand through my hair, skirting the edges of my scars. I hummed.

"I promise, this won't be like last time."

I froze. Every muscle in my body tensed and the lights and shadows vanished in a blink as my magic recoiled. I was left with bright spots in my eyes as I tried to adjust to the dimly lit corridor. I was still in the palace, the voidling was at my feet, curled up and purring, and the queen, Beatrice and Devereux were just one hallway over.

"Last time," I said. My mouth was dry.

Casimir pulled back, taking two steps away from me. He looked stricken. "Last time," he said with a nod. "It was...bad for both of us, I know, but this time—"

"We were...involved? Before?" I started taking deep breaths through my nose to try and calm my racing heart. No wonder he'd been appalled at my agreeing to marry Devereux. No wonder he'd been so harsh with me when I was training, trying to overcome what happened at Starfall Meadow. It all fell into place. And yet, I remembered none of it. I ached for those missing memories, a loss which suddenly felt insurmountable.

Casimir shook his head. "Of course we were, Astraea. Don't you remember?"

I bit my lip and shook my head. Tears filled my eyes to the point where I could barely see. "How could I? I remember *nothing*, so how could I remember that?"

"It's not a ploy," Casimir breathed. "Empty night, it's not a ploy." He looked horrified, truly and deeply, like I'd struck him with no cause.

I wiped the tears away with my good hand. "Why would it be?" I demanded. "I *told* you I'm not playing games! Stars above, Casimir, why would I lie about something like losing my memory? What sort of person do you think I am, to be so cruel, so self-serving? I cannot imagine why you wanted to be with me before, if this is what you think I am capable of."

I spun around and scooped up the voidling cub, stalking away from the hallway and from Casimir. I didn't dare cross before the entrance to the Queen's wing, instead fumbling my way through unfamiliar paths, twisting and turning.

"Astraea, wait!" Casimir called after me. I knew he

could catch up to me with ease if he wanted, but I kept moving. Hoping, maybe, that he would leave me alone. Hoping, maybe, that he wouldn't.

His hand caught my arm, and I stiffened. I gave him a scathing look, and he released me. "Just hear me out," he said.

"Why should I, when you obviously trust me so much that everything I say is suspect?"

He took a step back, then shook his head and took a step forwards. I refused to shrink away, instead reaching for my magic. The earth sang to me, but the plants and dirt were too far away, and the stone beneath my feet was too ancient for me to influence beyond a quiet rumble. The light and the shadow were silent. But the fire...oh, that seductive fire. I could just reach out and the torch on the opposite wall would come to my aid, wrapping itself around me until Casimir was forced away. It would protect me, serve me, adhering to my every whim. If only I asked.

The memory of my nightmare, of the searing pain that had accompanied my first waking, surged through me. I turned my head from the torch, cutting off the connection with that magic I refused to cultivate.

Casimir was watching me warily, as if he had seen every thought that burned through my mind. "You are, indeed, a changed person from who I knew before," he said, as if choosing each word with care. "But I never suspected that it could be possible. That *you* of all people could..."

"And why not me? Because I am the Chosen One? Well, see how much good that has done me. Seven people dead, essentially by my hand, an entire street of Altier terrorised and nearly destroyed because I couldn't control my magic, and now I prove myself completely incapable of killing a voidling—which is the entire purpose of my existence, is it not? As useless as I am, why should I not be susceptible to the injuries and maladies of normal people? Why should I not forget?"

Casimir grabbed my hand again, this time with that tempting gentleness of before. When I was blissfully happy.

I refused to look him in the eye.

"You could never be useless," Casimir whispered, and he drew closer again. "I am sorry, truly, for thinking that you were playing a game with everyone, including me."

I closed my eyes, feeling nothing but the touch of Casimir's hand on my arm and the gentle rhythm of the voidling's tail swishing across the stone floor. "Whatever we had before, it will never be as it was. I don't remember, and I'm *not* that same person. Perhaps we should..." I couldn't bring myself to finish my phrase, because the memory of being that free and happy, even if for a moment, was forefront in my mind. I *wanted* whatever this was with Casimir, no matter the consequences with Devereux and Raya and Beatrice. I wanted this in spite of being the Chosen One. And yet, it was surely doomed.

Casimir tucked a strand of hair behind my ear. "As it happens," he said, his breath on my ear, "I like this version of you the best."

Then, he kissed me again. There was no demanding, this time. No devouring, no getting lost in a haze of desire. It was just a touch, light and brief, and so much more intense.

"Lord Casimir!" The voice startled us both out of whatever trance we were in, and we leaped apart. A Void Runner, one of the ones who had escorted me into Altier the day before, was standing at the end of the hall, his eyes wide with terror.

"What is it, Malkis?" Casimir snarled viciously.

Just then, the world shook. It was like before, when I'd woken to the ground shaking and the world anything but stable. Only, this time, it was loud, accompanied by a desperate crash and the screams of people. And it wasn't to do with my magic. Malkis, the blood drained from his face, swallowed. He didn't even seem shocked at having caught us in a kiss, only terrified at whatever was making the ground tremble.

"Voidlings," he announced in a wavering voice. "A

whole horde of them, attacking from the south. From Starfall Meadow."

Casimir was immediately tense, at attention. "How many?" he barked.

"Lord Casimir, sir." Malkis swallowed visibly. He finally looked at me, and his eyes met mine as he spoke his next words. They were filled with horror. "The wall's been breached."

CHAPTER 11

Neither Casimir nor I hesitated; we ran after the Void Runner. The tiny voidling ran at my side, pawsteps in time with my heart beating in my ears. I scooped up the voidling cub, holding it close. My legs, despite all the training and exercising I'd been doing over these past weeks, were not truly up for running yet, and I quickly fell behind. Neither Runner looked back for me. It didn't matter. All I had to do was follow the sound of screams and roars and the shaking of the ground, and I would end up in the right place.

When I emerged from the palace into the night air, I froze. It was like being back in my nightmare, only this time the screams were louder, and the pain was enduring long past the time when I would wake. I couldn't breathe.

"To me!" Casimir cried, about twenty paces in front of me. Someone had handed him a sword, and he held it high, a beacon for the Runners and guards protecting the palace and Altier beyond. The wall—or what had been the wall—was lit by torches and arcane lights, but those were quickly being snuffed out as the voidlings systematically attacked the sources of their pain. I saw flashes of rubble and stone strewn across the earth, then the entire yard went dark as the last torch was extinguished, its holder dying with a scream.

There were shrieks from the voidlings as they advanced, barely visible except by their glowing eyes and their bodies that were darker than their surroundings. The cub in my arms wriggled and squeaked, obviously wanting to be free. I dropped him. If he wanted to return to his familiars, then who was I to protest. I had saved him once, but I wasn't sure I could do it again. Not with death and destruction before me. Not with monstrous creatures bearing down on anyone that moved. He pressed against my leg briefly, then I was too distracted to notice where he went as the battle raged on.

There were flares a few moments later, and I saw circles of light and magic springing up around the Void Runners. Arcane spells, I decided, meant to provide illumination in the midst of the void. How long would they last? It almost didn't matter, because they were drawing the attacking voidlings to them with dangerous ease.

"Keep position!" Casimir shouted above the snarls and screams. He raised his sword and brought it down in a swift dance, his movements precise and deadly. Each swipe of a sword felled a voidling, all of which were of the twisted and tortured variety I saw in my dreams. I didn't understand the difference between them and the sleek tiger cub I had rescued, but I knew they were different. There were creatures with antlers growing from their shoulders, spiny growths along their backs, some even with two tails or six legs, slavering for the people attacking them. All were splattered with blood.

A Void Runner not ten paces from me fell, a snake-like demon latched to her throat. She screamed until the sound broke off into a wet gurgle, and the arcane spell around her faded to black. A Runner and a guard on either side of her shifted position to cover the new gap in the lines. It wasn't enough. The Runners were fighting well, killing a great number of voidlings, but it was the dead of night and the monsters had the darkness to their advantage. They kept coming over the wall in numbers far beyond what the Runners had.

"Reinforcements?" the dark skinned Runner from the day before asked, her hands full with two large hunting knives that disembowelled and gouged with ease. Her face was splattered with ink-black blood, and some reddish blood of her own. She didn't seem to notice.

"Too far," Casimir replied. "They'd have to come from Runner's Landing, and that's clear across the city. If we don't stop this breach, all of Altier will be overrun."

Then, he looked at me.

I'd been standing there, frozen, unable to step into the fray of battle despite the earth singing beneath me, telling me where a Runner stepped or a voidling fell. Despite the screams that earned themselves a permanent place in my memories. Despite the people who fell around me. I couldn't bring myself to act. I wasn't prepared for this. I wasn't prepared to face what I was meant to face. My training was all for naught if I couldn't even bring myself to fight.

I hadn't even been able to kill a voidling cub that morning.

Yet Casimir looked at me as though I held all the answers. As though I only needed encouragement before I would stride into blood and gore and wield my power to save them all. He looked at me like I was a hero, when we both knew I was not. Maybe I had been, once. When he knew me, when he loved me. But not now.

Not anymore.

Casimir's brief moment of hesitation cost him. A voidling in the shape of a wolf yet larger than a man saw his distraction and leaped. The creature soared over the heads of two guards, aiming right for Casimir, as though it sensed he was the greatest threat. Casimir turned, sword raised, but it was too late.

I screamed.

And a wall of flame erupted before Casimir.

Everyone in the yard flinched at the sudden surge of light. I could not look away, though the light scorched my eyes. The monstrous voidling yelped and writhed, having moved too slowly to avoid the flames. They ate at its shadowy flesh until there was nothing left but bone, and then the flames ate those, too. I closed my fingers into a fist, and the wall of fire expanded, wending its way between the oncoming voidlings and the Runners fighting them. The magic in my blood would demand nothing less. *I* demanded nothing less.

They'd tried to hurt my friend, one of the only ones I had in this world I'd come to know. I was no hero, but neither could I watch as my friends were attacked. These things had done enough damage. I would not stand by any longer while those who swore to protect, to serve, to defend, died. I would not stand by while twisted creations of a shadowy world devoured and maimed. So I gave in to that seductive song in my blood, and I let the fire—my fear and my terror—free.

Soon, the entire yard was lit up bright as day. Void Runners killed the monsters, the fire moving with them as they fought, pushing the voidlings back. Immediately upon the death of one voidling, my fire leaped to turn the voidlings back the way they came. I felt the earth beneath my feet and called that up, too. Vines sprang forth, holding the creatures still while they died from the knives and swords at their throats. Dirt and mud clung to their feet, dragging them down.

I did not kill the voidlings caught in my magic, none but that wolf who attacked Casimir, but I gave the soldiers and Runners the chance to do so. Together, we fought back against the night.

The more magic I released, the less my mind tried to fight it. It was natural, easy, to let the magic forth in this way. Like a river that had been filled with the spring melt. What was usually a trickle of power in my blood now filled my entire person.

Then, as easily as it came, it was gone.

The flames snuffed out, plunging the yard back into darkness with a little light where the bodies of some voidlings still smouldered. The earth released its captives. My body, moments ago unstoppable, collapsed. The darkness of the yard became absolute, and I slipped away from reality.

"One part earth, one part the fire beneath, one part stolen light, one part shadow complete. With this touch, life I give, and where once was I, now you remain." The voice who spoke was soft, female, and ageless. In each syllable was an ache and a tremble, but I sensed no pain. Though I could not see, I knew I was safe, cocooned there in that warm space between moments. Then, there was a brush of a hand on my forehead. I gasped as air filled my lungs. Suddenly, I could feel my fingers, my toes, my face, my entire body. It was coarse and worn, yet smooth where the faceless hand had touched me.

"Daughter mine, awaken."

I sucked in a deep breath and spluttered.

"She is awake!" a young voice cried. I recognised Eloise kneeling over me, holding a sword in one hand, a shield in the other. She was bathed in arcane light, casting her features into a strange greenish hue. I tried to sit up and managed only to rise to my elbows.

"The battle," I rasped.

"Still rages," Eloise said grimly. "Reinforcements arrived ten minutes ago, thanks to the time you bought the Runners, but the voidlings will likely continue their attack until their numbers are completely gone. They are relentless, and the void pool which spawned them was vast."

"The Star lives!" The cry rang out from a nearby guard and echoed around the yard. I could see torches and arcane lights now, as well as some Runners who stood in their circles of arcane magic. The voidlings, though, were crazed for blood and the people could only last so long. At the shouting, though, people rallied, and the fighting grew more frenzied.

A whimper sounded to my right, and I turned. There, in the shadows, slunk the little cub I had saved earlier that day. He had his head hunched between his shoulders, his tail between his legs, and was dancing at the edge of the arcane light, like he was afraid.

"He won't leave," Eloise said. "Some of the soldiers tried to shoo him away, tried to get him to go and leave you be, but he won't go. He doesn't like me much, though."

"Eloise, you shouldn't be here," I said, pushing myself fully sitting. Around me, I could tell that the forces were rallying further. They'd secured the yard up to the wall, thanks to the space my fire had given them, and were managing to keep the remaining voidlings back. They didn't need me, now. Which was good, because I was completely spent. I felt no magic at all. My muscles screamed and my hands trembled as I reached for the cub.

He came to my lap, burying his head into my grimy skirts. A flare of understanding spread between us, tinged with fear and the taste of ash.

"I'm a Runner apprentice," Eloise said flatly. "I'd have to face the void soon enough, anyways. Protecting you is far safer than being out there."

She nodded her head to the wall, where a spidery voidling with eight glowing eyes tore the limbs from a hapless guard. The man died with eyes wide and mouth gaping. I turned away, stomach roiling.

"They're so different from the cub," I said, my thoughts too swift to calm and my emotions distant. Battle shock, I think Casimir had called it one day during training. It happened to many, when they couldn't process what was going on around them.

"There are different sorts of voidlings, ones we've seen before and can name, and others. The ones closer to the perimeter are almost normal, like regular animals. The ones deeper in are twisted, changed by whatever dark magic fuels the void. Some say they cannibalise each other and gain their traits, but we can't be sure. There are more new, twisted monsters appearing by the moon." Eloise shifted her weight, resting the shield on the ground for a moment. She looked at me out of the corner of her eye, then turned her attention back to the battlefield. "The records say that the voidlings always get more twisted in the time before the Chosen One comes. More desperate for life, for what remains of their need for light. Can you stand? We need to get you inside, away from the fighting."

My thoughts reeled at the sudden change in subject. I licked my dry lips. "I don't know. Everything hurts, and I've no magic left."

"Try," Eloise said with the voice of one used to facing life against death, and not looking away, for all she was twelve.

I shivered.

There was a yelp, high and sharp. That was all the warning we had before a voidling with massive, bat-shaped wings, soared over the wall and landed with a thud amidst the wounded guards and Runners. It had the head of a raven, the front legs of a raptor, and the body of a horse, and it shrieked loudly enough to split the ears.

"Malgrwm!" a Runner screamed, just before the dark creature raked its claws across his back, exposing bone. The creature took a look around, like it was *searching* for something. Where the other voidlings were mindlessly attacking, seeking out any spot of light and exterminating it, this voidling, this malgrwm, was searching. Its eyes, glowing and intelligent, landed on me. It shrieked again, this time with a note of triumph.

All of the Runners and guards, including myself, lifted our hands to our ears as one. Eloise had to drop her sword to do it, as did many others. In that instant, we were vulnerable.

The cub in my lap let out a tiny roar and leaped forwards, landing before the flying voidling. The malgrwm regarded the shadow tiger for a moment, then tilted its head back and croaked. Was it *laughing?* The cub roared again, then crouched and jumped into the air. It was impossible, surely, but its claws cut across the neck of the creature, letting blood the colour of ink flood to the ground. The creature shrieked again and tossed its head, one wing throwing the cub back.

I moved before I could think, just as I had with my magic before it gave out on me. My legs were still too weak to do more than lurch in the right direction. But I managed to crawl in front of the cub, standing before the creature, weaponless, without magic, without strength.

Fool.

The malgrwm stared at me with one large, glowing eye. It croaked again, though the sound was weaker for the slight wound at its throat. It raised a talon and aimed for me, but I stood my ground. The rest of the yard was silent, like the people couldn't quite believe what was happening. Either that, or they were too injured to move. Injured or afraid.

"Lady Star!" Eloise shouted from behind me. I couldn't turn my head away from the stare of the voidling, though.

It croaked again, then reared up, talons flailing. I didn't move. I wasn't sure if it was because I was truly out of energy, or if I had finally—impossibly—tapped into some well of bravery, or if I was just truly and suicidally foolish. The tiny tiger cub leaned against my leg, its fur almost warm against the realisation of what I was doing.

The voidling landed again without striking me, wings beating. It brought its head closer to mine. I looked into its eyes and did not look away.

The entire yard held its breath.

"Astraea! *No!*" Casimir screamed, voice shrill. He was the only one moving, but it was too late. He couldn't reach me in time, no matter how swift his sword.

The winged malgrwm huffed, then croaked again, lifting its wings wide. It let out a shriek at Casimir as he approached, then launched itself into the sky without a backwards glance. It hadn't harmed me, not once. It just left.

Casimir all but slid to my side, his armour covered in grime and blood of black and red. He had blood smeared on his face and it looked like he'd been scratched in the head. His arms were now fully dark, though it was likely more of that inky blood than whatever darkness had tainted him during his years of service. He didn't stop, though, but scooped me into his arms, where the last of my strength gave out.

"Eloise," Casimir said, and the girl was suddenly there. "Go fetch the healers."

"They won't come until the battle is over," Eloise said, as if this were a matter of course, and not some terrible breach of duty to the injured. "And there are no servants to be spared to carry her inside."

"Then I'll do it myself," Casimir growled. I licked my lips and tried to speak, but nothing came. All I could do was relive that moment over and over in my mind when I stood before the malgrwm and it turned away. "The battle is nearly over," he said, as if to reassure himself and Eloise. They both exchanged a grim glance, but Casimir continued his path inside, anyways.

Inside the palace, the world became muffled, quiet, like fierce battle wasn't raging outside. Yet surely I was still trapped in one of my nightmares?

Frantic steps drew my attention. Devereux raced towards us, a sword at his hip, expression alarmed. He skidded to a stop in front of Casimir, and his hands immediately went to my limp ones. "I was watching from a window. What happened? Why did the voidling leave? Are you alright, Lady Astraea?"

I tried to speak, but was still too tired for words, so I just smiled as much as I could and nodded.

Casimir spoke for me. "She is fine. She just burned through her magic too quickly and is now fighting magic sickness. She needs sleep, is all."

"Good, good. I'll take her to her rooms, then call for a healer, just in case," Devereux said, reaching for me. He didn't even seem to notice that Casimir hadn't answered his question about the voidling. The same question I had.

"She cannot walk; she is too weak." Casimir's arms tightened around me. I felt something sticky drip onto my face and realised that he was still bleeding from his head wound. Surely, he needed a healer, too.

Devereux hesitated, then nodded. "Alright, let's go."

I was carried to my rooms in arms that never once faltered, despite the fact that Casimir had been fighting demons but minutes ago. Eloise watched over me with silent surety, carrying her sword and shield as well as Casimir's. Devereux alone was anxious, babbling about the sights that he had seen while watching out the window.

"...and when you called on the fire magic, it was magnificent! My mother was suitably impressed, especially with your control over the flames. Beatrice said there hadn't been a Chosen One in all the records with such control, and that you would subdue the void with ease, despite the voidling you rescued. Er, tamed."

The voidling. Where was he? I cast my eyes about as much as I could without turning my head.

"He follows," Eloise murmured, nodding to a spot behind us. "Fear not."

Good. I blinked my thanks. At least one thing I had done turned out well, regardless of my good intentions. I couldn't even make it through a single pitched battle against the void. I might have fine control over the magic, but my endurance was pitiful. And any physical fighting seemed beyond me, if I froze at a moment's notice.

Nor, I recalled with a sick twist of my stomach, had I actually killed any voidlings apart from that wolf. The others had done that. All I'd done was push them back with fire, or hold them in place with earth.

I curled my fingers into Casimir's shirt, my movements so weak I could barely hold on. He looked at me, though, as if he could feel the touch, and something in his expression kindled a warmth in me. I shivered.

"Here," Casimir said. We'd reached my chambers. I was set gently on the bed, my muscles relaxing almost immediately. The bed was so soft, so warm, so safe. Compared to the fear and death that reigned outside, it was paradise. How much longer would the battle last? I was afraid to know.

The voidling cub climbed onto the bed and settled beside me. Devereux frowned. "Is it safe to let that thing sleep with her?"

"It attacked a beast far larger than it in her defence," Eloise said. "And she saved it in return."

None of us in the room were sure how that had happened, though if anyone knew anything, it would be Casimir. I looked at him, trying to convey my question in looks alone. He sighed and brushed some of my hair back from my face.

"Sleep," he ordered. For a moment, his eyes flicked to Devereux, as though wishing the prince anywhere else but here. Then, he nodded tightly. "I should go. There may be stray voidlings to hunt down, and I need to rally with the other Void Runners and clean up the mess."

"How bad was it?" Devereux asked, turning away from me. "Is the palace secure?"

"Yes, though I fear for Altier. We were the more difficult target; surely they wouldn't concentrate their attack here."

The city? It was under attack, too? I tried to rouse myself, needing to go and see, to help where I could, but nothing worked, nothing moved. Casimir murmured a few more things to Devereux, things I couldn't hear. The world around me went blurry. Then, trying to keep my mind from panic and horror, I fell asleep.

CHAPTER 12

When I awoke, everything was still. The air in my rooms felt stale, stuffy. The world was quiet, like it was holding its breath after the events of the battle at the wall. My mind was empty, as if my sleep had stolen all the thoughts from my head and given me true respite. Even my body was still, with no pain, no soreness, but no invigoration either.

Something stirred beside me, and just like that, the world began breathing again. I was weak, groggy, and couldn't quite get a grip on reality. I knew that terrible things had happened during the battle, but I didn't believe it.

The thing beside me stirred again. My vision was suddenly filled with the head of the voidling cub, his impossibly black fur sticking up in odd directions. He was, surely, twice the size of the day before, his paw already dwarfing my palm. He yawned, showing off those strange grey teeth, then began giving himself a bath. I felt a flutter of warmth from whatever connection we shared, a quiet joy at being together. I smiled and threaded my fingers through his fur.

"You're awake."

I started and sat up, wincing as my muscles protested. A servant had come, her arms full of wood for the fire. She gaped at me with wide eyes and open mouth. I waited for her to say something, for her to tell me what time it was, or what had happened while I slept, but she just stared.

"Are you well?" I asked, trying not to sound rude. My voice was hoarse. The girl winced, dropped the bundle of wood, then fled my rooms. The little voidling chirped at me. "I don't know," I replied. "Perhaps you scared her."

"It wasn't the cub." Devereux appeared a moment later, all smiles and fine clothes, this time of a deep red with hints of orange. Like fire. He bore a bouquet of hot-house flowers in an array of vibrant colours, which he deposited beside my washbasin. A gift, I supposed, though the sight of the flowers only reminded me of the vines I'd wielded the night before, and ineffectively. He sat on the edge of my bed and reached for my hand, taking it before I could summon the energy to move away. "The entire palace, and most of Altier, I suspect, has been talking about what you did last night. That wall of fire which pushed the voidlings back, using what darkness you control to send the malgrwm and the rest away. The entire city is in aware of you, Lady Astraea, and frankly, I cannot blame them."

I wasn't sure that my dark magic *had* been the cause of the voidlings fleeing from me. Nor did I think that losing my temper and control of my magic in the same breath was something to be proud of, even if it did save lives. I had vowed never to use those flames, the ones that sang so seductively in my soul, just as the earth sang in my bones.

The flames were dangerous. They had killed seven Void Runners already. They had branded me so that I would never walk through the world unremarked again. I did not mind the burns, but what they represented, what they painted me to be was difficult to accept. I may have managed to push back the monsters the night before, but I'd been barely in control. And I hadn't killed a single one besides the wolf. One voidling compared to the surely hundreds that had attacked? Awake, rested, and in the light of day, I could see how reckless I'd been.

"News of the Chosen One's abilities has spread," Devereux continued, as if my silence hadn't filled the air. "You're famous. People are clamouring for you. In awe."

"I don't want them to be in awe of me," I murmured, sinking my fingers into the voidling's fur. "I just want to push back the void and get on with my life."

Devereux squeezed the hand that he held. "Don't forget, Lady Star, that your life is now heavily involved with mine."

My stomach dropped. How could I have forgotten? I was betrothed to Devereux. I'd never have a peaceful, quiet life again. I would forever be enmeshed in politics and manipulations and people staring at me. After seeing the reverence on the faces of the Runners last night, and the near terror of the maid this morning, I wasn't sure I wanted to be the next queen.

I wasn't sure I'd wanted it to begin with.

I graced Devereux with as much of a smile as I could manage, then pulled my hand away. "Is there anything to eat? I'm starving."

"I called for a tray as soon as I heard you were awake," Devereux said. "Casimir says that you used up your magic last night, expending it too quickly. Your body is trying to compensate for losing all that energy, so you're going to be weak and hungry for a few days. To be honest, I don't know all that much about wild magic. Arcane magic was a required course in my studies, though my tutors despaired that I would ever master even the most basic spells. A

Void Runner, I am not. Still, I can manage a basic light spell. Wild magic, though, is so rare. There are maybe two Runners in the last twenty years with wild magic."

He was rambling. The smile that he wore didn't quite reach his eyes, and something about the way his hands fiddled with the hem of his tunic was disconcerting. Distracting.

"Devereux," I said. He looked at me with that charming smile of his. "What happened? What's wrong?"

"Wrong?" he scoffed. "Why would anything be—"

"Please do not treat me the fool."

Devereux's gaze fell. The smile faded. "The damage to the wall has my mother concerned. She refuses to allocate further resources to those suffering in Altier until after the wall is repaired and we are fortified against further attack. Just another excuse to keep resources under her control. No matter how I argue, there's always another excuse."

"How badly was the city damaged?" I asked. I hadn't been able to hear anything last night beyond the battle inside the palace walls, but Casimir had said something about the city, about other voidlings heading in that direction. I hoped that things were not as bad as I imagined them to be.

Devereux shrugged. "A few houses damaged on the outskirts of Starfall Meadow and Dark Mire, but nothing so far as the Trade Quarter and Mist Haven. The Runners at Runner's Landing were able to stop any dire incursions."

"That's good, isn't it?" I asked. A knock at the door interrupted us. The maid who had dropped the wood before now entered, carrying a tray of food. She didn't meet my gaze, only deposited the tray on the bed, curtseyed deeply, then fled again. The wood for the fire remained on the floor.

I sighed and began eating. Devereux snagged a crusty piece of bread from my tray and started tearing it to pieces. The cub started playing with the pieces, scattering them over the linens. At this rate, I was going to have to sleep in a bed of crumbs.

"Minimal damage is good," he said at last. "But it completely covers up the fact that the rest of the city is still suffering. Even now, there are refugees from other parts of the country coming here, regardless of the fact that there is no space. There are no resources to build, no extra food, and the harvest is already looking weak. Yet my mother insists on allocating resources to the protection of the palace and all the nobles within. People who can afford to pay for their food!"

I ate slowly, thinking. The voidling purred at my side, then batted a piece of sausage off the tray and scarfed it down. I managed to crack a smile. "Thief," I murmured.

"You should name it," Devereux said. "So that people don't go calling it something terrible when it inevitably follows you around."

"I'm amazed that he's even here, given how bright it is. I thought voidlings were afraid of the light." I stroked his fur, and he purred again, glowing eyes loving and joyful, despite what had happened to him before, what he'd done last night. He'd protected me, when it should have been impossible. I think I loved him for it.

"I don't know what to say about your mother, Devereux," I said at last. "She has been queen for many years, and surely she knows what she is doing. Even if she is trying to hold on to power, to protect the...prestige that ruling Baldarskiel gives her over all the other countries of Adhor, then letting her people suffer is hardly the way to do that."

"You know very little about my mother," Devereux scoffed. "She cares only for power, not for the people suffering in the streets. She controls my life, and that of my sister, though Beatrice enjoys the machinations and games. She wants to have absolute control over the fate of things, which means controlling you, too. Don't you *care?*"

I straightened. "Of course I care! All I want is to push back the void, to make things safe for people again. To fulfil my destiny. Do you think I want to be manipulated into performing for the Council of

Nobles, into using my supposed influence for the agendas of people I've only spoken with thrice? Do you think that I want to have my future dictated by the royal family, so that I'm always in the spotlight, always wondering if people wish to speak with me because I'm the Chosen One, or your betrothed, or just me? I don't even know who I am apart from the Chosen One!"

Devereux winced. He gathered up as many of the crumbs from his crust of bread as he could and deposited them back on the tray. "I'm sorry," he said to the pot of jam. "I see the suffering of these people and I can do nothing but sneak out in the night and liberate a few sacks of grain."

"Then find a way to do more. You're the Crown Prince! The heir to the throne! You say you have only one vote on the Council of Nobles, well use it. If you only control your grandfather's old land, then set it to farmland, sell the grain at a loss, do *something* instead of complaining to me about it. I know nothing of the world except what I have learned in these past two months. Do you honestly think that I can do more than you?" I was fuming, now, exhausted and weak and tired of being manipulated into schemes I couldn't even understand for lack of information.

Devereux still would not look at me, all his smooth charm and easy smiles gone. "Perhaps you can," he mused. "You are the Chosen One, after all.

Following last night's display, there is not a person alive who would refuse you."

"What?" I wasn't sure I liked where this conversation was heading.

"Come with me!" Devereux grabbed my hand again, holding it to his chest. "Come with me into Altier today, help me hand out bread and supplies from the palace kitchens. My mother cannot refuse if she thinks you arranged it. It would look badly on her."

"Devereux," I started to protest. There were a hundred reasons why I didn't want to go into the city, the biggest of which was that I did not want a repeat of what had happened last time. A clash between the guards and the people now, especially over me, would be devastating after the events of last night.

"I'll hear no refusal," Devereux said, but he leaned in and smiled at me. "Please, Lady Astraea, think of all the good you can do. Those people who are now without homes, who suffered at the claws and fangs of the voidlings. You can *help* them."

I wanted to help, I really did. But how much good would handing out bread do, when I should be pushing back the void and making all of this unnecessary? Making the suffering disappear almost entirely. I was weak, and tired, and what little spark my magic had left was flickering. My eyes were already drooping, ready to fall back asleep. And yet Devereux looked at me and pleaded.

How could I refuse?

Over the next several hours, he arranged everything while I did my best to crawl out of bed, bathe, and appear presentable. The voidling cub, whom I'd decided to name Dancer, pranced around at my feet during the whole process, lending me a strength I barely had. My muscles ached, and I was fighting exhaustion that showed in the circles under my eyes, but I was standing.

Devereux escorted me into Altier, surrounded by five guards, none of whom I recognised. All the Runners were supposedly busy, either recovering from last night or helping in shoring up defences against another attack. Casimir, to my disappointment, was nowhere to be seen. Though, I supposed he needed rest just as much—probably more—than I did.

Altier was not as badly damaged as I expected, even with Devereux's description of the mildness of the attack. There were a few buildings that had been destroyed, rubble and lumber strewn across the streets, but mostly there were just gouges to wooden beams, or a few slate shingles that lay in the street. Some thatched roofs had holes in them, but they were already being repaired. The people of Altier, though shaken, appeared perfectly healthy and hale, and were already well on their way to cleaning up the evidence of the night before.

"Here," Devereux declared, stopping the wagon carrying bread, and some smoked meats with a wave of his hand. He hopped down from the seat, then turned and made a show of helping me down. Dancer leaped to the ground and grumbled as Devereux nearly stepped on his tail. I grew increasingly anxious about this plan now that we were amongst the people. The sight of the prince, or perhaps the shadow tiger cub, caught the attention of those people in the streets. They started whispering, putting up their brooms and barrows to inch closer.

"Good morrow," Devereux said, smiling yet somehow still retaining a solemn demeanour. "We came to help you in your plight, after the terrors of last night."

"We had no terrors like the palace," a familiar voice said. I turned and recognised Tali, the dress-maker's granddaughter. She had her skirts tucked up into her apron strings for ease of movement, and her skin was smeared with dirt from clearing debris. Devereux spotted her and immediately smiled and bowed.

"Perhaps not," he said, "but the destruction of your houses is still no small matter. I have brought the Lady Astraea, as well as a wagon full of bread and meat for you."

At the mention of my name, the murmurs and whispers became cries. People surged forwards, their hands reaching, their eyes wide and eager. Tali turned her back on us and spread her arms, commanding the attention of the people.

"Halt!" she said, before the guards could even draw their swords. "Have you no shame? The Lady Star is not here to be gawked at, nor torn apart like some idol at the Temple on the equinox. She is here to *help* us."

The desperation remained in the people's eyes, but their reaching stopped. They shuffled closer, and were pushed back again by Tali. Eventually, Devereux managed to create some sort of order by shoving a loaf of bread and some meat into the hands of the Altian nearest him. After a bit more of this, people arranged themselves into a sort of line, accepting food and staring at me, then moving on.

I found myself handing out bread, Devereux meat, and Tali ladling out water for drinking. Dancer pounced on the scraps of food that people dropped, and though he earned strange looks, no one screamed at him. They just watched me.

"Maybe you shouldn't have come," Tali murmured to me once the crowd had died down a little, people shuffling off to their own secluded spaces to tear into their meal, eyes still following me as I moved. "Word has spread of what you did."

"So I heard," I replied. "His Highness thought it would be best that we get out, let the people see that I'm still just...me, I guess. Though, the food was his idea."

Tali shook her head, watching the eager Devereux out of the corner of her eye. "It's a dangerous thing, for you to be in the streets right now. The Temple has already declared you a hero, as well as the Chosen One. The people are, shall we say, fervent to get to you. Just to touch you. Your actions the other day were enough to set them off; this is just adding fuel to the fire."

Everyone seemed calm enough, though people were staring intently at me. I handed out another loaf of bread to a stooped man with a beard covering half his chest. He bowed deeply, touching his hand to his heart.

"May the blessings of the Earth Mother go with you, Bright One," he said. He backed away before I could ask what he meant, never once looking up from his bow. Beside me, Tali frowned.

"Earth Mother? Bright One?" I asked. The names tickled something in my mind, like they were familiar, but I couldn't place how.

"The Earth Mother is one of the old gods," Tali said in an undertone. "They were a pantheon of powerful, sometimes fickle beings. Their worship was displaced by the Temple of the Fallen Star, but you'll still find people who pray to them. Farmers, mostly, a few wandering sages. Their worship is more common away from Baldarskiel, in places where the void's touch is less known."

That seemed harmless enough. I knew that the gods were still part of the lore people followed, but the devotion to the Fallen Star seemed to displace everything, until they were little more than a curse, a passing story. I was about to say so when Tali seized my wrist. She was staring at something over the line of houses to our left. A cloud of dust, growing. A distant roaring grew louder, rising in time with the dust cloud.

"You need to leave. Now." Tali shoved me in the direction of a guard. The man nearly drew his sword on Tali, but she pointed in the direction of the dust cloud. The guard grew wan.

"I apologise, Lady Star," he said, then grabbed me around the waist and pulled me bodily away from the wagon and breadline. I was thrown into the saddle of one of the guards' horses. The guard leaped up behind me, then spurred the beast into action. I was unfamiliar with the layout of Altier, but I could see the palace moving farther away in the distance.

The dust cloud approached from there, pushing us away.

"Stop!" I struggled in vain against the grip of the guard. Even with my training, I was weak and my struggles were pathetic. "What are you doing?"

"I apologise, Lady Star," he repeated, "but we had to get you out of there. A mob was approaching."

I turned to look, and saw Dancer running after the horse, ears pinned to his head. Behind him, a second guard had Devereux in her grasp, the prince writhing as he tried to get away. Tali ran along beside, her skirts clutched in her hands. Behind them was a sight that set my blood cold. People, Altians, were running for the wagon we'd abandoned. They were squeezed together in tight quarters, their attention fixed on us, on the food. People reached for the bread. Others ran for the fleeing horses.

Then, chaos. A woman tripped, tumbling to the ground hard enough to snap her wrist. She screamed, but to no avail. The people behind her were pressed too close; they trampled her. Others fell. The wagon was soon torn to pieces. People fought over the bread and meat, tearing into those who had been faster than they. Some still ran for us, shouting.

"Bright One! Lady Star!" They called after me, their voices shrill with need and a hunger that no bread could ever quench.

The guard's face was grim, but he didn't turn

around, not even when the screams grew shrill and desperate, full of pain. "We'll go to the Temple," he said. "You'll be safe there."

I closed my eyes and turned forwards in the saddle. Their screams followed me all the way through the city, where they echoed in my mind.

CHAPTER 13

The Temple of the Fallen Star stuck out from the rest of the city like a glass shard. It towered above the surrounding houses and shops, drawing the eye to its stone-carved spires and detailed carvings, cut through with wide windows decorated with brightly coloured glass. From the outside, it managed to look both imposing and beautiful, an intimidating structure that cowed all who passed by.

The guard did not even bother to dismount from his horse, guiding the creature up the steps and into the open doors, shoving past a blue-robed priest with a shout of, "Make way!"

Devereux and Tali appeared a moment later, the prince still struggling from the grasp of his guard, who finally dumped him on the ground in an unceremonious heap. Tali bent over, breath heaving, eyes wide and watchful. The guards slammed the doors shut behind us, once again causing the priest to shout in alarm.

"What is going on here?" Beatrice appeared, looking disgruntled. Her veil was crooked and her expression harsh. As soon as she saw me, a graceful smile spread across her face, and she curtseyed deeply. "Lady Star!" she said. "After hearing of your exploits last night, I must convey the gratitude of everyone here. You saved us—"

"My apologies, High Priestess," the female guard said, her hand on her sword, "but we must ask that you keep these doors barred until the commotion dies down in the streets. A, ah, mob formed once it was discovered that the Chosen One was out and about."

Beatrice frowned. "Of course." Her attention snagged on her brother, who was still dusting himself off. He looked upset, but from the way that his eyes kept flicking to the closed doors, I had a feeling that he was more concerned with the people out there than those of us in the Temple. Beatrice reached over and touched his arm, a strange light in her eyes. "Brother. What were you thinking, bringing the Chosen One into the streets today?"

Devereux licked his lips, fidgeting with the edge of his tunic. What happened at the bread wagon must have really upset him, to be so distraught, even in front of his sister. I took a step forward, my legs shaking.

"The fault is mine, High Priestess," I said, my voice more smooth than I expected. "I wished to see the damage the voidlings caused Altier last night, and thought that it would be useful to hand out food to those affected by the attack. I underestimated their... interest in me."

Beatrice studied me for a moment, her eyes passing over Dancer leaning against me, the way my hands trembled slightly against my skirts, my face—which no doubt showed every particle of exhaustion I still felt. Then, she smiled, a look of pity. "It is generous of you to stand up for my brother, but he can surely deal with the consequences of his actions. You can barely stand, Lady Star! Am I to believe that you thought it wise to venture out so soon after experiencing magic sickness? I know little about wild magic, but surely—"

"Do you doubt my word?" I drew up, my shoulders back. My chin went up. I stared down Beatrice until she looked away, blinking hastily, already falling into a curtsey.

"No, of course not, Lady Star!" she simpered. "I merely did not understand the breadth of your compassion for the people of Altier."

Devereux stood by my side, threading his arm

through mine. He breathed a thanks in my ear, then let me lean on him. "Sister, now that we are to be here for some time, perhaps a tour of the Temple is in order? I understand that you especially wished Lady Astraea to see the murals?"

Beatrice's smile turned brittle as she turned it on her brother. "Of course! It wouldn't do to waste such a perfect opportunity. Please, if you'll follow me, I will show you the heart of the Star's gift to the people, as shared by her loyal servants."

The High Priestess spun on her heel, reaching up to straighten her veil as she did so. The blue-robed priest who had been shoved aside at our entrance ran up to her and took some instructions in his ear. He bowed once, looked at me and bowed deeper, then scurried off before Beatrice could do more than glare. Devereux squeezed my arm even as I tried not to tremble with exhaustion. A tour of the temple was absolutely not what I needed just then, but admitting my weariness would be just as problematic.

So, fully aware of the stares painting my skin with their desperate curiosity, I straightened my shoulders and walked after Beatrice.

The Temple was just as grand on the inside as it was out, with columns topped with exquisitely carved statues. The figures were of both genders, with veils covering their features, and not one reminded me of the Star, though I silently admitted I had no knowledge of such things. Indeed, the figures were draped with different items that reminded me more of Tali's Earth Mother instead. A basket of food, trees and flowers, a vase overflowing with water, a hunter's bow, a torch of fire. The forgotten gods, perhaps? An odd adornment for the star's temple.

I looked at the dressmaker and she smiled weakly at me. There were no answers there.

"Supplicants," Beatrice said, having noticed my attention. "These are statues of supplicants who came to the Star when the void first appeared, offering their goods and skills to her cause."

"Are there no images of the Star?" I asked, looking at the carvings that graced the high ceilings. There were creatures of all sorts, some of them monstrous, some of them not. Voidlings, perhaps. I quickly turned my attention away, memories of last night's battle too easily summoned.

"There are some that we think may be the Star, done after her disappearance." Beatrice shrugged one shoulder. "She was exceptionally modest, after all, and did not want effigies of her."

Devereux muttered something under his breath, which sounded quite rude towards his sister. I ignored him as best I could. Beatrice, though, stiffened and stalked farther on ahead.

"Come along, now," she said, voice tight.

We were led through the Temple, in all its carved

beauty, the coloured glass letting light shine on the floor in a myriad of patterns that looked like flowers on the stone floor. There were benches of simple carved wood for worshippers, and a raised dais where a pulpit stood, a large gilded book resting there. Presumably the teachings the Star left behind.

Beatrice ignored all of this, instead leading us through a door in the back wall, out to a room that was open to the skies. The floor was being cleaned by two young girls dressed in white robes, one sweeping and the other scrubbing with brush and water. The room looked as though it should have been full of plants, of life, spreading branches and stems to the skies, but instead it was empty of everything except a wooden scaffold set against one wall. Most of the wall was covered with a canvas, but I saw a design on the part that was clear. A mural, being dabbed on by a man who was definitely not a priest or priestess, dressed in rough clothing smeared with paint.

He took one look at me and froze.

"You may go for now," Beatrice told him with a dismissive wave. The man didn't move, his dark eyes fixed on me, a darkening of his brown cheeks signifying some high emotion. I swallowed nervously, glad for the comfort of my arm through Devereux's, Dancer at my side.

"What is this?" I asked, my eyes catching on the design.

"I *said* you may go!" Beatrice snapped. The man startled and ducked his head.

"As you say, High Priestess," he murmured. He quickly wiped his fingers on a rag tucked through his belt, then covered his paints and backed away from the mural. He approached me, ignoring a hiss from Beatrice, then bowed deeply. "It is an honour to meet you, Lady Star," he said. "I can only hope that my painting pleases you. Now that I have seen you, I will try to do you justice."

I recoiled, but before I could say anything, the man bowed again and walked off. I turned to Devereux, who was wincing.

"It was meant to be a surprise for our betrothal," he said. "Unveiled on the equinox. But maybe it's better that you see it now, if that's the look you're going to give."

"Nonsense!" Beatrice snapped. "It is an honour to be included on the wall."

With that, she tore away the canvas that was protecting most of the wall, the mural. With a self-satisfied smirk, Beatrice gestured to the larger-than-life painting that stretched the length of the wall. "What do you think?"

My heart dropped into my stomach. It was suddenly difficult to breathe, and the trembling in my limbs had less to do with exhaustion than with shock. Had Devereux not been supporting me, I would have sunk to the ground and buried my face in Dancer's fur. The mural was beautiful. It was more beautiful than any of the tapestries in the palace, and nothing I'd ever seen could compare. Even with my limited experience, I doubted anything I would see could compare. It was stunning. And devastating.

The mural was a depiction of the Chosen Ones. Seven of them, it appeared, all in different dresses and styles. They were all women, lithe and practically glowing with life. Their skin was fair. Two of them had freckles. Their hair ranged from silvery white to a reddish blonde. Their eyes were bright, blue or grey or even a shade of lavender. Every single one of them wielded the light of a star. It dazzled at their finger-tips, gave them an aura of divinity, sparking at their heels. Some had wind blowing their hair, or a storm in their wake, an indication of other magics they had wielded. The part that burned, though, was the image that wasn't yet complete. The eighth Chosen One. Me.

I had flowers at my feet, fire in my eyes, and a shadow tiger at my side. My body was indistinct, not yet complete, and the details on my grey gown were blurry, faded, almost the same colour as the stone wall upon which I was painted. In one hand, I held that same starlight that the others held. In the other, darkness. My face, though, was a terrible thing to behold. Burned and scarred, the beauty that might once have been there replaced with something fierce and dangerous. My darker skin and hair and green eyes may have looked little like the previous Chosen Ones, but none of them had any expression other than serenity on their features. In the middle of a company of fair beings, I was a tortured, horrid thing. Promising death and fire, not life.

Not hope.

"Stars above," Tali breathed, startling me so that I jumped. I had forgotten that anyone was there, that there were people to witness my distress.

"Lady Astraea?" Devereux asked, his arms suddenly around my waist as my legs fell away beneath me. "Are you quite well?"

"She is just a little faint," Beatrice said, sweeping in and grabbing my arm in her hand hard enough to bruise. She set me back on my feet and glowered at her brother. "Who wouldn't be, when faced with being immortalised in the Temple?"

"Perhaps some water?" I begged, wanting to turn my back on the mural forever. My request had the desired effect, the royal siblings all but dragging me from the open-skied room to a small, quiet chamber with a long seat and several shelves of books. Beatrice went and scolded some young priestesses into bringing us tea, then sniffed in disdain when the guards asked about my well-being.

"Are you well?" Devereux asked in a low tone,

keeping an eye on his sister standing at the door. "You look faint."

"I was just..." How could I put into words what I felt upon seeing that mural? "Surprised."

Devereux's frown deepened. "You looked more than surprised," he murmured. "We're friends, aren't we? You can tell me what's wrong."

I shook my head, not sure I could find the words to describe it even to myself. How could I tell him that I felt inadequate, that I wasn't sure I could be the Chosen One that he and his people so desperately desired? I wasn't worthy of being stared at as though I hung the moon. I wasn't worthy of being sought after, not like the people had been. I had managed—barely—to help during the battle the night before, but it took everything out of me. Even now, I was shaky, exhausted, barely coherent. I knew that I would collapse the moment I was allowed. But the way that those people had stared at me in the street? Had shouted and screamed for me? That was worse than any exhaustion. Much worse.

"My lady," Tali said, kneeling before me. Her eyes were bright, seeking, but I didn't feel like she thought less of me for my reaction. "I know this is all over-whelming. Perhaps things will look better tomorrow."

I barely hid a snort. "I doubt it," I murmured. "The people—the Altians, the Council of Nobles, the queen, the Void Runners—will still be expecting..."

"Expecting what?" Devereux asked. Tali's mouth pressed into a flat line. She squeezed my burned hand, hard enough that I felt it even through the deadened skin.

"They'll be expecting the person painted on the wall," the dressmaker said. "A legend. Not a person. Is that it?"

I nodded. Words failed me, and I feared I had nothing left to give. Dancer leaped into my lap, settling into my skirts with a purr. He eyed Tali and Devereux for a moment, eyes glowing brighter, then lowered his head and nestled into the fabric. My heart swelled, whether with the emotion that flowed through whatever connection we had, or with the reassurance that Dancer, at least, would not expect of me more than I was capable of giving.

"Finally!" Beatrice swanned back into the room, a procession of people bearing trays behind her. One held a small table, which was set on the ground and quickly adorned with a tablecloth. The trays were emptied, and in moments a full spread of food and tea was prepared before us. There were pastries and sandwiches and meats and cheeses, more food than could possibly be consumed by the four of us, or even the six of us with the two guards included.

"Did the Temple distribute any food to the people this morning?" Devereux asked. "After the disaster of last night, I would think that you and your people would be out trying to curry favour."

Beatrice laughed, the sound sharp. She poured a cup of tea and handed it to me, barely looking at her brother. "Curry favour?" she sneered. "Why would the Temple need to curry favour? We have living proof of the Star's divinity right here!"

I winced, pretending that it was the heat of the tea which made me flinch.

"The Star's divinity?" Tali asked. "I thought the gods were the divine creatures. The Star pushed them back, did she not? Wouldn't that make her anything but divine?"

Beatrice scoffed. "What do you know of theology...ah. Who are you?"

"Tali—"

"She's a friend," I said. Beatrice frowned and Tali blinked in astonishment. Devereux smothered a smile behind a sandwich.

"In any case, your *friend* is only partly right. The Star pushed aside the gods who had abandoned us, instead taking us into her care, giving us her wisdom and strength, even as she fought the void. Who needs the gods when the Star has given us the Chosen Ones? The only hope against the void?" Beatrice sniffed. I was suddenly anything but hungry.

"I wasn't questioning Lady Astraea's place in the world," Devereux said. "Only wondering if the

Temple was out doing good works, or hiding after the attack by voidlings?"

I stopped paying attention after that, my mind losing focus on the world. I knew only the meal in front of me, nibbled at, and the general sensation of Dancer's fur against my hand. I was aware, vaguely, that the Royal siblings were bickering politely, eyeing me to see if I would react to their words. Tali put her hand on my knee at one point, her expression concerned. But it was all I could do to stay upright. The image of the mural swam in front of my mind again and again until I was nearly insensate with exhaustion.

Finally, after what felt like an eternity, I became aware of the guard who had brought us here helping me stand, then finally carrying me to a carriage waiting outside. The streets, I thought, were strangely silent. There were no more screams. In fact, it appeared that there were no people out at all. I tried to piece out why, but knew nothing. Only that my eyes closed as soon as I sat in the carriage.

Someone's hands were there, warm, comforting. A voice spoke. "Why didn't you tell me of this fool plan of yours?"

Casimir. What was he doing there?

"She seemed fine this morning. Maybe a little tired, but—"

"She has magic sickness! If she doesn't rest properly, her body will never replenish the lost stores, and she will develop many illnesses. Her body is used to magic; to lose it forever could be enough to disable her entirely, or kill her if an infection settles in." Casimir's voice was cold, like ice piercing the skin, so cold that it burned.

"I didn't know," Devereux said, a snarl of defence.

"You should have asked me!"

I pried my eyes open, my mouth full of cotton. "No," I slurred. "I wanted to go."

"You, too, are a fool," Casimir said, but his tone was softer now. "Sleep, Astraea. I will wake you when we return to the palace."

"Promise?" I murmured, my eyes already closing.

"I promise," he said. I nodded, then lay my head on Devereux's shoulder beside me and slept, too tired to be grateful that no nightmares of attacking voidlings, or paintings of people long dead, disturbed my rest.

CHAPTER 14

"Fool!" The healer Eugenie leaned over me and checked my pulse. Her cheeks were flushed and her mouth was pressed into a thin line, eyes ablaze with anger. "I did not spend so much time healing your burns and broken bones only to have you expire from magic sickness. What were you thinking, getting out of bed, let alone throwing yourself into the middle of a riot?"

I winced. She was right. Every muscle in my body hurt, my bones ached, and if I tried to move, my nerves split into fire. Even with a tincture of pain medicine, I was hurting. Helping with Devereux's scheme of handing out bread and meat had not helped, nor had haring to the Temple on a horse.

"I didn't know how bad magic sickness was," I

managed, though my voice was hoarse. "Prince Devereux merely asked me to help him, and—"

"The prince is being chewed out by the queen. Consider yourself fortunate that I am the one delivering *your* scolding." Eugenie straightened and went to her pack of ingredients, rifling through bottles and leaves until she came up with the one she wanted. "Three drops of this in your evening drink, and you will sleep. Deeply. Do not even consider trying to get out of bed without assistance. Even to use the necessary! Rest until supper, then take this. Understand?"

"I understand," I said, and had no intention of disobeying. The healer sniffed, left the potion, then strode from my chambers without a second glance. Dancer, lying on the bed beside me, let out a confused mewl. "She means well," I said, lifting my hand enough to tangle in his fur. "I think."

I dozed fitfully for a few hours, the sunlight through my windows changing at each waking. Finally, at around supper, someone came through my door with a tray. It wasn't a servant, though. It was Casimir.

He wore bandages around his arms, and he had several cuts to his face that were scabbing over, plus bruises marring his features, but he was relatively whole. He set the tray on my bed, then sank onto the mattress beside me.

"What's this I hear of you getting out of bed?" he asked.

I huffed, pulling the tray closer. There was a crusty baked pie, with vegetables and meat inside, as well as various fruits drizzled with honey. Suddenly, despite my pain and exhaustion, I was starving.

"I didn't realise it would be a problem. Devereux came to see how I was, and he asked for my help. I thought—"

"You thought wrong." Casimir watched me struggle to cut the pie with a frown, then sighed and did it for me. I flushed. I was surely not that weak. Right?

"I didn't hurt this much this morning," I admitted.

"Magic sickness is very serious, Astraea. You can't just replenish the energy your body has used up. You have to rest, take time to recover. Once you've done that, *then* you can go into Altier."

"You're up and about," I grumbled, though I knew it was hardly fair.

"I'm a trained warrior, and I use arcane magic, which is an entirely different thing altogether. It is spells and incantations, not the life in your blood." Casimir sighed, then ran his fingers through his hair. "You scared me, Astraea. When I came to your rooms this morning and found you gone? I thought something had happened."

I flinched. It hadn't even occurred to me to ask after Casimir, or any of the other Runners and soldiers who had been in the battle. I'd just accepted Devereux at his word and run off to help him. I hadn't even thought that people would be concerned for *me*, at least not as anything beyond their precious Chosen One.

"I am sorry," I murmured. I shifted in the bed enough that Casimir could sit beside me, his legs stretched out alongside mine, his shoulder pressed against me. "I didn't know."

For a moment, we sat there in tense silence. I ate, the food disappearing far faster than I would have liked. Dancer tried to eat the scraps, but I pulled the tray away, pointing to the bowl of meat that a servant had left. The voidling made a sound and shuffled off to eat.

"In truth, I'm not angry at you. Nor, though, can I yell at Devereux. Even if I want to. Empty night, what was he thinking?" Casimir leaned his head against the headboard, looking truly exhausted. His wounds were fairly minor, certainly, but he seemed to bear a weariness beyond simple fatigue. It extended long and deep, and I didn't know what to do to help. So I lay my head on his shoulder and twined my fingers with his, trying to ignore the bandages.

"He wanted to help the Altians. Those displaced by the voidlings, who came here. He says that the queen will not release extra supplies to provide for them, so he thought that handing out bread and meat would be a start. He thought that if I were there, no one would question it. Would even be encouraged to help."

"Devereux..." Casimir sighed. "Devereux lives in a world of blacks and whites, and he walks around with his ideals at the forefront of his thoughts. A noble thing, and one to aspire to, but rarely practical. His cunning in politics and social charm is often overshadowed by his desire to help those he believes are not being helped. In this case, he is wrong.

"Those displaced by the voidlings are few in number, and they usually bring their own livestock and supplies with them, to sell if not eat. The queen has also ordered provisions to be purchased with the next void crossing, which will supplement those of the people for the winter. They are not starving. The grain stores which Devereux liberated not long ago— yes, I know about it, and so does his mother—were meant to be distributed during the harshest part of winter. We haven't even had the harvest, yet, and it looks to be a good one. Devereux's plan to distribute food would have been well received, but ultimately as just a kind gesture."

I studied my hands, where they lay on the fabric of my bed coverings, where they twined with Casimir's. Tears pricked the corners of my eyes. The screams of those injured in the riot, begging for help long after they stopped calling my name, rang in my ears. "It was all for naught?" I said on a croak.

"Kindness is rarely for naught," Casimir said. He reached over and brushed his fingers against my jaw, lifting my chin so that I looked at him. Deep in his eyes, that shadow still flickered, but it no longer frightened me. Instead, I felt a thrill, some part of me answering its call. I wanted to kiss him. Desperately.

"But then..." I leaned back far enough so that I could have a touch of distance, enough to clear my thoughts. "The riot?"

"For you. Didn't you hear what they're calling you? Bright One. A name not used since the first star." Casimir's expression went dark for an instant, then cleared. "They wanted to get close to you. To touch your hand, your dress, your shoes, whatever. They wanted your blessing. They wanted a word from your tongue, a lock of your hair, anything. You are their saviour, their Chosen One, and they would have torn down anyone in their way to get to you. Even themselves. The consequences they bear are their alone, as terrible as it is. Desperation for hope is a dangerous thing when poorly wielded."

There was a weight to his words that I did not understand, something in his eyes that told me of a previous me, who maybe revelled in all of that. What little Casimir had known of me before, it must have been enough to frighten him if he warned me this way.

"It's different now, isn't it?" I asked, touching my fingers to the ink-stained ones he bore. "From before?"

He let out a little breath. "Yes. More so than you'll ever know."

"Then trust me as I am now, not as I was."

"I trust you," he whispered, pressing his nose to my hair.

Before we could move further, either towards what now felt inevitable, or away, the door burst open. Devereux stalked into my chambers, his doublet unclasped, his shirt wide at the collar, hair unkempt and expression thunderous.

"My mother—" he stopped. Took in the two of us laying on my bed. We were fully clothed, and I was beneath the bedclothes, Casimir above. Dancer was leaping about the floor, playing with his food bowl, the very picture of calm. Yet, I knew that there was little doubt what Devereux saw.

Casimir and I froze, our hands still twined together. We said nothing. Devereux simply stared.

Something in his expression shuttered, then, and that warm openness I had known in him as my friend vanished. Immediately, he was the prince, charming and clever and unruffled by anything.

"I see," he said in a low voice. "Does our betrothal mean nothing to you, Lord Casimir?"

"You know full well that the two of you do not love each other," Casimir said, his voice just as even and cold.

"Devereux—" I started, trying to explain, to justify, even though I wasn't sure such a thing was needed. The prince held up a hand, cutting me off.

"It matters not, your justification," Devereux said. He drew himself up, shoulders back. "You have obviously forgotten yourself. The Lady Star is promised to me, as my wife, to be announced at the ball this coming week. You know this, Lord Casimir, and yet you have undertaken to, what, cuckold me? Or do you wish to claim the Chosen One for the Void Runners, to cement your control over the trade in and out of Baldarskiel. Perhaps you wish to gainsay her influence so that you might get more control in the Council of Nobles. Two votes rather than one? Three? Would you do away with the monarch altogether and put an electorate of Runners in its place?"

"Star above, Devereux!" I sat up as much as my weak muscles would allow, bracing myself on my hands so that I did not faint, despite the black spots that appeared in my vision. "Do you hear yourself? Thinking Casimir is, what, paying me attention because he wants power? It's absurd!"

Devereux twisted his lip in a sneer. "Is it?"

"It's only *your* family that wishes to control me for their own benefit," I snapped. "You've said so yourself."

He flinched. Casimir placed a hand on mine. I collapsed back against the pillows, exhaustion coming on me like a storm.

"I am not a fool, though my memories may only extend back a couple of moons," I murmured. "I heard you and your sister scheming about me. I know that my allure lies not in my beauty—" I gestured to my burned face, at which both men flinched, "—nor in my winning personality. I am rarely certain, rarely sure, and my achievements have all been wrought of cowardice and an inability to kill the very creatures I am destined to destroy. I *know* that you and your family want me for the influence I have, the ability to cause *riots* just by venturing outside the palace walls."

Devereux would not meet my gaze. "I thought we were friends," he murmured.

The fight went out of me. "So did I," I said.

"Why would you betray me like this, then?" he asked.

"She hasn't betrayed you," Casimir snapped. "Shame on you for thinking otherwise."

"Then you have willingly interfered with our betrothal. She *agreed* to wed me."

I had done. I had even been aware of the conse-quences of marrying someone I did not love. I knew that he and his family wanted me for their own power, though at least Devereux's intentions were altruistic. I had agreed because these people had helped me, because I owed them my life and more. Perhaps my gratitude was misplaced, or perhaps not. Either way, that did not mean I owed them my heart.

"Why are you angry?" I asked. "Did you truly think that I loved you?"

Devereux shrugged one shoulder. "Perhaps that you would come to do so."

"And I might have done. We *are* friends, Devereux. Did you think that as your wife I would be a friend bound to you forever, never to betray you as your family has done? Never to treat you as a pawn? I won't leave you, as much as it is in my power to promise such a thing, but surely you know that those ties you sought—your family sought—would be nothing more than chains, friendship or no. I do not want to be a pawn. I do not want the life that being the future queen will bring. I don't even want the foolish devotion of the people! I just want to push back the void. Then to make my own choices regarding how to live. Where to give my heart," I said. Casimir stiffened beside me, then relaxed, leaning into my touch. He brushed a strand of hair from my face and smiled.

"Truly?" he murmured, too quiet for Devereux to

hear. I nodded, as though some tentative agreement had been reached between us.

The prince watched this exchange vacantly. Then, his shoulders sagged, and he slumped into a chair. The fight had vanished from him, from us all. The lines were drawn. Now it was time to see what would happen next.

"My mother will be furious," Devereux said at last. "But I cannot deny that you are right, Lady Astraea. I did want to secure your friendship, truly. And I did hope we might one day have a love between us. But I also wanted your influence, as the Chosen One, as my wife. To help me build up a society of equal people and freedom for all, instead of the poverty I see outside my window. As I was informed this afternoon, however, my mother has already made plans for our people, ones years in the forming. I am redundant, useful only for my marrying power. You, at least, have a purpose."

"Fighting the void," I scoffed. "The one thing I have failed at."

"That fire last night was not failure, nor the way you used the earth to hold the voidlings in place." Devereux lifted his head and frowned at me. "Why would you think you failed?"

"Not one voidling slain by my hand, excepting that wolf who was attacking you, Casimir. No matter how I tried, I could kill no more," I said. "The seven

Runners dead that I remember only in my night-mares. However many more killed last night. Those injured. Those displaced. The void expands, and yet I lay abed, unable to do anything."

"None of it is your fault," Casimir said, that self-same heaviness in his words as before. As if he were begging me to believe it, when he knew it was a lie.

"You saved countless lives last night, even if you did just push them back," Devereux agreed.

"And you think you did nothing? I have never seen anyone care quite as you do. You have influence of your own. You should not forget it," I said.

Silence fell again, those words in praise of each other appearing to have taxed all of us beyond repair. We watched, waiting for someone to break the silence, but there was only Dancer, playing now with some thread on a tapestry.

"What do we do now?" Devereux asked finally.

"I don't know," I replied.

"We continue on as before," Casimir said. He sat up straight, taking charge as easily as if he were born to it. "You rest, Astraea, get your strength back, then we continue with your training, both magical and physical. At the ball this week, then, we act as though everything is normal. It is to function as her formal presentation to the court, no?"

"Yes," Devereux said. "And the announcement of our betrothal, which obviously can't happen now."

"No," I agreed. "Perhaps instead we could announce an alliance? An...accord? Something that would appease the court, if not your mother and sister."

"There is little that would appease them." Devereux rubbed his eyes, looking tired. As I would be, if I'd discovered that my plans and dreams were being achieved by another. "Unless you swore yourself into devotion at the Temple of Stars, in which case my sister would have her claws in you. Barring that, I imagine their fury will be terrible."

"She will not swear to the Temple," Casimir snapped. "Those pretenders, who do not even worship the gods whose statues grace their walls."

"You *are* old fashioned, aren't you? No one has openly worshipped the gods for nearly three genera-tions. Oh, yes, the farmers will have their harvest ceremonies for the Earth Mother. The shepherds still occasionally call on the Sky Farther in a storm. But worship them?" Devereux laughed.

I frowned. "Why would they not worship the gods? I know the Star pushed them back, but surely she would still have allowed worship to the gods." Especially if the Temple bore their figures, as Casimir claimed.

"They worship the Fallen Star, that is all," Casimir said, the words short and harsh.

"But the star wasn't a god." I felt like I was

pointing out something obvious, but both men gaped at me as though I'd spoken blasphemy. I shrank back into the pillows. Sensing my distress, Dancer leaped onto the bed and crawled into my lap, hissing at Casimir.

"No," Casimir said, his expression guarded. "She wasn't."

"It doesn't matter one way or another, the entire Temple is corrupt. They bow to the pressures of my mother and sister, getting people to agree to its edicts on tithes, on days of feast and fast, on how hard to work and when, on how to behave piously and act in a moral manner. Nothing short of your oath would please them."

I wrapped my arms around the voidling cub. "What do we do, then? At the ball."

"We inform my mother that the betrothal is off," Devereux said plainly. He stood and shrugged, shoulders no longer proud and straight. "There is little more she can do to me. She's already taken my purpose. My devotion to the people. Made it something...foolish. What else can she do?"

I leaned forwards, reaching out a hand. "Devereux, wait."

He turned and looked at me, something broken in his gaze. "Let me do this one thing. She would tear you to pieces, even if you are the Chosen One. Let me bear that burden, at least."

Then, he left.

I settled back against the pillows, suddenly weak. Dancer licked my face, and I tried to smile at the shadow tiger, tried to be happy and content that I was allowed to pursue this thing with Casimir, whatever it was. I'd told him he had my heart. Perhaps not in so many words, but it was true, if not entire. There was a shard in me that held doubt, bright and strong. Watching Devereux walk away had only made the doubt shine brighter.

"What have I done?" I murmured.

"Devereux is learning a lesson that all kings must learn, or be tyrants," Casimir said. He brushed my hair away from my face. "It is not your place to make the lesson less harsh."

"He is my friend." No matter what had passed in the last few minutes, I believed that much wholeheartedly.

"He is just a man." Casimir spoke the words with certainty, as though it meant something more. I shuddered, though I didn't know why. I took my goblet, dosed already with the potion to make me sleep, and drank the whole thing down.

"Goodnight, Astraea," Casimir murmured in my ears, then I gave way to the relief of oblivion.

I did not see either Casimir or Devereux again over the next week. I spent a great deal of my time in bed, recovering my strength. When Eugenie finally declared me well enough to be up and about, it was the day of the ball and I did not even have time to ask Eloise if we would resume training tomorrow before I was whisked away. Servants bathed me, scrubbing my skin raw, though they were more careful of the burn scars. They dried me, powdered me until my skin was an even tone, then started in on my hair.

I lost track over the next several hours of who was whom, only having the chance to talk when they brought me food and the polishing of my nails or the twining of tiny, silver beads into my fiery hair had to stop. I was brushed and painted and adorned with jewels, all in silvers and crystals and shadows. Then, I was dressed.

"Stunning," one of the attendants said as he draped my skirts artfully on the floor behind me. I stared at the black-flecked silver mirror and wondered if I dared agree.

Stunning, certainly. Fierce, even. Dangerous. Deadly. Any of those would suit better than the word I'd hoped would fit better. Beautiful. A foolish hope, perhaps, but one I'd harboured all the same. No, I would have to be happy with stunning. And I *was* stunning.

My hair was swept back from my face and pinned up, a few strands escaping and threaded with tiny crystal and silver beads. The silver and crystal continued as my hair cascaded down my back. My face had little in the way of paint, except around the eyes where I was decorated with shadow specked in silver. The burns had been smoothed and disguised with powders, but they were still impossible to miss, swooping across my cheek and down my neck and arm. I had a torque of the Fallen Star gems at my throat, cutting a stark swath across my burns. Then, there was the dress.

It was silver, the neck low enough only to show off the necklace and still hide the rest of my burns. The sleeves were long, again covering the burns on my left arm. The back dipped low, and the train brushed the floor when I walked. What made it so beautiful were the beads and crystals sewn onto the entire thing. Done up in shadow and silver, I looked like the night sky incarnate, gleaming and glistening and whispering as I moved.

But at the bottom, in tiny beads, were lines of gold. Just enough to hint at fire rather than stars.

"Are you ready, Lady Star?" the attendant asked me.

I was not.

I wanted to throw the dress away and crawl back into bed. Dancer was already there, sulking after having been told he could not attend the ball with me. The shadow tiger had grown in size again and was now at a height with my knee. He was too big to be subtle, and the presence of a voidling at the ball was likely to end in blood. Still, I wished with all my heart that I was remaining here with him.

A Chosen One who could not kill voidlings, whose prowess in battle was pitiful at best. Oh, yes, my magic was flashy and bright, but if I could not do anything with it, then what good was it? What good was I?

Before I could fall into the trap of my thoughts, once more spiralling downwards, there was a knock on the door. It opened and revealed Devereux, wearing a doublet of charcoal grey decorated with silver beadwork and a crown of dark iron and crystal on his hair. The colouring of his clothes was similar to mine, though darker, as if I were the emphasis in our matched set. I had no doubt that his mother and Beatrice had been behind the clothing choices for us both.

"You look..." Devereux's eyes trailed over me, lingering on my throat where the torque sat across the burns, marking them more than if it had not been there. He stared at the dress, at the line of gold at the bottom, and something in his throat worked. Finally, he met my eyes again, and he tried to smile. "You look stunning."

"Thank you." I inclined my head. Stunning. That was what I was meant to do, I supposed. Stun people with my presence. Blind them to the possibility that I could be anything other than the perfect Chosen One.

"How are you?" I noticed the smudges under his eyes, as if he hadn't slept the night before. Or the night before that. "How are...the people?"

Devereux's mouth twisted wryly. "If you mean to ask how the queen is after hearing of our failed betrothal, then the answer is that she is livid. Beatrice is perhaps the more vocal on the matter. She was practically screaming the temple down when I told her. However, if you *actually* mean to ask how the Altians are doing, how people are faring in the countryside where the void encroaches, then the answer is less simple. The plans my mother has made are long-standing and will not come to fruition swiftly. The people have begun receiving extra rations of grain, and makeshift settlements have grown around Starfall Meadow and the Mist Haven quarters. Altier grows, thrives, and I sit in this palace doing nothing useful but attending council meetings, reading books on agriculture strategy and animal husbandry."

I winced. He laughed, the sound caustic.

"Do I offend you when talking about my uselessness? I apologise, Lady Star, if I made you uncomfortable. It's just nice to be able to do so much for my family, for my people, even if it is only through marriage."

I reached out and grabbed Devereux's hand; it was his turn to flinch from me. He cast his eyes down, shoulders hunched. I waited until he looked at me. "Is that what you think?" I asked. "That you hold no value to Baldarskiel and your family except by virtue of your marriageability? That you hold no value to me?"

Devereux snorted and pulled his hand away. He went to where Dancer lay on the bed and tickled the voidling behind the ear. The tiger yawned, revealing those terrible fangs. Devereux didn't even seem phased.

"My mother was displeased at the fact that we are not to be wed, as I told you. I tried to offer help in other ways, perhaps taking on more of a role in the Council of Nobles, such as gathering taxes or distributing supplies between people. It was no use. She stripped me of my position on the Council, excepting the lands my grandfather gave me. Apparently, all the education and tutoring in statecraft I've had amounted to nothing." Devereux snorted. Dancer eyed him before stretching and turning around on the bed.

"Your mother," I said, crossing over to him, "is a spiteful woman if she thinks that your only value is in marrying me. I'm not some prize to be bought. Surely she doesn't think that you *need* my influence, not with everything that you've done to help your people? They know you as something other than your mother's puppet, at least. Right?"

Devereux shrugged.

"I'm sorry," I said. It was hardly fair, that his own family thought me more valuable than him, more worth pursuing. That they would punish him for not winning my heart.

"Don't be." He turned and smiled at me, the look full of arrogance and charm that did not quite shine in his eyes. Still, it was better than the sulking and despondent person I'd seen just minutes ago. "You deserve to be happy."

I snorted, fingering the skirts of my dress. "Is that what I am?"

"I hope that you *will* be happy, with Casimir or someone else if you choose. I hope that you'll be happy with your life," Devereux said. He held out his arm, and I twined mine through his. "One of us deserves to be happy, and if it's not the Chosen One, then I don't know who could be."

I smiled, though the movement felt tight. I was far from happy, though I'd stolen a few joyful moments with Casimir. I was a failure. My destiny loomed before me, and all I could do was illuminate it, not fight it, not defeat it.

"Let's go get this ball over with," I said. "Then I can get back to training to fight the void, and you can get back to doing your best to be a good prince to your people."

We both winced at my words, but neither of us mentioned it. Then, I was swept from my rooms and led towards the throne room. It was, apparently, the only room in the castle large enough to hold the ball. It also opened up into the gardens, so that the equinox ceremony led by Beatrice would take place here, rather than at the temple.

"Are there parties in Altier, for the equinox, I mean?" I asked, desperate for something to diffuse the tension climbing my spine.

Devereux shrugged. "Sometimes. It's harvest, so there are usually festivals and celebrations for that, but the equinox itself is more of a...purely religious holiday. Most of the people prefer drinking cider and eating meat pies to sitting in a temple and staring at the open sky."

I chuckled. "I can hardly blame them. I would choose that, too."

"If you had a choice," Devereux said. His charm, that sure expression, turned solemn. "If we either of us had a choice."

I nodded.

The closer we drew to the throne room, the more I could see how much the palace had pulled together all the tricks to show off. There were swaths of tree branches with leaves in a multitude of colours draped from the candles and arcane lights, twined with gold and silver fabrics to catch illumination. The tapestries had been dusted, or replaced, the scenes depicted within of heroic adventures and people whose stories I did not know. There were more servants and guards than usual, their uniforms gleaming.

And, of course, there were the people. Some I recognised from that disastrous Council of Nobles meeting, dressed in velvets and silks of bright, cheerful colours. Most people, though, I did not know. They lingered around the entrance to the throne room, watching others pass by and whispering in their companions' ears.

When Devereux and I appeared at the turn of the

hall, the whispering increased. Every eye turned towards us, towards *me*. I wanted to freeze, to run, to do anything but be here. Every step I took forwards was agony, like those first steps after my waking, when the entire world was new and unknown.

Devereux squeezed my hand, catching my attention. He straightened his shoulders, lifted his chin, and whispered, "All these people wish that they were as dazzling as you, Lady Star. Don't fear them. Never fear them."

I inclined my chin in the closest I could come to a nod, and wished I could say the same to him, to soothe those fears we both carried.

Now was not the time, though.

Now I was to put myself on display for these people who displayed such finery, such ease and care and grace. These people who depended on me to save them all.

"The Lady Star, Astraea, and Crown Prince Devereux," a steward announced, her voice thrown across the throne room so that no one could possibly pretend not to have heard. And if the eyes were staring before, now they were piercing.

I lifted my chin and stepped into the fray, the second battle I'd faced in a week. I wasn't sure which was worse.

Queen Raya sat upon her throne with King Consort Istir beside her, casually holding a goblet of wine and chatting with a few bejewelled people nearby. She cast a glance my way, her mouth tightening ever so slightly, then returned to her conversation. Beatrice was nowhere to be seen, though I had no doubt she was about, planning on making an entrance or already whispering in ears to turn heads in her direction.

That left Devereux and I to wander the room freely. I saw a banquet table piled with more food than could possibly be consumed, even by this large crowd. There were musicians in a corner, playing their instruments with great skill, but largely ignored by everyone. In another corner, a juggler spun knives through the air, surrounded by two dancers who got perilously close to the blades before darting away. They, too, were ignored.

No, it would seem that I was the entertainment of choice that evening.

A man with a full head of greying hair, his beard neatly trimmed, skin naturally dark, clothes of purple velvet, bowed before me. "I do not know if you remember me, Lady Star," he said in smooth tones. "I am Lord Ashcroft. We were introduced at the Council of Nobles, where you tamed your voidling."

I vaguely remembered his name, and face, but little else. That whole day was little more than a blur. "Lord Ashcroft, how good to see you again."

"I am all the better for seeing you, looking so

resplendent after your battle the other day." He held out a goblet full to the brim with wine. I glanced at Devereux and he nodded, so I took the goblet. I could not bring myself to drink.

"It was hardly my battle," I said. "Surely the Void Runners did most of the fighting."

I looked around, half-expecting to see Void Runners in their ivory uniforms, but instead saw only the palace guards along the walls, watching.

"You won't find any here," Ashcroft said, a cunning look in his eye. "They're not allowed in the palace proper, unless for guard duty or at the direct invitation of the Queen."

I blinked. "Oh, but Lord Casimir—"

"The exception," Devereux cut in smoothly. There was a warning in his eyes. "An Ambassador from Cortaesi, though we seldom see any of his countrymen this far north, and beyond the void as well. He is your personal guard and trainer, which grants a certain, hmmm, leeway? He is also a friend of mine and holds considerable land near the coast, making him a true lord."

Ashcroft smiled. "Indeed, Lord Casimir does rather capture the interest of everybody he meets. It seems a shame, though, that the Runners should be so shunned, when they do so much."

I had the impression that there were political undercurrents I was not understanding, so I stayed silent. Devereux, thank the stars, cut in again, looking bored.

"This argument again, Lord Ashcroft?" he sighed. "Everyone knows that the Void Runners would hold a great deal of political power if they were to be given voting rights. As it is, many of the noble houses have younger children training there. And diplomats from beyond the void, like Lord Casimir. If we gave them more voting rights in the Council, then every other member would be made null and void. There would be no point to the Council, then."

"And Baldarskiel would be ruled by the Void Runners. Yes, that is the argument," Ashcroft said, taking a sip of his own wine. His eyes twinkled, and I caught a hint of a smile. "Tell me truly, Prince Devereux, would that be such a terrible thing? The Runners know more about the lay of the land than any of us, as they are out there every day. And they're required to be educated, which is a mite more than can be claimed of *certain* members of the Council. Do you honestly think the people would suffer more under the Runners? Or less?"

Devereux clenched his jaw. Just for a moment, but it was enough to have Ashcroft smiling openly. He raised his goblet. "Don't think that rumours aren't spreading of your...dissent against the throne. Oh, the queen may have swooped in at the last minute to save face now, with the spreading void, but how long do you think it will last? How long do you think the goodwill can stand when the Runners are pulled from guarding trade convoys to fighting the void at every turn? How long will the grain last, then? We are northerly, here. Our soil is not ripe for growing. The citizens closer to Ynysfawr and the coast have already turned to Hunters for repast, those barbarians. No, our value lies in keeping back the void. But that fills no bellies."

Devereux's throat worked, his swallow nearly audible. I saw the faintest sheen of sweat break out on his brow. I knew that he felt the same, that he wanted to agree with Ashcroft, but he did not. Fear, perhaps, of his mother's reprisal. Or something else. I knew very little about the situation, and even less about the political web within the court of Baldarskiel. Still, even I could tell that this conversation grew fraught.

"This is pleasant talk for the equinox," I said, finally taking a sip of the wine. It was rich, thick, and too sweet. I lowered the goblet. "I thought we were meant to be celebrating."

Immediately, Ashcroft bowed. "Do forgive me, Lady Star. I fear that I think of politics and manoeuvrings so much that it is difficult for me to simply enjoy good company. And yours is, after all, the best company one can have."

I smiled, as sincerely as I could.

"When the ball is opened, would you favour me with a dance?" Ashcroft asked, already extending an arm. I saw several people around the room eyeing him with open interest, even jealousy.

"Oh, I don't—"

"Welcome!" The queen rose from her throne and lifted her arms. "The equinox is a day to celebrate the alignment of the stars and the remembrance of the past for the sake of the future! Before we open the ball, I would like to introduce to you the Chosen One, the Lady Astraea, whose magic defended us only a few days ago, and whose magic will defend us again against the encroaching void!"

Everyone looked at me. My face grew warm and the goblet in my hand trembled. Devereux took it in a swift movement before I could drop the thing. I tried to smile. I failed.

The queen looked at me and a slow, dangerous grin spread across her mouth. She nodded her head to me. My throat tightened.

"The Lady Star has told me herself that too long the void has grown closer, trying to steal our light, our life. As such, she feels it is time for her to go and face the void. In two days' time, she will venture forth to Ynysfawr, the place where it all began, and do battle with the void. My son, the Crown Prince Devereux, will accompany her, to bear witness to the

Chosen One's battle. May the First Star watch over her and guide her along the way."

Silence roared in my ears, even as I could see people's mouths moving, even as I was certain that someone had to be screaming in horror. Only, no one was. I wasn't ready to face the void. The battle at the wall had proven that. My sparing Dancer had proven that. Everything I'd done had proven that.

I locked eyes with the queen and she lifted her chin.

If I did not wish to marry her son, to give her my influence and power—neither of which I wanted—then I would have to prove my use in a different way. I would have to face my destiny. And, if I went now, when my training was incomplete, when my magic was barely contained, let alone controlled, then my chances of pushing back the void were very slim indeed. She knew it, I knew it, and yet now that such a plan had been announced, I could not refuse for fear of the world seeing my weakness. My failure.

CHAPTER 16

The lights were too bright, the world spinning too quickly. Only Devereux's arm in mine kept me steady, kept me from falling to the floor as I processed the meaning of the queen's words.

"Breathe, Lady Astraea," Devereux said out of the corner of his mouth. "We'll deal with the aftermath later. Right now, the eyes of everyone are on you and you must be resplendent."

Right. Of course. I took two deep breaths and bowed my head. The magic in my veins rumbled, reacting to my distress. The earth and fire twined together, pushing against whatever control I had on them. The light merely laughed in my ear.

Foolish, it said. *To think you could have everything you wanted.*

I lifted my head to smile at those around me and mentally shoved the power down, down, down, hiding it away until it was bound with that fire and earth, nothing more than a furious whisper. The shadows remained silent, watching, waiting, pooling in the small of my back like some armour. Its weight was the only comfort I could draw.

"You are braver than I thought," Lord Ashcroft said, tipping his goblet at me. "To face the void, almost alone. It is my understanding that Chosen Ones in times past have had armies of Runners at their backs."

I let out a laugh and desperately hoped it didn't sound as strangled as I thought. "I would rather no one else get hurt in the quest to push back the void."

At least that much was true.

"Lady Star," Devereux said, still with that bored tone, as calm as ever, "I hate to interrupt, but there is someone I really *must* introduce you to before the ball opens."

Without a backwards glance at the political Lord Ashcroft, I was whisked away. We crossed the room, past several other members of the Council, past people who stepped forwards to greet me, hands outstretched to touch me, to possess me. Devereux deftly sidestepped them all with polite smiles and greetings, but never stopped. Not until we were near the buffet table, near a woman old enough to be my great-grandmother, her golden skin more wrinkled than smooth, her white hair piled on her head in a truly ridiculous ensemble, complete with beads and feathers. Her dress was garish and ill-fitting, just a little too loose in the shoulders and bodice, just a little too short in the hem. But her eyes, they were dark and cunning and fully aware.

"Am I to be her rescuer, Prince Devereux?" the crone asked, popping a fig into her mouth. She leered at me while she chewed. "I saw you trying to escape Ashcroft, the conniving fox. And your reaction to the queen's announcement. A shock to you both, though you will surely claim otherwise."

Devereux smiled wryly. "Lady Astraea, this is Dame Winters, the official seer of the Baldarskiel court."

"A seer?" I blinked. I'd never heard of seers, only of arcane magic and wild magic. Dame Winters chuckled.

"Oh, yes, a seer. True seers held a wild magic known only to them, but I am a close enough facsimile. I know arcane spells that have been forgotten for generations by all but other seers. We guard them closely, for they have the power to look to the future as well as the past." Winters held out her hand, a myriad of rings dazzling on her fingers. "Would you care to look?"

To see my past. To see who I was, before I forgot.

The temptation was strong enough that I reached out to take her hand. Then, the woman laughed loud enough to draw the attention of several others around us, and snatched her hand away.

"Only fools rely on magic," she said, eyes twinkling. "You can learn everything you need by watching people. By seeing the things they wish to hide. Like I saw you, just now."

"So you cannot use magic?" I frowned. I desperately wanted to know what I might have seen about who I was, and yet she pulled away so swiftly. So easily. Teasing me.

"I can," Winters said. Her expression darkened for a moment, turning the ridiculous costume she wore into a darker, more sinister raiment. "It is not for you, though, Lady Star. Other Chosen Ones have tried, in times past, to cast into the future and see the outcome. See how to succeed, see how they would be beloved by the ones they saved. See the joy that was surely due to them in the future. Always, there was a cost they could not comprehend."

I did not want to see the future. "I want the past," I murmured. "I want to know my past."

Interest sparked in Winters' eyes. "Ah, yes, I'd heard that you were without memories."

"Can you restore them?" Devereux asked, taking note of the conversation for the first time since introducing us.

"No." Winters plucked another fig from the table, rolling it through her fingers. "Even if I could, I would not. The gods took your past for a reason, and I need no magic to tell me that. Now, stop hiding over here by a shunned woman and mingle."

"I would rather not," I admitted, eyeing the courtiers who were lingering nearby, not close enough to hear and therefore interact with this Dame Winters, but close enough to claim my attention as soon as I stepped away.

"Politicians and snakes, the lot of them," Winters sniffed. She grinned at a young man who drew too close. His cheeks turned bright red, and he scurried away. "All of them afraid of what I might see. The only reason the queen keeps me around. Still, hiding here will bring no one any confidence in you. And if you are to face the void, alone, then you will need everyone here to have confidence in you. So that they will not die hopeless deaths."

Without so much as a by-your-leave, Dame Winters popped the fig into her mouth and strode away to the other end of the banquet table, where she leered at a hapless young woman and her mother, both of whom immediately leaned away and started looking about for their own rescue.

"Why would you introduce me to her?" I asked Devereux, unable to look him in the eye.

"Because she's the only one no one else will talk

to. I thought it would give you some peace. Not..." he hesitated. "I'm sorry. This whole night was a mistake. As soon as my mother learned of our broken betrothal, she's been...I'm sorry."

"It is hardly your fault."

Devereux studied me, something in his expression hardening. "Perhaps you're right. Perhaps all of this is a mistake."

Before I could ask what he meant, Casimir appeared, bowing his head to Devereux and myself. "Your Highness. Lady."

I smiled, unable to help myself. Here was a good thing in the midst of all this chaos. Casimir wore his armour, polished and gleaming in ivory, with black clothes beneath. The black on his fingers and in his hair looked intentional, rather than a result of prolonged contact with the void. With his dark eyes and the strength of his stature, he looked more regal than I could claim, with all my borrowed finery and hours of preparation. Even Devereux, gilded and full of charm, could not quite match the assuredness of Casimir.

"I thought you weren't coming," Devereux said, and there was only relief in his voice. "I don't think I could make it through my sister's ceremony without you there."

Casimir winced. "Ah, yes, the equinox ceremony.

At least we don't have to traipse to the temple this year."

"What's so bad about this ceremony?" I asked. "I thought it was some sort of guidance for how the winter would fare, or the harvest or something."

Devereux scoffed. "Hardly. It's all nonsense. My sister and her acolytes pretend to read the stars and cast our fortunes—entirely unlike what Dame Winters can do—and then there's some chanting and begging for the First Star to return and purge the void from us entirely. If the star does return, it won't be because we chanted for her."

Casimir flicked his eyes to me and his mouth tightened. "It used to be that the harvest was the purview of the gods, Lady Earth in particular, but the rise of the religion surrounding the First Star has pushed that aside. No one has heard from the gods in nearly two generations."

Devereux nodded. He started picking over the banquet table. "The devotion to the gods has waned and the Temple of the Fallen Star has risen, which solidifies my sister's power as a leader of the people. It's just one more way to control people."

"But if it's real, wouldn't that be a good thing, then? Guiding people?" I asked. "Helping them live a better life?"

"That's not what the Temple does," Casimir

murmured, as if he were apologising for something. "They worship the Star as a god, which she is not. Some say that is why the gods have abandoned us. Why the prayers of the people go unanswered. All the while, the Temple gathers control by reading the stars for answers to any problem, taking people's money and their prayers, buying their devotion with false words and promises."

Devereux coughed pointedly, looking around us. People were still trying to approach, but they remained a discreet distance off, as if they could sneak up on me. No one was likely to overhear us.

"Careful, Casimir," Devereux said under his breath. "You can get away with a fair bit, given your status, but even blasphemy against the Temple is dangerous, even for you. And to say such things to the Chosen One; if anyone heard, you would be flayed personally by Beatrice. I may not agree with the Temple, but I am not foolish enough to decry it to that degree."

Casimir growled something rude, but said nothing further on the matter. I, on the other hand, felt like I was swimming and barely able to keep my head above water. Already, I'd been thrust into a world of politics that I did not understand, one pitting the Runners against the royal family and its court. Then I'd been introduced to a seer, who kept my very past from me. Now I was told that the religion of the people, the one that claimed undying devotion to me—whether I deserved it or not—was false. I had barely heard of these gods until a few days ago, and now I was to blame for their silence. At least, me and the other Chosen Ones before me, those who were born of the Star and pushed the void back.

Who stole the devotion of the people.

"I think I want some air," I murmured. Casimir's hand shot out to grab my wrist before I could walk away. There was a pained look in his eye, more of that apology I didn't understand or require.

"You had better wait," Devereux said, eyeing the dais where his mother sat. "It looks as though the ball is about to open. You'll be required to dance."

I felt my face grow warm. "I...I don't know how to dance."

Devereux scoffed. "Surely you do! I remember teaching you myself maybe four months ago, one rainy afternoon."

His expression softened. "Oh."

"I'm sorry," Casimir said, frowning. "I have spent so much time devoted to your training that I did not think of this. I should have foreseen that this would be an issue."

"Can't I just stand in the corner?" I asked. "Surely someone will come by to speak with me. Keep me company. The courtiers, if no one else, simply because they want to talk with me."

"Unfortunately, you will be expected to dance,"

Devereux said. "My mother will demand it. And those who are your chosen partners will be greatly favoured in status and will claim your ear, try to win your influence. It's all part of this political dance of ours."

I looked desperately to Casimir for help.

"Devereux will open the ball with you," Casimir said. "Then I will dance, and hopefully that will last long enough you can claim fatigue for a bit. And we'll try to steer those who actually know how to dance in your direction. No one will care if you don't know all the steps, only that you're dancing."

Somehow, I doubted that. Still, I appreciated their attempts to cheer me up.

As predicted, the queen rose a few moments later to announce the opening of the ball. The musicians in the corner, previously ignored, straightened and put their fingers to their instruments. Devereux held out his hand for me and I slipped my fingers into his.

"I promise, I will not let you flounder," he said, smiling. Then, without further preamble, we began to dance.

The music was like nothing I'd heard before, not that I'd heard much music in my short memory. This was smooth and joyful, yet somehow elegant and calm at the same time. It was cheerful enough to hint at new beginnings without forgetting the past. It was wonderful.

Devereux was a deft dancer, his hands placed on my back and holding my hand. He put pressure on me when he wanted me to turn, to step, to dip, and in each beat of music, he knew exactly what to do. I'd heard Casimir tell me that Devereux was an accomplished politician, one skilled at manipulating things to his advantage. So far, I had seen no evidence to that fact; in truth, Devereux seemed charmingly naïve, idealistic, hopeful that the right thing would be done, always.

But tonight, when he danced, I knew what Casimir meant.

Each movement of Devereux's feet and hands and face were designed to draw attention. A simple smile at me had two ladies nearby start whispering as we passed. A glance of significance at a man perhaps ten years older than the both of us, wearing green velvet trimmed with bronze, had the man growing pale and start fidgeting with the buttons at his cuff. A turn that had me spinning very nearly out of control, my skirts brushing at the shoes of a trio of nobles in shining finery, had several interested glances turning towards me, towards my clothes and my gems. The stares that were on my burns but moments before now looked at my gilt and gleam. And I knew that this dance, the way Devereux moved, was carefully calculated to have everyone looking at me, not at my burns, at the face that would never be beautiful, only dangerously stunning, but at the fact that I was the Chosen One, the power of a fallen star somewhere in my veins.

One dance, and I had transformed from awkward and nervous, damaged in their eyes by the burns and my reticence at killing voidlings, into something more. Something of legend.

The idealistic prince, who stole grain from his family's own stores to feed the hungry, was indeed a cunning politician.

I wondered what he had shown me that I had seen as he wished, and not as it was. I wondered how much of his railing against his mother, his disappointment at having his schemes dashed, was true. How much was misdirection? I wondered who, exactly, would be travelling with me to Ynysfawr.

My mouth went dry just as the last music note echoed through the throne room.

Applause sounded quickly afterwards, and judging by the looks that everyone was giving me, it wasn't for the musicians. Devereux bowed to me; I gave him a curtsey in return, my legs trembling as they had not done since my waking. Then, he smiled and kissed my hand.

"There, that wasn't so bad, was it?"

"You are quite the dancer," I admitted, and wasn't lying. Never once had he let my steps falter.

"I've had years of tutors teaching me about everything from which fork to use at a formal dinner, to the art of dance." Devereux waved a dismissive hand. "It wasn't the most entertaining of educations, but it has its uses."

As we stepped off the dance floor, several people swarmed us. One was Lord Ashcroft, his eyes gleaming with renewed interest. Another was the man in green velvet who had seemed so disconcerted at Devereux's looks. There were more, none of whom I recognised. And all were clamouring for my next dance.

"I apologise, but the Lady Astraea is promised to me for the next dance." Casimir cut through the gathering crowd with ease, his chin held high and his eyes never wavering from mine. Devereux delivered my hand into his, and then I was whisked away once again to wait for the music to begin.

This time, the musicians plucked out a faster, more lively song. It was one of open fields and running brooks and growing things, so alive with it that my earth magic started singing in response. That familiar darkness flared in Casimir's gaze as he settled his hand on my back.

"None of that, now," he murmured, tugging me closer and immediately turning us both into the throng of dancers on the floor. "We don't need a garden sprouting beneath our feet."

I flushed, my earth magic stuttering. The darkness in his eyes seemed to delight in my reaction. Something in me loosened, feeling happy for the first time that evening.

Then, we danced.

Dancing with Devereux had been a performance, meant to display me to the crowd. Dancing with Casimir was something else entirely.

There was no second-guessing my steps. Where he moved, I moved. When he bade me turn, I turned. When he pulled me close, I revelled in the feeling of his form pressed against mine. The movement of our bodies matched the music exactly, so that where the song began, so did we, and where it led, we followed. It was impossible to notice the people around us, either watching or dancing. I could not bring myself to look away from Casimir.

From that seed of darkness in his gaze.

One that spoke to a similar seed living in my heart, right next to that radiant light.

A crescendo in the music had Casimir turning me so that my back pressed against his chest. He leaned in, his breath warm against my ear.

"I never said how beautiful you looked this evening," he murmured, and I could have sworn I felt teeth nipping at the tip of my ear.

My breath hitched, and that kernel of light sighed, leaking out a little, warming my skin. Casimir's hand tightened in mine and he spun me around again, my dress swirling and catching the light that now spilled from me.

"You look magnificent in silver," he said, pulling me close once more. "But you would look even more resplendent in black."

I shivered, that light inside me flaring for a moment before settling back into silence. The shadows that lived beside it shifted, filling the space the light had just left. Casimir's eyes widened in surprise, and he smiled widely.

"My star," he murmured.

Then, before he could move in to kiss me, before he could satiate the need that was rising in me right alongside those shadows, the music ended.

Casimir stepped away, bowed, and began clapping for the musicians, not giving me more than a cursory glance. My magic faltered, pulling in on itself, remembering that we were amongst people, amongst those who might see and remember.

The rest of the evening, though, I felt that call between Casimir's shadows and mine, and the light that lived in between. And I feared it, for what it might do to me.

CHAPTER 17

"She can't do this." Devereux threw a pair of boots into his bag. Casimir immediately unpacked them.

This was the first time I'd been in the prince's chambers, and I was surprised at how tidy they were. Well, they had been tidy until Devereux had begun packing. I was there, ostensibly, to discuss our travel arrangements. Casimir had joined us mere minutes later.

"She is the queen, and your mother," I pointed out. "She can do this."

"Sending you, *me*, to Ynysfawr? I know she made the announcement to punish me, but she's actually making us do this. She's only hoping that I'll be able to convince you to change your mind while we're away. That's what she said, at least, before dismissing me to pack," Devereux growled and pulled out three tunics, which Casimir allowed to be packed. "It's at the other end of the country! The void is strongest there. We'll be torn apart by voidlings."

"We will not." Casimir snorted. "You complain frequently at being a poor swordsman, but I happen to know you've been trained in the blade since you were a boy."

"Ineffectively," Devereux muttered. "I am not even allowed to join the training sessions for the royal guard."

Casimir cast his eyes to the ceiling, as if asking for strength. "We will be travelling by day and sheltering at night. We will have fires. We will have other settlements around. For stars' sake, we have Astraea!"

My muscles tightened, and I sat up straighter in the overstuffed chair by the hearth. I swallowed.

Devereux brightened considerably at this. He smiled at me. "Of course! Forgive me for worrying, Lady Star. I've never been away from the palace for more than a day or two, excepting a few summers spent at my grandfather's estates. It was not meant as a challenge against your abilities."

I shrugged and picked at the threads on the chair. Dancer reached up with a paw and batted at the strands, claws catching. He'd grown again, and I could feel his concern at my apathy radiating from his fur like the shadows that sometimes dripped off of them.

"Astraea?" Casimir was suddenly before me, a finger at my chin prompting me to look up. His expression was clouded, a line between his brows. "You've been awfully quiet on the matter. What do you think of this pilgrimage to Ynysfawr?"

I shrugged again. "It had to happen at some point."

"That's hardly a ringing endorsement," the Void Runner said. "I know the manner of our departure is rather abrupt, what with the queen springing it on us, but surely—"

"Surely what?" I snapped. The fire that lived in my veins flared for a moment, reaching for the candles on the wall, aching to light them and make them burn. I reined in the desire, and that of my earth magic to rend the palace to pieces. The light and shadow magics were, thankfully, silent, as if watching. Waiting.

"I would think that facing the void would be a relief," Devereux said. I was half-tempted to snarl at him, but instead leaned back in the chair. "After all this time, with everyone telling you that you're going to face the void, push it back, save us all, surely you would want to get it over with. It's your destiny; there can be no question of your success."

"No question?" I scoffed.

Casimir frowned. He knelt before me, careless of the soot on the hearthstones, instead grasping my hand. I wanted to pull away, but did not. "There *is* no question of your success."

"Truly?" I was losing my grip on the earth magic. I could feel it reaching for me, in the ground far beneath my feet, in the stones that made up the palace, in the dirt tracked in by careless shoes. It had been growing, ever since I unleashed it at the battle of the wall. It terrified me.

Now, though, my temper outweighed my fear, and I let some of the magic slip. Outside the window, a climbing vine began sinking its tendrils into the mortar, pulling itself towards me. Other plants begged to do the same, but I pushed them back. Instead, I stood, and the marble beneath my feet rippled.

"Truly?" My voice was quiet, deadly. "When I could not slay Dancer? When I could not kill more than a single voidling at the wall, despite people's *lives* being at risk? My physical training has resulted in me being able to hold a sword correctly, but that is very nearly all. I cannot fight, I cannot kill voidlings, so how am I expected to push back the void itself?"

Devereux flinched away. Casimir did not, but he saw the ripples in the stone and a muscle worked in his jaw. He looked up at me. "You have more wild magic than anyone I've seen. You turned the tide at the wall against a Malgrwm, a more dangerous voidling remains unknown. Yet you think you failed?"

"People *died* because of me!" I clenched my fists and the vine outside thrust its tendrils deeper, clawing mortar from between stone, taking its place. "At the wall, at Starfall Meadow—"

"We do not know what happened at Starfall Meadow," Casimir interrupted. "It's possible that your magic hadn't awakened then. And you only had six months of training, which is hardly enough to take on a void pool alone."

Dancer nudged at my hand, purring gently.

I relaxed, letting go of my magic. The vine stopped growing, the stone beneath my feet smoothed over. The fight in me vanished. "Exactly. I had six months of training, then. None of which I remember. This time, I've spent more time recovering from my injuries than training, and the time has been considerably less. If I face the void as I am, then I will fail. This world will be doomed to live in darkness until a new Chosen One is born, and who knows how long that will be."

Something dark and terrible flickered in Casimir's eyes. He coughed and turned away. "I won't let that happen," was all he said.

"I believe in you," Devereux said. "You accomplished more to turn the tide at the wall than any

Runner with years of training. We'll keep practising on the road, too, help you build up your endurance."

I nodded. What else could I do? My entire life since waking seemed to have me asking that question. What else could I do but agree when a betrothal to Devereux was sprung on me? Now I was bound to go to Ynysfawr because of my refusal. What else could I do but go out among the people and try to help them? A riot followed in my wake. What else could I do but agree to the queen's demands, again and again and again? No matter how I spun the situation, the answer was always the same.

Nothing.

I could do nothing. I was the Chosen One. All she did was ask that I push back the void. It was my destiny, no matter how foolish it seemed that I, who had faltered at every step, would be chosen for that impossible task.

"This is what you were meant to do," Casimir said, standing. He reached for me. I flinched away. "You were born to it, Astraea. The power of a star is in your veins."

I desperately hoped he was right, because if he was not, then we were all doomed.

"You need to have faith," Devereux said. "The gods sent us the First Star, just as they sent us you. They would not have done so if you were doomed to failure."

I didn't think the gods had sent the First Star, not if the stories I'd heard about her pushing them aside were true, but I didn't want to argue with Devereux about theology. I didn't want to argue about anything.

"What gods would possibly send me?" I asked flatly. Then shook my head. "It doesn't matter. The path is laid. I'll go pack and see you both in the morning."

I didn't bother with a backwards glance at either one of them as I left Devereux's chambers, Dancer pressed close to my side, my arms wrapped around myself and that fragile hope held close in my chest. That hope that I was chosen by the gods. That I did have the power of a star in my veins. That I was *destined* to do this, no matter my training.

It seemed like another failure would send that hope shattering into a thousand pieces.

✦

I f I expected fanfare at my departure, then I was to be sorely disappointed. The only people who were in the courtyard at dawn while Casimir, Devereux and I prepared our horses for travel were a few guards, two Runners who were watching the repairs on the wall with care, and Eloise. Not even Beatrice had come to see her Chosen One off, which was surprising after her many verses and chants the night of the equinox. I had hardly paid attention to all the verses, given that they were mostly repetitions of supplication to the stars, only with different constellations named in each version. My mind had been too taken up with my dance with Casimir.

Still, it seemed odd that neither Beatrice nor the queen and her king consort were here to bid Devereux goodbye, even as family. I studied him, but he was intent on the straps and saddle bags of his horse, his expression stony.

Eloise stood at the reins of my own horse, smiling widely. "I wish I were coming with you," she said to me, dancing from foot to foot.

"Your time for adventures will come," I replied, though I doubt I was very assuring. She was a child and far more eager for this than I.

"But you get to go with Lord Casimir! And Prince Devereux," Eloise said. She eyed the Prince with a faint blush to her cheeks. "And you'll have to pass through open country, and I hear there are Hunters just about everywhere out there, and bandits besides. It's so exciting Besides, very few people even get permission to go to Ynysfawr. It's sacred, and carefully guarded. There's an entire *ring* of void surrounding the island."

That did not make me feel any better, to have to venture to this sacred site when I wasn't sure of my own ability, even disregarding bandits and Hunters, whatever those were. Especially now.

Eloise waited, holding the horse steady. It was a great beast of a creature, considerably taller than I, brown with white at its hooves and eyes that shone with a dangerous gleam. It snorted at me, tossing its head.

"Titan was the only horse we could find who would tolerate being around Dancer," Eloise said, eyeing my shadow tiger as he groomed himself on the flagstones. She winced as the horse tried to bite her while her attention wavered. "He's...testy."

I shivered. "I don't actually know how to ride."

The admission was a whisper, but it must have been loud enough to have Eloise whipping her head around and seeing if anyone else heard. The nearest guard was thirty feet away and looking bored. "Truly?"

Dancer, now with his head at the height of my hip, sat up and licked a paw. He and the horse eyed each other, then pointedly looked away. I sighed.

"Truly. If ever I knew, I have forgotten." I was sure I could figure it out, given how at ease Devereux and Casimir appeared in the saddle, but something told me it would be uncomfortable.

"Maybe your muscles will remember for you," Eloise suggested, though we both knew it was a pointless thought. My muscle memory had been useless when trying to learn how to fight, so why would riding be any different? The girl held one of the stirrups steady for me. I tried to replicate the movement that Devereux had performed moments ago, grabbing onto the saddle horn and pulling myself up. It was less than graceful, and I was certain my face burned by the time I was fully in the saddle.

Eloise smiled widely at me. "See, that wasn't so bad, right?"

I winced.

"Your sword is behind you, and there's two daggers in your pack, just in case. Dancer can catch his own food, but there's some dried jerky for you, and—"

"Thank you, Eloise," I said, reaching down to tussle the girl's hair. She smiled up at me with all the impossible hope of childhood. "I could not have done this without you."

"I'm only disappointed that I couldn't be a full Void Runner, riding with you to push back the void."

Then, before I could refute it, before I could tell her how terrible that would be, Eloise gave me a swift bow and ran off to go stand by the other two Runners. Titan shook his head and stamped his front hoof. Dancer showed his fangs. I tightened my grip on the reins.

"Come on, Astraea," Casimir muttered, clicking his tongue. His horse started on ahead and Titan immediately followed behind, tossing his head at me one more time before settling into a steady walk, Dancer alongside. Devereux made up the rear, and I saw him turn his head to watch the palace recede, as if waiting for his family to appear. When he turned back around and saw me staring, he flinched.

All in all, our journey was not off to a great start.

We went through the outskirts of Altier, sticking to the river road and moving through Mistward before anyone realised it was us. Those few who poked their heads out of their doors quickly fled at the sight of a voidling in the streets, even though the sun was quickly rising above the horizon.

Then, before I could even really take in the sights, Altier was gone. A city I had hardly known, with people I couldn't name, but which had somehow made up an integral part of my life for as long as my memory existed—gone.

"Right," Casimir said, circling his horse around. It shied the closer it came to Dancer, but he held it in hand with practised ease. "We need to make it as far as we can before nightfall. I don't want to linger in the countryside unless we have to."

"Agreed," Devereux said. "We ride hard for the nearest village, then? Stop for lunch there."

Without my input or advice, our journey was set.

As it turns out, riding a horse is something that requires a great deal of practise. Within twenty minutes of starting out, my legs were starting to grow sore from gripping the saddle. My rear bones felt like they were grinding together, and I was certain that my back was going to start screaming. It evened out some as the day wore on, but the first watering break had me falling over in the dirt as I dismounted.

Dancer was immediately standing over me, his glowing eyes concerned. He growled at Devereux as the prince approached, his claws digging into the earth.

"Easy, Dancer," the prince said, raising his hands. He looked at me, concern gleaming in his eyes. "I was just going to ask how you were doing."

Casimir leaned over the stream, filling the water-skins. He watched me with a frown, as though my pain was something unusual. To a highly trained Void Runner, I supposed it was. The thought did not make me feel any better.

"Dancer, enough." I pushed the shadow tiger aside and sat up, groaning. "Perhaps we should have added horse riding into my training. Along with how, exactly, the other Chosen Ones managed to push back the void. And perhaps some geography. I'm completely lost."

Devereux winced. "Ah, yes. Sorry. We hadn't considered...well, it's just that—"

"We thought there was more time," Casimir said, walking over to me with a hand outstretched. I waved him off, perfectly content to sit on the ground for a few minutes, at least until the burn in my muscles abated.

"It would appear we were wrong," I muttered. Then, in a desire to do anything but meet Casimir's gaze, I looked about.

As we'd left Altier, the landscape had changed. The hills became more prominent, rising up from the rivers and spreading across the horizon like gentle giants. I could feel their vastness, their ancient lives, like an ocean to my magic. They were covered with short grasses and clovers, bent down by the wind and made stronger for the exposure. Any trees were sturdy, their branches twisted and grasping for the sun. It was open and empty and wild, and it may have been the most beautiful thing I'd ever seen.

"The world is vast, is it not?" Casimir asked, something in his voice incredibly sad.

"It's wonderful," I answered. Devereux shifted uncomfortably. "Are all the lands like this, beyond Baldarskiel, I mean?"

"Some are flatter, some with more trees, some have jungles, others mountains. There are lakes and deserts and much more besides," Devereux replied as if listing a dry collection of facts. He shrugged. "It's hardly remarkable here. The land is fertile, yes, but the wind won't let any true crops grow. And we could graze livestock here, but they would be under constant threat of the voidlings. It's just empty space on the hills. Only the valleys are generally populated."

I was beginning to grow annoyed with the prince, though I knew it was hardly fair. "All I've known in my life are the stone walls of the palace and the enclosed gardens. Or, the two times I ventured into Altier, the backs of guards' armour. Just let me enjoy the wild for a minute."

Devereux scowled at the ground. "My apologies, Lady Star. I just don't see what use I can possibly be here besides listing off facts."

"What do you mean?" Casimir asked, something dark in his tone. I shivered at the sound, and even Dancer pricked his rounded ears. "Is fighting the void not worthwhile?"

"Oh, it's the most worthwhile thing anyone could do," Devereux scoffed. "But *I* am not the one who will be doing the fighting, unless I've mistaken the way of things. I am poor with a blade, have no experience with the void, and have no magic—arcane or wild—to speak of. I am trained in politics, in social niceties, in campaigns and strategies and court intrigue. None of which, I might remind you, we will find out here. All I see is useless land, which is perfectly suited for a useless prince."

Something in me wilted at his words. I thought he'd enjoy travelling with Casimir and myself, even if we were marching to our doom. I knew that this was a punishment from his mother, but I didn't realise that he took it as such.

Foolish me, I thought we were friends.

"I won't hold you to your mother's instructions," I murmured, burying my fingers in the grass. "If you can be more use somewhere else, then that's where you should be. Your people's welfare depends on it, after all."

"I can hardly just ride back to Altier." Devereux turned his head back in the direction we'd come, and I could hear the longing in his voice. "My mother would never forgive me."

"Are there other cities you could visit?" I asked. "Gather support there? Or perhaps you could join one of the parties that crosses the void and act as diplomat to another land."

The prince's eyes shone with hope for a moment before he looked at me. He shook his head. "No. I gave my word that I would accompany you, and so I shall. I'll just have to find a use in some other way."

With that, he went to his grazing horse and mounted, walking off into the distance. Casimir helped me stand, and I groaned, leaning somewhat on Dancer.

"What should we do?" I asked under my breath.

"Nothing," Casimir said. "He is fully capable of deciding his own path. He has not done so up until now because of his mother's interference. It is time for him to make up his own mind."

Something in the earth rumbled under our feet, ancient and terrible. My magic recoiled from it, and as I pulled back, I noticed something else. Hoofbeats, regular and quick, approaching us. There was no time now to worry about Devereux's frustrations, or my own worries.

"Someone is following us," I said. "Coming from Altier. Fast."

CHAPTER 18

I thought the trap that Casimir set up for our tagalong was excessive. I'd told him that no one would bother harming me, as I was their only hope to push back the void. He'd merely glared at me like I was naïve and pushed me down into a slight dell with Devereux.

"Don't take it personally," the prince muttered, glaring at the mud that now spattered his boots. "Casimir is incapable of not exercising his protective instincts. He was born that way, or so I assume."

I snorted. "That explains a lot, actually."

Devereux cracked a smile, the first I'd seen from him in days. I thought about asking him about his fears, his insecurities, thinking that maybe I could help him see that he was far from useless, but now didn't seem like the right time. I doubted that being squashed against a rock and crouching under the cover of some scraggly bushes that tore at my hair and skin was a great time for many conversations.

We both looked up the hill, waiting. The horses were tied in a line, meant to make it seem like we had stepped away for just a moment. Casimir was hiding, sword bare, just beyond the stream, while Devereux and I crouched in the dell. Dancer remained with the horses, the voidling a better guard for them than any of us, even with magic at our disposal.

After a few minutes of silence, my earth magic started prickling the back of my neck. I could feel the hoofbeats getting closer. Whoever the rider was, they pushed their horse hard. When they drew close enough, a scuffle started.

Dancer let out a roar, startling the horses—even Titan. I could see them rearing and plunging, trying to break free of their ties. The rider was thrown from their horse, falling to the ground in a heap while the creature bolted. Casimir leaped from his cover, sword immediately at the intruder's throat.

"Stars and stones, don't kill me!" It was a woman's voice, one that I recognised. Casimir straightened and signalled to Devereux and myself. He did not look pleased.

The prince and I emerged from our poor hiding spot, brushing ourselves off. I knew I should be frustrated, by the delay in our travels if nothing else, but

I couldn't keep a smile from my face as I brushed off my skirts.

"Tali," Devereux said, as stern as I'd ever heard him. "What are you doing here?"

The dressmaker's granddaughter propped herself up on her elbows, her hair coming loose from its braid. She huffed. "I was attempting to find you, to come with you."

"Well, you found us," Casimir growled. "The question is why?"

"To help, of course," Tali snapped. She held out a hand, and I immediately reached to pull her to her feet. She wore loose trousers that were tight at the ankles, a worn tunic with a mantle of fur over her shoulders. Travelling clothes. She knew what she was doing.

"We do not require your help," Casimir said. He looked at me and must have seen something in my expression, because he softened slightly. "Though your company will not be unappreciated."

"If I'd known you wanted to come, I would have made them wait for you," I said. "Now I won't be the only woman along."

Tali laughed, tossing back her head. "If you were that starved for company, you should have sent for me weeks ago! Being stuck with these two will test any woman's resolve."

"I don't understand. Why, exactly, are you here?

And please, don't give us that line about wanting to help. You and Lady Astraea met but twice, and those meetings were hardly long enough to develop the sort of friendship that has you running straight into the void." Devereux's words were sharp, pointed, and unfortunately logical.

I'd liked Tali from the moment we met, but he was right. She and I were basically strangers. I had spent more time with Eloise than with Tali, despite us being similar in age. The palace walls had stood between us, no matter my decree that the people could come to me. My injuries and magic sickness had stopped that plan before it began, and my departure for Ynysfawr had destroyed it completely, no matter my intentions. The dressmaker's granddaughter surely had some ulterior motive.

Everyone seemed to have some ulterior motive when it came to me. With Devereux and Casimir at least, we'd got past that. With Tali...

She shrugged one shoulder, playing with the ends of her braid. "Can't a girl wish for adventure every now and again?"

"Surely," Casimir drawled. "Yet picking this exact moment to depart on one is a bit coincidental. You knew we were leaving for Ynysfawr today, yet you weren't outside the palace gates when we left. Why follow after us? Did you plan to hunt us the entire way, staying just beyond our vision? Or were you hoping to come across our fire this evening, in a mere chance encounter?"

Tali flushed, her brown skin taking on a darker hue. She kicked the dirt. Tossed her braid over her shoulder. Then, "Very well, Runner. If you *must* know, I'm a *dharangui*. A—"

"Wandering poet?" Devereux spluttered. He fairly gaped at Tali. "You're a poet of the gods?!"

"I don't understand," I said, looking between the two. Tali's scowl deepened and Devereux seemed too stunned to do more than gape. Casimir sighed, wrinkling his nose in distaste.

"The *dharangui* were chroniclers of legends, back in the days when the gods and their heros walked openly among us. They recorded divine will, setting it to poetry or song. After the fall of the First Star, when the void entered the world and the gods disappeared, the poets largely became priests and priestesses of the Temple of the Fallen Star, turning their taste for legend into devotion for the only legend remaining in the land. They're sycophants."

Tali curled her lip and jutted her chin out. "Those fools who turned priest, perhaps. Some of us remained true to the *dharangui* calling. We record important events—not just legendary ones, thank you—so that the true history of things may be passed down through the generations. We're the only ones with the true story of the ages, rather than the people who rewrite things to suit themselves."

Casimir rolled his eyes. "We have no need of a wandering poet. Return to Altier. Now."

"No," Tali said. She folded her arms. "It is my sworn and divine duty to record the history of what happens here, on this journey. Last time a Chosen One appeared, we were thwarted in our attempts to record the truth, and the method of her defeating the void was lost. So much about the nature of the world has been lost. I'm not going to be the one to lose this!"

I wanted to shrink into myself and support Tali at the same time. Instead, I wrapped my fingers into the fabric of my skirts and said nothing, once again forgotten in the argument.

"Is our word not worth enough?" Devereux asked, and he genuinely sounded hurt. "When we return—"

"You are not trained in the taking of events," Tali said. "I am."

Casimir looked like he wanted to say more, to disagree and fight and push her away, so that our journey might be taken in peace. Devereux, too, looked as though he wanted to say more, though I decided his was more academic interest than frustration. Tali, though, looked at me, her eyes shining defiantly.

"Why don't you ask your Chosen One what she

thinks?" she said, as though daring me to look away. To give in. "It is *her* journey, after all."

"Is that all I am to you? The Chosen One?"

Tali's mouth worked, indistinct sounds spluttering forth. She winced. "Of course not!"

"Liar." I was tired of being useful only as the Chosen One. I was tired of being best known for the failures that had haunted me so far. People rested all their hope on me, on my pushing back the void, and no one seemed to actually care what I thought about things. About my role in the world. I was glad to fulfil my destiny, but a small part of me wanted to be known for something else, at least to one person. To be known as Astraea, not the Lady Star.

More fool me, I supposed.

I turned away from my companions and found Titan. He had calmed some, but still looked liable to bite. Good. I felt like biting, too. At least no one would get near enough to him to bother me. With more ease than I'd felt that morning, I pulled myself into the saddle, ignoring the protest of my sore muscles.

Tali was still spitting out apologies and denials to Casimir and Devereux, wringing her hands and looking truly alarmed that she might not be allowed to accompany us.

"She can come," I said, surprising myself with the

coldness in my voice. "Her horse is just over there. Let her fetch it and let's be off."

"Astraea, you don't have to do this," Casimir said, taking a step towards me. Titan snorted and tossed his head, making the Runner pause in his approach.

"Don't I? Isn't it my duty that my success—or failure—get recorded so that the next Chosen One will know what to do? After all, I'll only ever be able to push back the void, not defeat it. Someone has to make sure that my story gets told. That my deeds as Chosen One are never forgotten." Then, without waiting for anyone to mount their own horses, I turned Titan in the direction we'd been riding all morning, then urged him forwards. Dancer followed at my side, tail twitching all the while.

I stewed for much of the remainder of the day, keeping to my own company. Dancer seemed to pick up on my mood and kept the other horses back by showing his teeth or growling whenever someone tried to draw near. Eventually, they all got the message and left me in peace, though Casimir kept throwing worried looks over his shoulder.

Tali and Devereux spent much of the ride conversing. I could hear Devereux asking questions of the wandering poet, about her thoughts on the history of his family, on her collection methods for information, and eventually about past events that were either battles or treaties or other significant things that were complete mysteries to me. As much as I longed to learn of things that I must have once known, I stopped listening, happier in my own mind. Casimir watched me, and the world in turn, keeping an eye on the road and any potential threats.

We passed only two groups of people on the road. One was a family with three young children, the mother on the wagon seat, the father leading his mule. The back of the wagon was packed to the brim with their belongings. They watched us warily as we passed, the children even crying at the sight of Dancer. I wanted to reassure them, to tell them that I was going to make it right, that I was going to push back the void and they could return home soon, but I kept silent. There was no need to give them false hope, after all. And I was tired of being the Chosen One.

The second set of people were far more jovial. There were three men, travelling without horses, carrying the carcass of a deer between them. They stared openly at Dancer, but didn't back away in fear, instead turning their gaze to the four of us. I could feel their eyes linger on my burns, and on Casimir's armour, but thankfully they didn't stop us to even exchange news.

As the sun started towards the horizon, though, we saw no one else. The road was well maintained, but it was empty. I had a feeling that I knew the cause, and if I failed in my duty, the road would be empty for a while longer.

The burden of my task was beginning to weigh more heavily on my shoulders.

I felt like I was suffocating in silence by the time Casimir called a halt to the day's journey. Tali rode up next to me as we stopped in the slight dip in the ground, sheltered by some large rocks and a few scraggy trees.

"I thought we were aiming for the nearest village," she said, loud enough for the whole party to hear.

"We were," Devereux said. He eyed Casimir with a frown. "At least, so you said this morning."

"We passed it." Casimir swallowed, his throat bobbing. "Or did none of you mark the remains of the houses? Burned. Torn to shreds."

We had passed a collection of scrap wood about an hour past, the timbers no larger than firewood, but there had been no indication that it was a village.

"The voidlings," Tali whispered, looking at me. My stomach dropped.

"They destroyed the entire village?" I could barely get the words out.

Casimir shook his head. "Voidlings don't care about buildings, only living beings. Most likely the villagers fled after a particularly nasty attack and bandits burned it down after sacking it. Fewer people ask questions about missing objects when the villages are nowhere to be found. We'll camp here. Tali, you collect as much wood as you can. Devereux, help me move some of these rocks into a perimeter."

"What about me?" I was desperate to be useful. Casimir gave me a weak, half-smile.

"Gather your fire magic. We'll need to heat the rocks as bright as they'll go."

"That'll draw any bandits in the area right to us," Tali protested. "We should be lying low, keeping the fire as contained as possible, not announcing ourselves with beacons! You might as well set an arcane light spell off for how unnatural it will look to be bound by a perimeter of glowing rocks."

"The bandits are but human," Casimir snapped. "Voidlings are far worse. Dancer is tame, sane, not driven mad by the years trapped in the darkness, desperate for a lick of life to give brightness to the gloom. Why do you think so many of those monsters are twisted? Why they bear the forms of more creatures than you can count? When there is nothing of the light, you grow accustomed to consuming what else resides in the dark."

Tali grumbled and held up her hands. "Fine! I understand. There's no need to bite my head off."

She stalked off to go find firewood while Devereux just shook his head and went about moving the rocks. Casimir grumbled under his breath and set to work on preparing the camp. I saw to the horses as much as I knew how, giving them food and water, then untying the various bedrolls and setting them out.

Finally, the silence was too much for Casimir. "What?" he snapped. "What is it?"

"This journey isn't easy on any of us," I said, my voice equally frigid. "But I don't think touting the danger so baldly is helping anyone."

Casimir exhaled slowly. "Least of all you, is that what you're saying?"

"No. I know what we face. What I face. The rest of you..." I shrugged. "I think you're the only one who willingly chose this."

"I would choose it a thousand times over if it meant being here with you, Astraea," Casimir breathed. He stood to reach for me, his expression all tenderness, when I stepped back. He paused. Hesitated. "What's wrong? Is it the void?"

I wrapped my arms around my waist. "Some. I just can't bear the thought of failing again."

"You're not going to fail again." He sounded so sure.

"Perhaps. Perhaps not. It's more than that, though. It's Tali."

"I knew we shouldn't have let her come!" Casimir growled, glaring off in the direction she left.

"She needed to come," I countered. "Just as I

need to face the void. I just...I don't want to only be known as the Chosen One. As a cautionary tale or guideline for the next one. I don't want all my achievements to be boiled down to that. I want—"

I couldn't breathe, let alone continue. Suddenly, Casimir was there, his touch as gentle as I'd ever known it. He brushed his fingers along my chin, lifting it so I looked at his eyes. I wanted to shy away from the depth of emotion there, for fear that I would just let him down. But I didn't. I kept still.

"What do you want?" he breathed, his words soft against my ear. "Tell me, and I will make it so."

I closed my eyes. "I want to be a person. I want to know if I'm a cheerful person, or if I prefer solemnity. I want to know my favourite food, my favourite colour, whether I like travel or if I prefer to stay in one place. I want to experience life outside of the stone walls of the palace and see if I like it. I want to know what talents I have, whether I'm good at drawing or sewing or singing. I want to be someone *other* than the Chosen One, but I haven't been allowed to even think about such things because I've spent every day of my known life training for my destiny. I don't even know if I *like* training, because I haven't done anything else besides to compare it with besides your politics. I want...I want...I want to be *real*. Being with you is all that I have that's mine, and I want it to be enough, I really do. I'm just not sure it is, anymore."

Arms wrapped around me, their weight strong and heavy. "You are real, my star. You are more real than you can possibly know. All the rest of it are details, ones we can discover along the way."

I wanted to believe him. I wanted to accept the safety that being in his arms brought. And yet those details seemed blindingly important.

We didn't have any more time to consider such things; Tali returned, sprinting, her arms empty of firewood. Devereux was not far behind her, a single rock cradled in his arms.

"We were wrong," she panted, sliding to a halt in the slick grass. "The bandits haven't fled the area."

CHAPTER 19

The bandits came just as the sun fell behind the horizon, our pitiful fire lighting up the hills. We hadn't had time to get more than a few sticks thrown onto it, then lit it with a touch of my fire magic. Devereux had protested, but Casimir insisted, claiming that we would need all the protection against the voidlings that we could get, bandits or no. So we'd taken the five minutes we had and started a fire. A beacon.

Dancer prowled just beyond the firelight, eyes gleaming in the dark, letting out low rumbles in his chest as the bandits grew nearer. The horses were increasingly nervous, tugging at their tethers and eyeing the tiger. Tali shifted nervously, holding a dagger in her hands. Casimir held his sword with a sort of boredom that told me he'd done this before.

That didn't make me feel better.

"Now, look at this! A prettier party of travellers I've rarely seen." The woman who spoke was large, built heavily, and with a patchwork of clothes that was old and ragged. She had an axe in one hand and a round, wooden shield in the other. Behind her were several others, both men and women, all wearing ragged clothing and carrying weapons that looked well used. They looked hungry.

"I would advise you to move on," Casimir said evenly. Devereux drew his sword and pointed it at the bandits, though he looked decidedly less sure of himself. "We do not wish to harm you."

The woman laughed, tossing back her head, the sound echoing off the rocks. "Oh, my, pretty and funny! You honestly think that you could do us harm? We outnumber you, dearie, or haven't you noticed?"

Indeed, they did outnumber us, perhaps eight or nine of them to the four of us. I wanted to reach out to the earth and hold their feet fast, but Casimir had told me not to use any grand displays of magic, in case they were needed later. I kept still.

"I am a Void Runner," Casimir said, "and I have faced far worse things than you."

The man closest to the woman, his beard a tangle of red, sneered. "You think we haven't faced voidlings out here in the empty lands? Where no one cares about the little people like us?"

Devereux tensed, his jaw working. I begged him not to speak, not to tell them who he was and how much he did care. He could help them in some other way, some other time. Not now, when we needed to stay in one piece for the duration of our travels.

"Hey, Rin, look at this." A short woman with a war hammer in her grip gestured to the horses, still guarded by Dancer. The shadow tiger noticed the attention and let out a growl that was loud enough to shake the stones under our feet. The horses showed the whites of their eyes, but they seemed to understand that he was protecting them and stayed still. "They got a gods-dammed monster with them."

"Dancer, be calm," I murmured, hoping that he would listen to me. After a moment, he did, though quieter growls emerged from him.

The bandits all looked at me like I'd grown two heads. The woman, Rin, stood straighter, her axe raised. "That's not natural," she said. "No one tames voidlings, not unless they want their head ripped off in the middle of the night."

I raised my hands. "I can assure you—"

Dancer let out a roar, covering up anything I might have said. I whirled to scold him when I saw them. Glowing points in the dark. Dozens of them. Moving our way.

"Voidlings," I said.

"Kill it, she can't control—" Rin started.

I grabbed Casimir and spun him around, pointing. "We're under attack."

The bandits grew quiet, the sharp tang of fear filling the air. Devereux cursed. Tali muttered what sounded like a prayer.

"They must have seen the fire," Casimir said. "And heard Dancer. Thought he was attacking us, calling for aid, not protecting us."

"You brought this upon us," the bearded man said, his steps wavering as he tried to back away. "We need to run!"

"You can't run," Casimir snapped. He pointed, at the glowing eyes that were surrounding the slight rise where we had camped. The bandits were trapped with us.

"This fire won't keep us safe for long," Tali said. She was right; already the flames were dying, the few sticks we'd added barely tinder.

The voidlings drew closer, enough so that I could see some of their forms. Many were whole creatures —deer, a wolf, two beavers, all made of shadow—but there were several that looked to be a terrifying nightmare of spikes and fur and antlers and large, dangerous claws. One of the nightmares licked its muzzle, glowing eyes eager.

"Truce?" Rin asked, already turning her back on us to face the creatures.

"Indeed," Casimir agreed. He looked at me once

then turned away, sword at the ready. "Any time, now, Astraea."

This was what I'd saved my magic for.

I reached inwards, grabbing at the power that came to me first. The earth beneath our feet rumbled, already shifting where I sank my mind into it. The voidlings let out shrieks as their feet were trapped in the ground. Casimir didn't wait for anything more, just lunged at the nearest voidling, sword flashing. Devereux did the same, his movements jerky, almost ineffective. The bandits realised a moment later what was happening and they, too, started slaying voidlings.

But the ones I'd trapped were only a first wave, those most eager for prey. And the ones behind were smarter. They managed to avoid the grasp of my earth magic by leaping swiftly from place to place, never holding still long enough for the slow-moving earth to grab them.

I heard a scream as one of the bandits went down, a many-toothed muzzle in his leg. Rin cried out as well, staring at her fellow. She didn't notice a large, hound-like creature lunging for her. Devereux did and stepped between the bandit and the fangs. But, as he'd claimed all along, he was no great swordsman.

The fangs sank into his shoulder.

He screamed, the sound splitting my ears. It was the scream of one who had never known such pain, unlike the screams of the Runners and soldiers at the wall. They knew what they were doing, they faced the fight willingly; Devereux did not. What little innocence he had left was shattered in that moment, and the entire hillside knew it from the sound of that scream.

Rage, burning, terrible rage, filled my veins. That was *my* price, not his. I was the one to pay the void, to push it back, to take on its suffering. Not Devereux. Not my friends.

I lashed out with a single thread of fire, so white-hot that it was cold. Incandescent. Like starfire. It sliced through the air with a fierce scream, the temperature difference making the air part around it with a thunderous snap. The voidling hound that had attacked Devereux fell to the ground, its head rolling another few feet.

Every battling force on that hill hesitated for a moment, each staring at me. I clenched my fists and let out a snarl to make Dancer proud. The voidlings hesitated for one more beat before lunging for me.

I grabbed each and every one of my four magics and lashed out into the night. The light and shadow resisted me at first, until they began to taste the dark blood of the voidlings, then they leaped and cut through the air with abandon. The earth and fire were easier to control, but less eager. Within moments, the hill was lit by flashes of light and fire, while my earth bound the creatures, and shadows poured themselves into the eyes of the enemy, dousing them from within.

The bandits killed off those voidlings that were incapacitated with my magic, and Casimir slew those that escaped my grip. Tali knelt by Devereux, brushing his hair back from his head while he let out moans of pain, oblivious to the battle raging around him. Dancer kept guarding the horses, dispatching voidlings that were foolish enough to attack him.

Then, there was silence. The voidlings lay dead or dying on the ground. One more bandit had been struck down, but otherwise everyone was whole. Not even a scratch—excepting Devereux.

Wings beat overhead.

I poured the last of my magic into the rocks around us, illuminating the land with impossibly white light. Above us, wheeling about and clicking its beak, flew a malgrwm. It tilted its head, and I caught its eye, the glow somehow familiar.

"No," I murmured. "It can't be."

The malgrwm from the wall. It was here. And it took in every detail of the destruction I had wrought. I didn't know what it wanted with me, why it was following me, except that perhaps all voidlings had an innate sense of the Chosen One. It didn't matter, not now.

I jabbed a finger into the air. "See this? This is

what lies in store for all of you! I am the Chosen One, and I come to push back the void. If you stand in my way, you will die."

And right then, for perhaps the first time, I believed every word.

The malgrwm clacked its beak, as if it were laughing at me. Then, with a shriek, it flew off, leaving the night as empty as before.

That silence fell again, heavy and dark. Slowly, the rocks I had filled with light dimmed, then went out as the magic faded. I wavered and sank to my knees, exhaustion thrumming through me. It wasn't as bad as at the wall, perhaps because I had some sort of control now or perhaps because I hadn't used as much of my magic. I could move, though it hurt, and I didn't feel like I would sleep for a week.

"Astraea!" Casimir was at my side, his hands against my face, searching my eyes. "Are you well?"

I nodded, too tired to bother forming words.

"What in the blazing stars was that?" Rin asked. She stood before me, axe hanging limply in her hand, her clothes spattered with voidling blood. "Who *are* you?"

"This is the Chosen One," Tali said proudly. She lifted her chin at me as if daring me to stop her. "She saved us all tonight, and she will save us all again. We go to Ynysfawr to push back the void."

Rin, and all the bandits, fell to their knees and

prostrated themselves on the ground, their heads brushing the earth. "Stars above, we are saved," the bearded man said, voice thick with tears.

Disquiet twisted my stomach. Then, pushing Casimir aside, I vomited into the grass. Casimir brushed my hair back from my face, murmuring to me. I chose not to listen. Not to hear his soothing.

I'd killed voidlings.

I should have been pleased. Should have been proud of my accomplishment. It was what I was destined for. What I'd been training for. My magic had responded to my will, precisely and with great destruction. I was closer now to being a proper Chosen One than ever before.

Before my eyes, though, in a vision that seemed never ending, I saw the shock in the eyes of the voidling hound as I tore its head from its body. I saw the blood, great shadowy founts of it, that appeared at the slightest will of my magic. I saw the pain I had caused, no mater that these creatures were in turn causing me pain.

In my ears, I heard the cry of the malgrwm. And I knew it judged me.

"I did what I was meant to do," I muttered to myself. Casimir's hands on my head, my neck, holding me, hesitated.

"Astraea?"

I rose, ignoring the blubbering of the bandits, and

went to Tali. She leaned over Devereux, trying to blot the blood that welled from the wound in his shoulder. Beside him was the bandit who had been taken in the leg. He was muttering, half-coherent, his eyes crazed.

"Can you help him?" Rin asked, moving closer to me. I shook my head.

"I do not know how."

"There is no help for him," Casimir said, once again at my shoulder. As he ever seemed to be. "The beast tore into his main artery. He'll bleed out before we can do anything."

"You won't even try?" Rin looked desperately between Casimir and myself, her throat bobbing. "You're the Chosen One!"

I shook my head again. "That's not how it works. I am meant to push back the void. Healing is not my gift."

I wished it were.

"It will be quick," Casimir said. The bleeding man was shivering, now, his mutterings slow and the light in his eyes a bit dimmer. He looked as though he were going to sleep, if you didn't account for the leg. "And he will feel very little pain."

Rin let out a sob. She and the others knelt by the dying man, and soon his hands were held and he was being comforted by words that had the sound of ritual. Of community.

I turned away, moving instead to where Tali knelt

by Devereux. He was panting, teeth ground together and eyes squeezed shut. His shoulder still bled where the hound had ripped into it, but it was slowing.

"How is he?" I asked. Tali started.

"Gods! You're so quiet. You need to wear a bell or something." Tali held a hand to her chest. I tried not to note the blood that covered her skin. "He's doing well enough. The voidling missed anything vital. I've cleaned it out as best I can, but it'll need consistent care over the next week or two."

"Should..." I swallowed, not wanting to say the words out loud. "Should we send him back to Altier?"

Devereux's uninjured arm snaked out, touching my ankle. He opened his eyes and stared at me. I winced at the pain there. "Don't. Send. Me. Back," he gritted out, each word an effort.

"You're seriously injured! Being on the road with us is only going to be more dangerous. You could get the proper care at the palace, from Healer Eugenie even. They..." I choked back a sob. "I don't want you to get hurt for me."

Devereux shook his head, mouth working, but the pain was apparently quite high. He breathed, "Don't. Please."

I nodded. "Alright."

Tali's shoulders relaxed, and she went back to dabbing away blood from Devereux. "I'll wait until it stops bleeding, then put a wrap on it. It would be better if we had an arcane healing spell, but my knowledge runs only to simple light. My grandmother thought it better I learn history and herblore and religion, not magic."

"I don't know any arcane magic at all." No, my training had been too short, too narrow minded to consider that I might need a healing spell. I looked to Casimir, where he stood, watching.

"I know a healing spell," he admitted, "but it's excruciating. It would be better if you could heal on your own. Can you manage it?"

Devereux nodded. "Be fine," he slurred.

"Sleep," I said. His eyes slid shut, and for once, he did as I asked. Even as I said the words, I felt my own exhaustion on me like a mantle. The dregs of my magic flickered weakly at me. I blinked blearily at Tali.

"I'll stay up with him, Lady Star," she said. "You sleep. You saved us all, tonight. You deserve to rest."

I frowned, something about that not quite right. I couldn't think of an argument to the contrary, though, so nodded and turned away. I found my bedroll and wrapped myself tightly, laying so I faced the fire. Casimir knelt, already tending the weak flames. No one seemed to mind the bandits that were sharing our camp, and a couple of them even brought wood for the fire.

Their friend must have died, then, if they were helping.

I blinked back tears.

"I killed voidlings tonight," I whispered.

Casimir sat back on his heels. I noticed that the inky spots on his fingers seemed larger, stretching to cover almost his entire hand, disappearing up his sleeves. "Yes. And you'll likely kill many more before this is done."

"I know they're...the enemy. That many of them are insane with their desire for life, for light." I wasn't sure I could say any more.

"Do you regret what you did?" Casimir sounded awed, astonished beyond anything he'd ever been before. That stung.

"Yes," I said, and meant it. "What was I like before, that you would be so shocked at my unwillingness to take life."

He turned his face away, staring into the flames as he built up the fire so it would burn brightly all night long. "I don't know what you mean, Astraea."

"Please," I said. "Just tell me."

"You're different now, that's all that matters."

I propped myself up on an elbow, pulling on my last reserves of energy. "It matters to me."

"You're making yourself anew, forging yourself if you will. You don't need to know what you were like before to do that. All you need to know is what you're like now." Casimir jabbed a stick into the flames and it broke with a crackle.

I lay back down, pulling the blanket tighter. "Very well."

"That's it?" Casimir asked, that same shocked tone in his voice. "You're giving in, just like that?"

"Just like that." The words came out bitter, sharp. "After all, your reluctance to tell me says that what I was before was uncaring about who or what got in my way. And yet you claimed to love me, even then."

I turned my back on the fire, on him, and closed my eyes, ready to fall into the oblivion of sleep.

"I have loved you since the beginning," Casimir murmured, his words following me into my dreams. "And I will love you when the skies grow dark and all the other stars die. Cold. Alone. You and I, we will endure. As we always have."

I shivered, and it was not from cold. It was from fear of an emotion that big, that impossible. How could I possibly deserve it? How, when I wasn't even sure anymore that I could feel that deeply? When I wasn't even sure I could be that brave?

CHAPTER 20

We parted ways with the bandits early the next morning. Rin offered to travel with us, to lend her fighting skills to our cause in protection of me. I had firmly refused. Casimir tried to convince them that news of my being about the countryside would do no one any good, but we all knew that the information would be spread far and wide by the next afternoon. Then, without examining the slain voidlings whose bodies seemed withered in the light of day, we left our camp and went on our way.

The next two days were fraught with tension. Casimir was alert for any sign of movement, be it animal or human or voidling. Dancer kept close by me, hackles up at any slight sound, which in turn made Titan nervous and harder to handle. Given my inexperience as a horsewoman, I ended each day in more pain than the last.

Tali kept close watch over Devereux, who was barely able to sit upright in his saddle. He grew increasingly pale over the course of the next two days, despite changing the dressing on his wound and treating it with herbs and potions to dispel any infection. The prince tried to remain in good cheer, keeping up most of the conversation in our group, but I could see the exhaustion creeping up on him. By the end of the second day, he wasn't talking at all.

We passed one village on the road, and I was so bombarded with interested parties who had heard my description—there weren't many women travelling who had full-thickness burns on the face and neck—that we quickly left, riding as hard as we could, Dancer snarling at any who dared to follow. We hadn't even been able to stop for supplies. After that, Casimir said it was too dangerous to stop at any villages at all, unless just he or Tali went in to buy supplies.

With that news, our travelling party stopped talking altogether.

On the morning of the third day, I was warming my hands over the dregs of the fire that we had built. No more voidlings came to attack us, but Casimir insisted we build a massive fire each evening just in case. I was certain that no more voidlings would come until we reached the void itself. I didn't know why; perhaps the malgrwm had warned its brethren off. Or perhaps they were biding their time. Either way, I was glad of the reprieve.

Devereux twitched a bit in his sleep, breath hitching. Tali lay nearby, her bag of herbs within reach, but she was dead to the world. She'd lain up several times treating him, so it was no surprise that the *dharangui* was exhausted. I was grateful, though, for her vast knowledge that she used to help Devereux, even if it did remind me of things I didn't know.

Casimir was off hunting, trying his luck in the nearby stream to see if he could find fish or perhaps a muskrat, anything to add to our dwindling rations. That left me, alone with my thoughts.

"Nnngg." Devereux twitched, his muscles spasming. I went to him, cradling his head in my lap.

"Devereux? Are you well?"

He opened his eyes, and I nearly recoiled. The right one was luminescent, almost glowing orange while the left remained the same. I quickly undid his jacket and pulled back the dressings on his shoulder. Emanating from the wound were several strands of black, just like the inky darkness that coloured Casimir in various spots. As I watched, the strands grew, spreading their tendrils further, wider, even deeper.

"Tali!" I fairly screamed it.

She was immediately awake, crawling towards me. She took one look at Devereux and cursed vividly in several languages, some of which I imagined were long dead. "This is bad, very, very bad."

"What's happening to him?" Surely she had to know, all that knowledge in her head. She rocked back on her heels and shook her head, trembling. "Tell me," I commanded.

"There are some poems. Old, ancient poems, half of which have been forgotten due to their age. They speak of a...changing. A transformation. I think that's what's happening to Prince Devereux." She looked so pained, afraid, even.

"What do you mean, a changing? Surely you have more specific information than that!" I was beginning to panic, my earth magic delving deep into the ground beneath, as if sinking roots to hold me steady.

Tali shook her head, her dark hair wild first thing in the morning. "Only the poems! And the translations are barely coherent."

"Please," I begged. "He's my friend."

Tali winced at that, no surprise to me. I had treated her poorly since she joined our expedition. She may have wanted to follow me to gather knowledge for her keeping, but that didn't mean I had to be cruel to her. She could have been a friend, had I tried harder and set my own disappointments aside. Now, she was just Devereux's caretaker. And not that much longer, if things went as I expected they would.

"Please," I said again, quieter, trying to convey my apologies with that single word.

Tali nodded. She sat and crossed her legs, setting her hands on her knees. She closed her eyes and began rocking gently back and forth, a steady motion that soothed. After a minute, she opened her mouth and began chanting.

Dark lies beyond the gold,
Where stars once fell
Dancing with the stars so cold,
The gods' own creatures bayed and howled
At the music of the wild
One so bold, heart wandering, felt a call
Deep and strong
To the dark that lay beyond the light
Beyond the gods' song
Called he was, and so he went
Into the void so deep
Where wild things once forgot
Sought the light that still lived
And so he slipped away, the stars and gods distracted
Becoming voice of the dark,
The song with him did come
Until the creatures danced in the void, and out upon the plain
Their king now free to seek a queen

Among the stars that remained

T ali's words faded away and left me in disquiet. It sounded like an epic poem of some sort, with heros and monsters and happy endings, but this was real life, not some story told over a fire. Devereux was going through this change, whatever it was, and the poem Tali had offered made no more sense now than before.

What was worse: it offered no solution.

"Is that it?" I asked.

Tali shrugged and nodded, eyes watering. I brushed my fingers over Devereux's wound, testing it with my magic, but it didn't respond. Whatever was happening to him, I couldn't help.

"What's going on?" Casimir returned, three fish on a line in his hand. "I heard you shouting."

I gestured helplessly to Devereux. "Something's happening to him. Tali says it's a change of some sort, but how? I don't know what to do."

My words came out in a rush and I feared I was babbling. Dancer came closer and sat beside me, pressing his now-massive shoulder into my side. He eyed Casimir, then Devereux, and let out a low purr that rumbled through my bones. Casimir hesitated.

"The voidling bite must have been poisoned," was

all he said. No emotion crossed his features, nor no shock in his voice. He was, to all onlookers, calm. I wanted to scream and rail at him, my magic already rising to do so.

"What do we do?" Tali asked, her own voice cracking. "He is the Crown Prince! He cannot die, not like this."

Wasn't that why his mother had sent him out here, so she could be rid of one useless heir and replace him with his sister? Or had she hoped that he would win some honour and return home a hero? I hunched my shoulders and shook the questions from my head. They helped no one, not now.

"You have done all you can," Casimir said. "The poultices have fought off infection, and we have no way to draw the poison from his body. Not now that it's reached his eye. The void calls to him."

"No." I straightened. "Your healing spell. You said it was painful, but would it not do the job?"

Casimir winced. He dropped the fish by the fire and rubbed his hands together. The shadows there looked just like the shadows on Devereux, only starker against the pale skin rather than the prince's golden brown. "It would only halt the poison's progress. It wouldn't heal him."

"Isn't that a good thing?" Tali demanded.

"It may not be. The change is already well upon him, and has consumed a good portion of him, to have changed his eye. He already feels the call to the void. Stopping the poison now will only..." Casimir drifted off and looked at me, pained.

"Will only what?" I pressed.

"It may break his mind, to resist the call."

"It may not! Devereux is not weak, not so much as you believe. He is strong enough to resist." I was sure of it, so sure that it tasted like desperation. I held my ground, meeting Casimir's gaze without fear or hesitation. Finally, he lowered his head in a slight bow.

"Of course," he said, and it didn't feel like he was agreeing to save his friend, but because I had asked it of him. Because I had commanded him.

Casimir stood over Devereux and began sketching something in the air, following the motion in the earth with his boot. It hardly made an impression in the earth, given how hard the ground was this time of year, but the air hummed with potential, regardless. His mouth moved, the words impossible for me to hear, to understand. His fingers crossed a point in the air and the earth began to glow beneath Devereux, marking the points of the spell.

The prince started screaming.

Tali reached for him, but I held her back, knowing instinctively that if she interfered, things would shatter into pieces. Not just Devereux, either, but Casimir for casting the spell. Devereux kept screaming, his eyes staring unseeing at the sky, his fingers curled into claws and tearing at the ground beneath him. Casimir continued his spell, speaking the casting over and over again, tracing the pattern in the air, his toe following suit.

This went on for what felt like an eternity. The prince's screams grew hoarse and hollow, quiet enough to no longer echo in the open air. He seemed to lose energy, no longer able to dig into the ground, his fingernails broken and the tips of his fingers bloodied. Still, his multi-hued eyes stared at the bright blue of the sky, seeking something that could not be found there. Tali was sobbing quietly as I held her back. Dancer pressed against me, lending me what strength he had, though a low growl rumbled in his throat.

Finally, Casimir stepped away, slashing his hand through the air in a violent motion that broke the spell. Devereux slumped to the ground, heaving for breath, his eyes mercifully closed. Tali went to him, her hands hovering over the wound in his shoulder, the lines of shadow snaking up his face. I felt my own burns, and while mine were on the left and Devereux's injuries on his right, I couldn't help but feel we were a matched pair.

Both marked.

Both unable to be fixed.

"Did it work?" I asked as Casimir sat beside me,

his breath thick and worn. "Did you halt the progress of the poison?"

"We shall see."

I wanted to tell him that it wouldn't be good enough, that we needed to know now. I held my tongue and instead reached for his hand. "Thank you."

"You need only ask."

I turned away, watching Tali put more poultice on Devereux's shoulder, unwilling to see the abject devotion in Casimir's eyes. It didn't feel right, not now, not after all that had passed between us on this journey. Yes, I would admit that I loved him, but what did I know of love? What did I know of anything?

I certainly knew I wasn't deserving of that blind adoration he bestowed upon me. The way he looked at me, I wasn't certain anyone deserved it.

"How far are we from Ynysfawr?" I asked, grasping for any topic of conversation that would cut the tension from the air.

"Perhaps another fortnight. It depends on how the villages fare along our way, whether we can stop for supplies, or if we need to fend for ourselves." He stretched his fingers, wincing. The shadows there had spread, or so it seemed. But when I looked again, they were as they had ever been. A trick of the light, surely.

"And the void, it will get thicker the closer we get?"

Casimir brushed a strand of hair back from my face. "Devereux will be fine," he assured me, though based on what he'd said before, I wasn't so sure. "The poison has been stopped and when he wakes, you'll see that he's himself again, apart from a few cosmetic differences." Here, he touched the burns across my cheek. I flinched back.

"Please don't. Don't pretend that everything is going to be alright. I am not a fool, nor do I need to be coddled." I couldn't bring myself to meet his gaze.

"I never suggested that." Casimir's voice was sharp, almost hurt, but I refused to think that my simple words could have triggered such a thing. There was something else going on, something from before that he wasn't telling me. Again.

Fine. Anger wrapped around me, its arms reaching into my bones and holding tight. I straightened, then stood, brushing off my skirts and pulling my woollen shawl closer. It was still reasonably warm during the day, being just past the equinox, but the nights were getting cooler, and the first brush of winter was fast approaching.

"Astraea?" Casimir asked, frowning up at me. "What is it?"

"You refuse to tell me what I was like before, saying it doesn't matter, that I'm starting over.

Perhaps that is true, but the way you treat me isn't new, it's tinged and tainted with the old." I held up a hand to silence his protests. "Don't pretend that it's not. You loved me, as I was then, and perhaps you love me the same now, but I don't think you do. I think you still love the idea of what we were, what I was. Sure, you've marked my differences, but you still treat me as though…as though the past rules my decisions, my actions."

"You're wrong," Casimir growled, rising as well. He looked down at me with such a pointed, furious stare that I very nearly felt the scream of hollow shadows rushing around me in response. "I love *you*, Astraea. I don't know what's brought this on—"

"What's brought this on is that you are treating me like a fragile piece of jewellery. Something precious, to be shown off, but protected and polished. You treat me like I'm going to turn feral at any moment if I don't hear exactly what I want to hear, if things don't go exactly my way. You don't help alleviate my fears, you dismiss them. When I asked about Devereux before, you said it might help. *Might*. But after the spell, you were so certain that it worked. And you've been doing it for so long."

His eyes turned to stone, his posture stiff. "I see. It's nice to know what you truly think of me."

"Empty night, Casimir!" I cursed, borrowing one of his favourite phrases. He flinched. "That's not what I think of you. I think you're strong and caring and so, so good that it burns and comes out cold. You know the world needs you to be the fearless Void Runner, so you are, but I've seen you, how you care. I love that, without reservation. And I love *you*. But when you treat me like the past is holding me back, like I can't handle the present, then it stings. Because you don't trust me."

His breath fluttered, sharp and jagged. In that moment, I knew it was true. He loved me, but he *didn't* trust me.

I took a step backwards, threading my fingers into Dancer's fur.

"He's awake!" Tali said, interrupting. I was grateful; whatever came from my tongue next would likely be irreversible. Instead, I went to Devereux and knelt by his side. His glowing eye found me. I wrapped my hand around his.

"Lady Astraea?" he rasped. "Stars above, my head. It's splitting."

"What do you remember?" I asked.

Devereux winced, squinting against the sun. "I was dreaming. There were voidlings everywhere, but I could understand them, and they weren't trying to hurt me. They were searching for something, something they'd lost so long ago. They thought I was the answer, that I could help them. Then there was pain and then I woke up."

Tali helped him take a few mouthfuls of water, which he spluttered up.

"Easy," I murmured. "You've been poisoned by the voidling hound that bit you. The infection in your wound is gone, but—"

"But I have voidling blood in me now." It wasn't a question. Devereux nodded. "I can still feel it, I think, even when I'm awake. It's…whispering to me."

"What does it say?" Tali asked, and for the first time in a while, I remembered that she was here to take our story, not just as a friend and travelling companion. I didn't want her to know this.

Devereux shook his head. "I can't hear the specifics. It's too quiet. But it's there."

"Once we get to Ynysfawr, maybe we can purge it from you. Maybe there's something at the temple there that will be able to help." It was an empty promise, made so easily without basis. Yet I couldn't help but make it all the same. Devereux squeezed my hand.

"We had better hurry, then," he said.

It was as close to a call to arms as we were going to get. I helped Tali prepare the horses, tying the saddle bags back on and throwing dust over the remains of our fire. Casimir helped Devereux to stand.

I mounted Titan and was just about to turn and

see if the others were ready, when I heard Casimir talking quietly to Devereux.

"Are you truly well enough for this?" he asked. "My healing spell only sealed off the wound. It did nothing to stop the poison."

"I know," Devereux murmured.

I pretended to fiddle with the saddle and stirrups, brushing my skirt flat and signalling Dancer to my side.

"The whispers, then," Casimir continued. "How bad are they?"

"I can feel the void, out there. It's far more vast than we ever knew, Cas, stretching almost into another realm. It's more than just a darkness, a shadow. It's a barrier, a gateway."

"You know this?" Casimir's question was hissed.

"I know this," Devereux replied.

I couldn't bear to hear any more. I clucked my tongue at Titan and nudged him with my heels, riding to where Tali waited. She smiled tentatively at me. I tried to return the look, but I certainly failed.

"Let's go," I said, strained. "Destiny awaits."

Over the next week, we travelled steadily east, sticking to the road as much as possible, and taking what felt like deer tracks when the road veered away. The entire time, I kept my eye on Devereux, waiting to see if he would do something untoward. All I received for my trouble was a jumpy reaction to almost everything.

There were no more voidling attacks as we went, as if they were biding their time, and we managed to avoid meeting any people as well. In fact, the entire countryside felt abandoned, despite the lush greenery and beautiful scenery. There weren't even shepherds grazing their sheep or cows. Any wild animals were scarce and even jumpier than me, vanishing out of sight before we could see them. The only beings that remained were the fish in the rivers and streams, and birds.

Tali passed the time by telling us stories of people in other countries, beyond the void. We learned of the rain forests of Cortaesi and the volcanic island of Kinbreck. I liked especially hearing about the nomadic people of Llyn Rhosalwyd, who followed the great herds of wild horses across the plains. Occasionally, Devereux or Casimir would request a specific story, usually something to do with adventures or exploring. I didn't even know what to ask for, though I had questions about the other Chosen Ones on my tongue a hundred times. I kept silent, listening instead.

Casimir tried to keep close to me, doing little things to show his affection. I found a wreath of wildflowers beside my bedroll one morning, likely the last of the season. I wore it all day until it fell apart and was snatched away by the wind. Sometimes, he would give me an extra portion of tack, or a bit of honey in my porridge. I wanted to refuse all of this, to say that it was unfair, but I couldn't do that without causing him more pain than I already had, and seeing the hurt in his eyes after our words was bad enough.

He tried to ask me questions about what I thought of things, like what colours I liked, and whether I preferred skirts or trousers, or if I enjoyed travel, but they were all perfunctory. Never once did he touch on deeper issues, like the social strata of Altier, which was Devereux's topic of choice when we all ran out of conversation.

Despite the shadows on his face, which were growing by increments daily, Devereux tried to remain cheerful, goading Tali into discussing court politics and the distribution of wealth in the city. They delved into economics and social welfare, and all the things that his mother was doing. Tali appeared to have a vast knowledge of the queen's reach in Altier, and even what her influence over the Council of Nobles was doing. To Devereux's eternal disappointment, it appeared that cunning, sharp Queen Raya was encouraging the schooling of all children through the Temples, with the full backing of Beatrice as High Priestess. There were roving healers that were paid with royal coin, who ventured to places where few others went. There were even open courts for those with grievances; they were gathered throughout the week and then judged upon by selected magistrates. Those grievances which could not be easily solved were taken before the queen herself, mediated by various Council of Nobles members. Not the prince, though. Never him.

Devereux grew more agitated the more he heard of his mother's doings. I wondered if it was because he realised how mistaken he had been in his raging against his family, or if he was coming to understand how blind he had been to their actions. One night by the fire, I tried to reassure him by saying that I still didn't like Beatrice, no matter her involvement in the schools, but all that earned was a scowl from Devereux and a few grumbles from Tali on the pervasiveness of the Temple, and the fall of the gods.

"Tell me about the gods," I said, picking at my bread. Dancer lay at my side and pricked his ears up at my question, as if he, too, were interested in the answer. Casimir, across the fire from me, his shoulders hunched and eyes focused on his food, tensed.

"What do you want to know?" Tali asked.

"You keep mentioning how the current Temple has pushed the gods aside, letting people forget them, but you never mention the gods themselves." I shrugged, dipping my crust into the shallow bowl of fish stew. "The only name I know is Mother Earth, or Lady Earth."

Tali nodded and shifted, folding her feet under her. It was the pose she took when she delved into her *dharangui* knowledge. She set her bowl of stew, half-eaten, on the ground; I knew then that my question was not a simple one, easily answered. My stomach twisted, and I gave the remainder of my food to Dancer.

"The gods, it is said, were here before the world was born." Tali took in a deep breath from her stomach. The fire crackled and spat forth a burst of sparks. Devereux flinched, squinting at the sudden brightness.

"They ventured forth from the deepest depths of the sky, bringing with them light and dark, earth and water, fire and air, even life. Mother Earth was their queen, crowned each spring in a glorious offering of flowers, which she shed for a mantle of frost each winter. Her consort was Father Sky, who bathed the earth in brilliant sun and soft moonlight, who brought wind and rain and snow and sun, each an aspect of his changeable moods. The Oceans Deep was their first child, a being so vast that he had to dwell at the bottom of the deepest oceans, for there was no space for him elsewhere. He inherited his father's moods, and his mother's steadiness, some-times dashing ships upon the rocks, but always following the currents of his ocean home. Mother Earth's sister, the Eternal Flame, lived beneath the crust of the earth, and in every fire upon its surface. She is the Consumer, the Devourer, and in her jeal-ousy of all that grew and thrived under her sister's care, she hatched a plan to take her revenge. She tricked Father Sky into lying with her, and gave birth to the stars, vast and numerous and bright. In his rage at discovering her treachery, he brought forth the blackness that lives between the stars, keeping them separate and alone, able to only call out to each other across the distance."

Casimir shuddered at this, his hands reflexively squeezing his bowl of stew. He flashed me a look of pure longing for one, desperate moment, then went back to staring at his food. I bit my lip and smiled at Tali, silently encouraging her to speak more.

"There are many, many other stories out there of other, lesser gods. Children of Mother Earth and Father Sky, they say. Or of the stars, even. There is Uro, guardian of doors; and Itax, keeper of trees. There are gods for the North Wind, and gods for the West. They say that the stars bore the first dragons, gifting them with their mother's fire, but no one has seen a dragon in aeons. Gods of mountains and rivers and horses and hunting." Tali shrugged, picking up her bowl again. "You name it, and there has probably been a god. Some say that these lesser gods are just creations of humans, but it's hard to prove. You'll still find people offering at shrines, but it's more rare now that the Temple has spread, giving people the hope of the First Star to worship."

"No one doubts the existence of the star, but they doubt the gods?" I asked, shivering.

"Only the lesser gods," Tali said. She shovelled up a mouthful of stew on her spoon. "No one doubts Mother Earth and Father Sky, or even the Eternal Flame. People claimed they heard the whispers of the gods up until about fifty years back. Then, as the Temple rose, the whispers of the gods ceased. Some say they're angry for defying them, some say they've gone to sleep until they're called on again. Either way, it would appear that they've left us to fend for ourselves."

Devereux nodded. "That, I would believe."

"What do you think, Casimir?" I asked. He jerked his head up at my question, bowl fumbling in his grasp.

"About the gods? I think maybe they grew tired of the world, all its troubles, and left it to their creations until a better time comes." He stared at me while he said this, his gaze intense enough that the hair on my arms stood on end. It was like he knew that his words were truth, though that was surely impossible.

Devereux broke the strained silence that descended on our camp. He stood, stretching, his sudden motion making Dancer jump. "I've had enough storytelling for one evening. I think we should get some sleep."

We all murmured agreement, our responses subdued. Casimir added wood to the fire, Tali and I cleaned up from our meal, and then we crawled into our bedrolls. The night fell upon us with a howl of cold wind from the north. I wondered if it was the voice of one of those lost gods speaking to us. Perhaps warning us.

I woke again sometime in the middle of the night, when the world was at its darkest. The fire had banked some, but not enough to put us in any danger. Everything seemed fine. Mostly. Dancer lay at my side, his head lifted and his teeth bared in a quiet snarl. He had his ears pinned back, his eyes fixed on a point in the darkness. I looked and found Devereux's bedroll.

Empty.

Grasping some of my magics in my mind, I stood and wrapped a cloak around me, ready for whatever would throw itself on me from the darkness. Dancer rose as well, massive paws silent as we crept away from the ring of safety and after the prince. He had a few minutes' head start, enough so that I relied on Dancer to lead the way through the darkness, the shadow tiger's nose our guide. I could have lit up the country side with the light magic that sang at the tips of my fingers, but something told me to keep to the shadows.

Devereux's path was winding, as though he were following a wayward spirit. We climbed over rocks and ducked through gorse bushes that tugged on my clothes and Dancer's fur. Once, I even splashed through a stream that had water soaking into my stockings. I should have taken the time to put on my boots. Then I remembered the words between

Devereux and Casimir after the healing. No, this was far more important than my comfort.

Finally, I caught sight of Devereux, a few buckles on his jacket catching in the faint starlight. He was standing straight, upright, and proud, as though this meandering were purposeful, intentional. That was all I could make out, though, for the rest of him was shadowed. In fact, he was so dark that he seemed blacker than the night.

His change had spread.

How had he hidden it from me? I thought I was watching him carefully, but now I realised that he sat to my left, so I could only ever see the right side of his face, the side that was already in shadow. I would have missed that the rest of him was changing, as well. And he kept back from the fire, as though it was too bright. Or had it been because he didn't want light cast on his changing features, so Tali and Casimir would remain ignorant, as well. Or had they seen and thought I already knew?

Now, he walked through the night with ease, like the voidling at my side. Unafraid of the darkness and what lingered there.

He moved towards a slight dip in the ground, at the edge of a forest of pines that had made a home in these inhospitable windswept hills. The closer we came, the more my magic itched to break free, some instinctual part of me knowing that we walked to danger. That Devereux walked to danger.

He stopped at the edge of the forest, not bothering to look around him for the threat I knew was there. I sent my earth magic into the ground, sensing, but found nothing. Only emptiness.

My breath hitched.

I never felt emptiness. There was always *something*, even if the rocks slumbered so deeply as to be barely moving, barely alive. But this was true emptiness. True nothingness, as if my magic couldn't comprehend what lay beyond the darkness.

I realised what it was a moment too late. A creature, equine, with a pointed horn of impossible shadow, stepped from the forest. Its pelt was charcoal grey, its hooves shining like obsidian. Its eyes, though, glowed golden, a match for Devereux's after he was poisoned by the voidling hound.

Devereux had come to a void pool at the edge of the forest.

The unicorn lowered its head in what looked to be a bow.

Devereux copied the movement in a smooth motion. Then, "I heard your call."

The unicorn nickered, tossing its shadowy mane. A noise, almost like a voice, rasped through the air in a language I couldn't understand. I wanted to clasp my hands to my ears, but was still, unable to move.

My fingers tightened involuntarily in Dancer's fur, and he pressed against my side.

"I did not choose to be changed," Devereux said, sounding annoyed, "but once I understood what was happening to me, I accepted it. I come willingly."

The unicorn pawed at the ground, and again there was that voice, terrible and powerful. My breath nearly froze in my throat.

"The ones I travel with know nothing of this. They would have tried to stop me."

The unicorn spoke, and I began to understand with creeping horror that these creatures, these beings, were intelligent. I knew that Dancer was more clever than any other animal I had encountered, doing as I asked with little more than an instruction. But he had never tried to *speak* with me, and I began to think that he was just uncommonly capable. Now, though, hearing the horse voidling speak, hold a conversation with Devereux, I knew that they were not just simple animals, desperate for food—for light and life. They were intelligent.

Perhaps not those ones, the twisted beings who were too many things melded together. They were mad, insane. But the malgrwm? The shadow tiger at my side? The horse with the shadowy horn that now studied Devereux with interest in its gaze?

They were sentient.

Bile rose in my throat at the enormity of this

knowledge. The implications for fighting the voidlings, for fighting the *void*, were staggering, so much so that I couldn't comprehend them all without my knees buckling beneath me. Dancer seemed to sense my distress; he leaned against me and nudged me with his muzzle, breaking me out of my stupor.

"...the *dharangui* is of no danger to you. She is no roving Temple worshipper, just a poet." Devereux fingered the cuffs of his jacket, and for the first time that evening, I sensed a hint of unease in him. "The Void Runner will prove a difficulty. He is uncommonly attached to the star's heir. And void touched, though he resists it."

The unicorn hissed out a phrase that had me wanting to scrabble at my ears. Dancer's ears went flat, and even Devereux stiffened.

"The star's heir? She..." He hesitated. A hand went through his hair. "She has powerful magic. And she believes in her destiny. She did rescue the voidling cub, but when I was attacked by the hound, her true colours came through. She will do as the star was meant to do, for my sake, if nothing else. You'll have to stop her."

The unicorn snorted and tossed its head. Then, it turned and looked past Devereux, up the hill a bit, to where Dancer and I stood, half-concealed behind a rock. It looked at *me*.

Devereux whirled, and I saw the extent of his

transformation. His eyes now both glowed with a deep gold, their centres so bright that I could barely stand to look at them. His skin was uniformly shadowed, his hair a grey only slightly lighter than his skin. Only his clothes remained unchanged.

He had become a voidling.

"Astraea," he breathed, and I thought I saw a glimmer of shock and horror there.

That was the first time he had used my name and no title. The first time I think he saw me as a person, even as he betrayed me.

The unicorn let out a furious cry and lunged forwards, hooves digging into the ground and propelling it towards me with impossible speed. Dancer leaped in front of me, snarling, the sound almost like that terrible language. Giving a toss of its head, the horse gored Dancer with its horn, throwing my beloved companion aside.

I couldn't breathe. My magic fluttered.

It bore down on me, eyes blazing. One step, and the rock beneath my feet cracked. Another, and all the living things in several hundred feet died at my hand, feeding my fear. A third, and the unicorn was above me, its expression one of pure victory.

I raised my hand to cover my face, my magic roaring to life. The unicorn let out an angry scream, then backed away. I opened my eyes, only to see my hand engulfed in fire so bright that it was almost white, almost as bright as the light that I bore. The unicorn reared, pounding its hooves on the ground. I couldn't move, couldn't fight, could only stand there, burning.

Devereux appeared between us, his hand on the unicorn's chest, holding it back. "Not now. Not like this," he said, and if I didn't know better, I would have said he was begging.

The creature let out an incredulous sound. Its nostrils flared, then its eyes widened. It took in another deep breath and snorted.

Impossible.

My ears ached, pressure building inside my head. I was fairly certain that my nose was bleeding. My vision turned blurry and the edges of the world faded away.

"What is impossible?" Devereux asked, making no move towards me, his hand still held gently against the voidling's chest.

Do you know what she is? The unicorn pawed the ground, digging divots into the earth. Devereux said nothing, though his expression was sad. He turned his gaze away from me.

You know some, the voidling guessed. The more it talked, the harder it was for me to stay awake, to stay upright. My flames began to flicker around my hand. *But not all. She is not what you think.*

"Leave her," Devereux said. "Not like this. Let her live a little longer."

"Devereux," I begged. "Why are you doing this?"

He didn't look at me when he answered. "They need me. They need me in a way that no one here ever has."

"But I—"

"Never needed me," he spat. His hands curled into fists at his side. "Never once needed me like I needed you."

"What of all our talk of friendship? All the time we spent together? Does that all mean nothing to you?" I was sure that it had, that it wasn't a lie, and yet he stood there, eyes glowing with a bright spark of anger and disappointment. He was prepared to throw me away, as easily as his family had done him. "I thought you a better man than this," I breathed.

He recoiled at that, and that spark of anger became a riot of fury, all the injustices in his life coming to a head. Bearing down on me. "You know *nothing* of me," he hissed. "Nothing of what I've been through. Poor, lost, Astraea. Who remembers nothing, but is so desperate to do her duty."

"I know that all you wanted was to help your people," I said. My vision faded for a moment, and I could have sworn that my fire flickered. I licked my lips, mouth dry. "I know that you were in agony when you thought that they were being ignored or abandoned by your mother. That you risked yourself to help them. To help me."

Had he, though? Helped me? He had guided me through some of the court politics, but just as often he had begged me to use my influence, my position, to help him. I thought we were friends, but perhaps I had fallen prey to the very thing that Casimir warned me about. Devereux was a master of facade. Charming, cunning. Insincere.

His jaw was tight as he stared at me, and I half expected him to defend himself. Instead, he just shook his head and turned towards the unicorn, waiting with wicked interest in its gaze.

I tried to sit up straight, but my energy was waning, drowning. "Then we are to be enemies?"

Devereux sneered, then shook his head. His eyes softened, and he looked at me for a brief moment. I almost thought I saw sadness there, but it vanished into emptiness a moment later. "We are only enemies if you refuse to see what it before you. What has been laid out for you to see, painted in masterful strokes, since you were brought in from Starfall Meadow, the star that burned. What has been before you this whole time, *Chosen One*." To the voidling unicorn, horn dripping with Dancer's blood, Devereux said, "Come. Let us go. We have much to do."

The voidling ducked its head in a nod, that

piercing horn slicing the air. Then it, and Devereux, turned and walked away.

My flames flickered and died, leaving me in blackness, the afterimage of my fire emblazoned on my eyes. I crawled in the direction I thought Dancer had fallen, my hands grasping. Eventually, I came across his fur, sodden with his blood.

"Don't leave me," I murmured, laying beside him. "Please."

Not like Devereux had left, without a backwards glance. Gone to join the voidlings, our friendship, such as it was, broken with a single moment. Though, I thought as exhaustion crept upon me, perhaps it had been broken for a while. After all, it was my destiny to save the world. And his, when he so desperately wanted it to be, was not.

CHAPTER 22

I was found just before dawn, Tali rushing down the hill towards me, calling for Casimir. She skidded to a stop and dropped to her knees, hands roving over the blood on my limbs, though never touching. I stared at her dully.

"Astraea," she breathed, "what *happened?*"

"Devereux is gone," I said.

"Are you alright? Are you hurt?" She looked to Dancer and her hands flew to her mouth. "Stars above! What happened to him?"

I didn't have a chance to answer. Casimir appeared, stumbling over rocks and shoving through gorse bushes. He, too, fell to his knees beside me, gathering me up in his arms, the pressure soothing and constricting at the same time.

"Empty night, don't scare me like that again." His

voice was broken, pleading. "I thought I'd lost you. I can't lose you again, not now."

I brought my hand up to touch his jaw, then flinched at the voidling blood that stained it. "Casimir," I begged, though I didn't know what for.

"Shhhh, it's okay." He rocked me gently, pressing his nose into my hair and breathing deeply. "You're not hurt, are you? What happened? It's going to be okay; I'm here, now."

"She said that Devereux is gone," Tali offered, looking on with a sort of distant confusion, as if she couldn't quite understand what was happening. I could not, either. "And Dancer..."

Casimir flicked his eyes to my injured friend, his mouth tightening. He looked again at me, this time noticing the blood on me. Carefully, so as not to jostle me, he pulled back. "What happened?"

"I woke in the night. A dream. Or a nightmare. Devereux wasn't there. Dancer and I went after him. He came here, to the edge of the void pool, and was met by...by...a voidling. It was a unicorn with a terrible horn, and it *talked* to him." I shuddered, the memory of the creature's impossible voice filling my head.

Casimir baulked. "A unicorn? You saw a unicorn? A voidling unicorn?"

Tali shook her head. "I didn't know such things *existed*. They're supposed to be myth, like the dragons. Not voidlings. And certainly not capable of speech."

"Devereux said he went willingly, and then they talked about..." I trailed off, closing my eyes. "About what sort of threat we each posed. They saw me, and attacked, and I held the horse—unicorn—off with my flames, but it...it said that I was impossible, that Devereux didn't understand what I was."

I opened my eyes just in time to see Casimir flinch, the muscles in his jaw working, as if he were holding in words that would answer my unspoken question. It was another of those things he wasn't telling me. I remembered, then, the way that Devereux spat out the words, *Chosen One*, as if it were a mockery of my title, my purpose. All the things he said, about the truth being laid out before me. About me being the star that burned. Had he known something as well? What wasn't I being told?

"I've heard stories," Tali said, almost excited, "about voidlings negotiating with people before, offering them riches or their heart's desire in exchange for something, usually their soul. But those are ancient stories, older than the poem I told you, Astraea. My grandmother says those are some of the first things the *dharangui* collected when they wandered the world, given to them at the behest of the gods."

"They can talk," I murmured. They were intelligent, excepting those of them that were insane, twisted by whatever force in the void bound them there. "They called to Devereux, seduced him with promises of being useful. This changes everything."

Just as his betrayal changed everything.

"It changes nothing," Casimir snapped. He reached for the waterskin at his belt and unstoppered it, hands shaking. Wetting a handkerchief, he washed my hands clean of blood, though there was nothing he could do for the stuff spattered on my clothes. "We press on to Ynysfawr and push back the void from there."

"What?!" Tali leaned back, aghast. "You just want to *leave* Prince Devereux, the heir to the throne, in the claws of those things? He—"

"He was void touched," Casimir snarled. "He chose to leave. He could have resisted and yet he chose to leave us behind, and attack Astraea. He is our enemy, now."

I flinched, recalling Devereux's parting words. It didn't seem right to bring it up now, not when I knew that Casimir was keeping things from me, not after all that had happened. The truth was, I didn't know what to think. I was certain that the voidlings were not just mindless monsters, but did that change what I had to do? I didn't know.

"We go to Ynysfawr," I murmured. "Maybe there's information there about how to rescue Devereux."

"This is a mistake," Tali said. "How do we know we can find him again? How do we know he'll still be Devereux?"

"I don't even know if he was still Devereux last night." I tried to stand, my knees buckling as I did so. Casimir was there again, steady and strong, ready to hold me up. But not ready, it would seem, to offer me the truth.

"What about Dancer?" Tali asked, her voice quiet.

My throat tightened. "I can't leave him behind." The words came out in a rasp.

"He is severely injured," Casimir said, hand on my back. I knew what he was asking, what he was suggesting. Not that we stay here and save him, wasting precious time and resources to heal what was, essentially, a creature hated by all of humanity, but that we put him out of his misery. That we kill him swiftly and bury him here. That we abandon my friend, perhaps the only true one I had, to a wave of my hands and a flash of magic.

Tears filled my eyes, but didn't fall. Wouldn't fall. I had nothing left in me to give after last night. I would *not* give up Dancer.

"I will not leave him behind." I crawled back to him, where he lay, breathing shallow and eyes glazed in pain. At my hand on his fur, he let out a low moan. His side was split, wounded muscle nearly giving way to bone. His blood, grey and sticky, oozed slowly out of the wound like shadows fleeing the dawn. I knew, too, that his strength would fade more as the day progressed and the light grew stronger.

Maybe, though, I could do something to help him. I had to.

Reaching deep, I nudged that heart of shadow that lay inside me and coaxed it to the surface. It didn't want to act without the light that I possessed, but I held it down. The shadows spilled forth, liquid and somehow living. They met Dancer's wound and my voidling let out a groan. I could feel his pain through our weak connection. Tears filled my eyes, but I continued flooding him with magic.

With a flash of fangs and a weak batting of his claws, Dancer tried to protest, tried to pull away from the touch of the shadow. But the more I poured into him, the more he relaxed. His muscle began to knit, his blood stopped seeping forth, and soon there was nothing but a weeping wound on his flank. A pain in my side flared, as if I were the one now injured. I pressed a shadowy hand to my side, but felt no blood, no gash, only the phantom pain. It flared as I moved. A price, perhaps, for pouring away my shadows. Or perhaps Dancer and I were now linked as we had never been before. I didn't care about the pain, only Dancer. He was far from healed, and travelling would be a strain, but I knew with absolute certainty that he would not die.

He would not leave me, or lie to me, or use me. He would be there for me, as I swore silently to be for him.

My shadows, though, did not belong in this world of light and life. And we were perilously close to the edge of a void pool.

The void pool, less threatening in the light of day, seemed to stretch forth, as if reaching for Dancer, for me. I flinched back, even as Casimir cursed and tried to inscribe the arcane spell for light on the ground. The pool moved too swiftly, reaching in tendrils. I had lost too much to this pool already, though, and I would not lose any more.

I screamed at it, throwing my fire and light into the blackness with every piece of magic in me. The void shrieked, like ice cracking under boiling water, and retreated. I threw more of my magic into it, more and more and more, pushing back the blackness and burning whatever emerged until the pool was nothing more than a sliver clinging to a long-dead tree, its husk charred and twisted.

My fire guttered, then went out. My magic was gone, nothing but a tiny seed of earth remaining to keep me from magic sickness. I turned my back on the newly empty ground, dry and barren and free. Devereux, unsurprisingly, was nowhere to be found. Gone, likely deeper into the void.

"Let's go," I said. Something in my voice was

different, even to my own ears. There was a hardness there, now. A sharpness, a coldness. An absence of trust and innocence that had carried me through the unknown.

Good, I thought. It was about time that the Astraea who woke with no knowledge, no idea about the world and people, about anything, learned how things worked. It was about time that she grew up.

✳

Walking away from the place where Devereux had abandoned us was one of the hardest things I had ever done. I felt a tug in my chest, pulling me back towards him, towards the spot where the void pool had been. I had to strain not to turn my head, but keep riding forwards. My hands dug into Titan's reins, my knuckles white. The pain in my side flared every now and again, usually when we climbed and Dancer slowed his pace, tongue hanging out and eyes dull in the bright light of day. Tali and Casimir seemed to sense that I didn't want to talk; they rode in front of me, occasionally murmuring between each other. They didn't look back at me, but I could feel their attention all morning.

That evening, when we stopped to camp, I caught Casimir by the horses. "I want you to help me continue my training."

He blinked. "What?"

"My combat training. I haven't done any since the wall, when I blacked out from magic sickness. Eloise said we would start up again when I was recovered, but the queen sent us away and...I want to keep learning. I have to."

Casimir brushed the corner of my jaw with his fingers. I wanted to lean into the touch, but did not, holding my ground. "Is this because of Dancer? There was nothing you could have done, love. That he survived at all is testimony to his strength. And yours. You have to be content with that."

"Dancer lives, and he *will* continue to live, but he was hurt because of me. He leaped in front of me, because I was helpless except for my magic. Magic fails. I need another option. I don't know that I could have stopped the unicorn, or Devereux. I have to do something!"

"Fine. Of course. We can start right away."

Placating me. He was placating me, with that tender smile and the gentle caresses. And I wanted to give in, wanted to believe him, but couldn't. Instead, I grabbed the sword he gave me and settled into my fighting stance.

My arms trembled as we warmed up, going through the motions of various attack forms. My legs were burning as I slid from form to form, trying to keep light on my feet and yet balanced and planted firmly into the ground. My side twinged now and again, but since Dancer was resting, it ached less and less as I warmed up. I did my best to remember all the lessons that Eloise taught to me in her infinitely patient manner. But when Casimir faced me after our warm up, that gentle smile across his features, I promptly forgot everything that Eloise had shown me, and leaped for him instead, furious.

Casimir backed up in shock, obviously not prepared for my onslaught. He recovered quickly enough, blocking me with the ease of practise. I struck again, and again, never breaking through, never even so much as making him take a step away from centre. My exhausted muscles quickly caught up with me, and I was soon panting for breath. Casimir thrust his sword forwards, tilting it under the guard of mine, and with a flick of his wrist, I was disarmed and unbalanced, stumbling backwards until I fell on the ground.

"That was..." He trailed off, helping me to my feet.

"Horrible," I huffed. Embarrassment burned across my cheeks and I tried to rub it away. The burns on my face caught my fingers and that same rage filled me again. I wasn't going to fail. Not anymore.

"Enthusiastic," Casimir returned. "You need to have patience. Your muscles take time to build up knowledge. We should just stick to the forms for now."

"The forms won't save Devereux," I snapped. Casimir stilled.

"Is that what this is about?" A quiet question.

"No." I scrubbed at my eyes, ignoring the dirt on my hands. "Maybe. He walked away from us, Casimir. Without a second thought, a second glance, he just walked away. Like we weren't his friends. Like we were nothing."

"The Devereux you knew isn't there, anymore." Casimir picked up my sword from the ground. "You will have to stop thinking that he is. The void changes people. Even Runners, who know how to travel through it, are not impervious."

He flexed his shadow-tinged fingers.

I nodded to his hands. "Devereux told the unicorn that you were void touched. That you resisted it."

Casimir looked away as he put the swords in their sheaths and set about tending the camp. Tali watched all of this with quiet intensity, stirring the soup over the fire. I wondered if having her here made Casimir more reluctant to speak, if he would tell me the secrets he was keeping were we alone.

No. He had been keeping these secrets for far longer than Tali had been with us. If he hadn't told me before, he was unlikely to do so now.

Surprise jolted through me as he spoke, his words careful and precise. "I have been closer to the void more than most Runners. I have led more parties through the void, spent more time patrolling the edges, fought more voidlings than most. My hands, my hair, the other parts of me that the void has touched, it is not the same as what Devereux experienced. That was a poison, spreading through his body. He could have tried to resist, but he would have failed. He would always have failed."

"You resist!" I insisted. "Surely—"

"I have studied the void and its ways for most of my life. And, as I said, my—infection, if you will—is completely different. It's not as invasive. It's more like a whisper in the back of my mind. Devereux would have experienced a symphony, to the exclusion of all else." Casimir kicked at a rock, the biggest display of temper from him that I'd seen. He glared at the ground, though I knew that the look was meant for me, but he would never actively glare at me. No, I was too precious to him for that.

It was infuriating.

"There has to be a way to save him!" I snapped. Dancer let out a snarl, echoing my sentiment, and I felt a tinge in my side. It was almost like a thought, a swirl of emotions that were not quite my own and yet mirrored my mind. I ignored it.

"Lady Astraea," Tali started formally, still stirring

the soup. "I think Lord Casimir is right. The Prince Devereux that we knew isn't there any longer. Something else exists where he did, now. The transformation poem, that passage I recited to you, doesn't suggest that the changed person is the same. Only that they change."

Being devoured by the void wasn't enough? Being turned into a voidling wasn't enough?

I refused to believe it.

"Tell me about the void," I growled. "I want to know everything. I want to know those ancient stories about the void negotiating. I want to know how it formed, how to fight it, how it thinks. I want to know it all."

"We would like to know that, too, I think."

Out of the darkness, perhaps fifty people appeared, all bearing weapons, most clad in fur mantles with streaks of paint across their faces. They bore the hardened expressions of those who had seen too much and experienced more. They made the bandits that we had encountered a week ago look like children playing a part.

The man who spoke was tall, taller than Casimir, with shoulders like a blacksmith. He had a pelt draped across his back, mottled in black and grey, so dark that it blended in to the night. My stomach turned as I realised it was a voidling pelt, likely from a creature very similar to Dancer.

Even as I had the thought, Dancer rose to his feet and let out a rumbling growl. His wound was hardly healed, evidenced by the pain in my own side. I pressed a hand to my ribs, hoping to keep the pain in. My magic was barely returning, a trickle compared to the river I'd had that morning. I would be useless against these people.

"Who are you?" Casimir demanded, already on his feet, sword drawn. His eyes were darkened with that shadow, his features twisted in a snarl.

"We?" the man asked, sweeping the air to indicate his band. "We are the only ones keeping this part of the country safe from the likes of that monster there. Or do you fancy folk think that those precious Void Runners of yours are going to come riding out of Altier and raze the countryside, freeing us from the void? No, I didn't think so."

"You're Hunters," Tali said, a harsh emphasis on the title. She looked disgusted.

"So named!" The man bowed, the others around him laughing. "And you, my dear girl, are a wandering poet. Or am I mistaken? After all, your friend here seems to think that you have some vastly important information on the void."

Tali let out a string of curses in several languages. Another man, short and stout, came up behind her and put his hands on her shoulders. She struggled, but he was too strong. Dancer growled, the sound deep enough to send shivers down my spine. The Hunters just laughed.

"Well, well, a tame voidling! We'll bring it along, too. Maybe we can have some fun before we skin it alive."

"What about the rest of them?" a woman with dark skin and only one eye asked. She fingered the scythe in her hand, rasping against the blade. "Should we kill them?"

"No," the man said. He considered Casimir and myself. "They may be of some use, if only in getting the poet to talk. Bind them!"

Once again, my rage was for naught. My fighting was for naught. My magic was for naught. Before I could even attempt to fight, or draw on my magic, someone knocked me over the head, and I fell into the comforting darkness of unconsciousness.

CHAPTER 23

I woke to an uncomfortable heat on my face. The burns I had were more numb to sensation than the rest of my skin, but even these were uncomfortably warm. I opened my eyes and found myself facedown on the ground near a cooking fire. A cauldron full of some pleasant smelling food was set low over the flames, which danced and leaped towards the sky with gleeful abandon. My own fire magic reached forwards, still greatly depleted from pushing back the void. It was barely enough to coax a spark into being.

This knowledge prompted the events of the night before to rush back to me. The Hunters. Tali. Casimir.

I struggled to sit up, but discovered that my hands were bound behind my back. My side was sore where I had bound myself to Dancer—something I still did not understand, yet knew to be true—and I ached in various other places, presumably from being dragged to wherever this place was.

Someone grabbed my bound hands and pulled me upright, wrenching my shoulder in the process. It was the short, stocky man from the night before. He smiled at me, a wolfish sort of look.

"Awake at last. Your friends have already enjoyed the pleasure of our company for breakfast. Alas, we have none left to spare." He chuckled, then hauled me to my feet. I stumbled over the rough, rocky ground, and barely noticed the well-established camp around us before I was thrown down again, my shoulder nearly hitting a large rock.

"Astraea." Casimir's voice was strained. I managed to sit up and found both he and Tali beside the rock as well. They were both bound, smudged with dirt, and with dark shadows under their eyes. Dancer was nowhere to be seen.

"Where are we?" I asked. "Who are these people?"

Tali hunched her shoulders. "They call themselves Hunters. They're sort of unofficial Void Runners for the more desolate parts of the country, only they demand payment for their 'services' as they call it. A lot of the people coming into Altier have been fleeing these people as much as the void."

I vaguely remembered Hunters being mentioned a few times, but hadn't thought much of it. Perhaps I should have.

"These people are not Void Runners," Casimir growled. "They're thugs who hunt down voidlings and force people to pay their protection money or be taken by the void. They wouldn't be allowed to operate, but we have few Runners to spare for this part of the country. Most of the population is in Altier, and what Runners can be spared are on patrol. Runners would *never* exploit people the way that these Hunters do."

These last words were spoken loudly enough for our hosts to hear. The leader laughed as he stomped his way over to us. "Exploit people?" he asked, chuckling. "We *save* them. A few coins, some food, that is surely a fair price for protecting people from the void."

Casimir met the man's gaze evenly, but said nothing.

"Now that your friend is awake, I think it is time that we were introduced." The man sketched a deep bow, his voidling-fur cloak falling over his shoulders. "I am Ilar, leader of the Hunters. May we have your names?"

"Tell them nothing," Casimir said evenly.

"Now, now, is that any way to treat an honest man?" Ilar pouted. "Very well, don't give your names.

I have enough information to paint a general picture. You, my dear, are a wandering poet. That means you're on a journey to gather information, gather a story to pass on. Which, in these parts, means you're on your way to Ynysfawr, as it's the only place around that could possibly hold any information of value. Not unless you wish to disappear into the void itself."

Tali struggled against her restraints, glaring at Ilar. He smiled at her and continued, turning to Casimir.

"You, obviously, are a Void Runner. Oh, what a treat it is to see one of Altier's finest warriors out this way. It is so nice of you to care for the people here, who are so often forgotten and mistreated, who live so close to the void itself. We aren't nearly so fine and fancy as your wealthy merchants and nobles who live out in the city, but we make do."

"And how do you know I'm a Runner?" Casimir asked, his tone mocking.

"Simple. Your armour." Ilar drew close, grabbing a strand of Casimir's two-toned hair with his fingers. "That, and the fact that you're void touched. It's hardly a mystery for those who know what they're looking for." He dropped Casimir's hair and shook his head, clicking his tongue. "A shame, really, that you refuse to help us. We could use someone trained in the ways of the void."

Casimir took a deep breath through his nose and

said nothing. He sat up straight, that earlier flash of temper I'd seen now nothing but calm annoyance. Ilar clicked his tongue again and turned to me. He crouched and studied me closely.

"Now, I understand the poet, and her Void Runner escort. But you...you're a true mystery indeed." He brushed a hand over my burn scars. I jerked my head away. "You don't seem like a warrior, certainly not a Void Runner. Nor do I think the wandering poets like to send two of their kind together, being so few in number. So what is it, my dear, that makes you so special?"

I flashed a glance to Casimir, who clenched his jaw. When I looked at Tali, she shook her head minutely. Ilar, though, just watched and waited. I had nothing to lose, not with my friends bound and my magic nothing more than dregs. Dancer was nowhere in sight, though the dull ache in my side told me he was not dead. I needed to make it Ynysfawr, and escaping these Hunters would take more time—and skill—than I had. So I bargained with the one thing I had left.

The truth.

At least, the truth as I knew it, though everyone's secrets kept swirling in the back of my mind.

"The Void Runner is my escort, not hers," I said, lifting my chin.

"No," Casimir growled, struggling to reach me.

"Really?" Ilar asked, sounding pleased. "And the poet?"

"Here to document my story, my success." I did my best to sound assured, arrogant, even. And why shouldn't I? I was the Chosen One. I had vast amounts of magic at my disposal, had bound a voidling to me, had pushed a void pool back until it was nothing more than a sliver. I had faced a malgrwm and a unicorn and survived. That none of those things had been planned or well executed, or even successful, was none of Ilar's business.

The Hunter raised his brow, waiting for my explanation. I straightened my shoulders as best I could, and said, "I am the Chosen One, and I go to Ynysfawr to push back the void."

Immediately, Ilar and those Hunters within hearing range began to laugh uproariously. Ilar even fell backwards where he knelt, clutching his stomach.

I glanced at Tali, who shook her head and seemed just as confused as I was. Casimir was frowning intensely, as though the laughter were some insult against me that he needed to remedy.

"You doubt me?" I demanded, still trying to maintain my arrogant persona. Even I could tell it wavered, though. "Why?"

Ilar sat up and wiped his hands of dirt. "You'll excuse me, your *ladyship*, but you're the seventh Chosen One we've had come through these parts in the past year. All trying to make their way to Ynys-fawr. All died screaming when they encountered the void. Now, I'll admit you've made it farther than most, what with having an actual Void Runner attached to you, as well as a wandering poet. And a pet voidling. What, is it some mountain cat you've had spelled with arcane magic to look like a shadow tiger? I'm impressed, even if you are a fool."

Seven Chosen Ones? False ones, apparently, but still. I wasn't aware that people would willingly pose as a Chosen One, given that the price was facing the void. The likelihood of my surviving the journey was slim, at best, though I intended to take the void with me when I went. Something gnawed at my stomach, a doubt that hadn't been there before.

What had possessed those people to call themselves Chosen One? And why had they risked death?

"She speaks true," Tali said.

"Oh, that she's managed to convince you, I have no doubt, though I never thought the wandering poets fools. Her command of her 'voidling' surely. And the presence of a Void Runner. What, Runner, did she persuade you to come along by offering her heart? Something more? The riches at Ynysfawr, perhaps? What riches lie between her legs?"

Casimir snarled wordlessly and threw himself at Ilar. Even bound, he was formidable, managing to regain his feet and strike out at Ilar with kicks and ramming his shoulder into the man. Ilar, though, was bigger and free to move. He soon had Casimir on the ground, pinned with a knee. My throat grew tight.

"Please, Runner, don't fight. It's so dull, fighting you. Not when we could be fighting something more...interesting." Ilar waved a hand and three of his people dragged something forwards by thick ropes, the thing screaming and writhing all the while. A large circle quickly cleared around the thing, leaving Ilar, Casimir, Tali and myself with the creature and its handlers.

Only when the handlers moved did I realise that it was a voidling. It was lupine in looks, with two curving horns on the top of its head, and a mouthful of slavering fangs. Its thick, black fur was shaggy and dripping with grey blood. They'd baited the creature into a frenzy, or it was already insane. Either way, this was bad, especially with my magic at its weakest.

"I'm sure you know what this is," Ilar said, gesturing to the beast. "A wilfkin, one of the fiercest voidlings known to us. We use this one to train our warriors, and let me tell you she is quite fierce. She won't hesitate to rip out your throats. Unless, of course, you are who you say you are."

This last was directed at me, said with a sneer and a twinkle in his eye, as if he wanted nothing more than to watch this wilfkin tear me to shreds.

"Astraea," Casimir breathed, struggling further as

Ilar rose and came at me with a knife. In a swift motion, the Hunter sliced my bonds, picked me up, and threw me in the direction of the wilfkin. As one, the handlers released the ropes, moving back to the perimeter, where the Hunters waited with hands on swords or spears or scythes.

The voidling snarled at the retreating forms, snapping at the air where they had been. Foam, flecked with grey blood, flew through the air. Then, realising that I was unarmed and weak, she turned to me and let out a low, rumbling growl.

"Astraea!" Casimir screamed. He was being held back by two of Ilar's men, and the darkness in him was growing. He was becoming more panicked, more frenzied, the closer the creature got.

I smiled at him. "It's alright," I said. If I died here, it would surely not be alright. But perhaps then a Chosen One could be born into the world that could actually do some good, instead of failing over and over and over.

Casimir screamed again, the sound something more than rage. I looked away, not wanting to see the pain on his face, that darkness spreading as he lost control. The wilfkin licked its muzzle, taking a few steps towards me.

I raised my hands in the defensive pose that Eloise had taught. In the brief moment as the wilfkin leaped, I felt my doubts and fears slipping away.

There was no concern over who would die if I failed, no fear over not being able to fulfil my destiny, no thought of the looks and whispers of people playing games I didn't understand. There was only me, my heart beating strongly in my ear.

My magic whispered as it tried to rally, tried to muster strength and fight as it had done before. But there was nothing left.

The wilfkin slammed into me like a boulder, her teeth latching into my arm with ease. I screamed my pain, but pushed against her anyways. She almost seemed to laugh at me as I fell to the ground and rolled away.

My wounded arm brushed against the bare earth, and suddenly, life speared through my veins. I screamed again, my throat turning raw as pain shattered my body apart. Vines, roots, tendrils of growing things, settled themselves into my bones, just as stones and earth moulded themselves into my blood. My magic as it was vanished, swallowed by the raw power that surged through me.

I slammed a hand into the ground, levering myself upwards, and the resulting shockwave knocked the wilfkin from her feet. She yelped and scrabbled backwards, ears pinned. I dug my fingers into the ground, and she was pulled forwards by a wave of rock.

Still bleeding, I stood, my legs supported by the beginnings of a tree that sprouted from the ground and held me high. Flowers bloomed in my hair, vines wrapped around my arms. There was no fire, no shadow, no light. Just the vast enormity of the earth beneath my feet, willing to do my slightest bidding.

I pointed a finger at the wilfkin and she cowered, whining piteously.

A black blur leaped into view, and suddenly Dancer was there, a leather collar around his throat, his claws stained red with blood. He stood before me and roared at the wilfkin. She pressed herself as far into the ground as she could. Dancer looked at me, ears flicking as he appraised me, as if making certain I was alright. I nodded, and he approached, licking my blood from my arm. The connection I had forged yesterday by healing him with my shadow magic became stronger, a bright light leading from me to him in the depths of my mind. He was mine, and I was his, bound together.

Then, as one, we took a step towards the wilfkin. As one, our voices split the air. *"Bow."*

The language of the voidlings mixed with my own tongue, reverberating across the camp. The wilfkin, trembling, lowered her gaze from mine and swept into a deep bow, her muzzle scraping the earth. With a nod, I released her.

"Astraea." The word, the name, snagged my attention, and I turned to where the void touched man stood. Casimir. His hands where wholly dark, and the shadows slid up his chest, touching his neck. As I watched, the vines and flowers curling around me, his shadows retreated until he was as before. Until he was nothing more than an ordinary Void Runner.

"What have you done?" Tali asked, drawing my attention from the man with many secrets. She watched me with wonder and a hint of fear. The Hunter's hand rested on her shoulder, though without any force or intent. It was as though he had forgotten who he was, why he was here, as he watched me claim what was mine: the power over voidlings that I needed only to unravel.

"I am the Chosen One," I said. Ilar nodded weakly. He fell to his knees. The whole camp followed suit, bowing to me as I stood with wilfkin and shadow tiger at my sides. I met Casimir's open-mouthed look. "Do you doubt me, now?"

He swallowed, and in a movement so fluid as to have been done a thousand times, he prostrated himself on the ground in a bow. His hands were still bound, but he pressed his face to the earth, regardless. "Never, my star," he said.

I flinched, and my magic retreated. The tree supporting my legs grew brittle and dead, snapping into twigs as I moved. The vines at my back withered, the flowers in my hair died. The land grew still. I still felt my connection to the earth, but it was dormant, slumbering as a mountain after a rockslide. Dangerous, but waiting. The remnants of my fire and shadow and light were nowhere to be found.

I took wavering steps to Tali and Casimir, untying their ropes with fumbling hands. Ilar, head still inclined to me as he refused to meet my gaze, helped.

"My deepest apologies, Lady Star. I was foolish to doubt you. We have had so many imposters, you see, and I could not be certain that you were who you said you were. I will never doubt you again. You will have a full escort to Ynysfawr, through the void bridge that protects it, and against any voidlings that cross your path. Whatever you need, only ask and it will be given to you, even unto my life and the life of my people."

"No." Did he expect me to execute them for defying me? "I want nothing from you."

Ilar recoiled, growing pale. "Nothing? Lady Star, it is my sole purpose, and the purpose of my Hunters that we face the void until the First Star returns and—"

"I want nothing from you!" I snapped. Tali rubbed my shoulder, even as she reached for my injured arm. "You took me and mine hostage. You would have killed us for sport had I not been what I said."

Ilar crawled towards me in supplication. "Lady Star! It was a mistake, an honest mistake! We are wary of any travellers and you were travelling with a voidling and—"

"No!" I pulled back and turned away. "Just give us our supplies and let us be on our way."

Ilar's mouth flattened into a grim line, but he just nodded. "Very well. May the Earth Mother smooth your path and the Sky Father light your way."

I curled my lip and turned away, wanting to never see these people again. A part of me, some deep and dangerous and alien thing, wanted to lay them all bare for daring to defy me. It whispered there with the slumbering depths of my earth magic, more colossal than ever before. I closed my eyes and silenced that desire. Despite these people's crimes, I was meant to save them, not harm them. The void was my target, my enemy, not the greed and arrogance of humans.

No, that was an altogether more difficult foe, one I wasn't sure I could face.

Within minutes, we were mounted and galloping hard for the eastern horizon. Tali had bound my arm with a linen strip and the murmured promise of more care when we stopped. Casimir only brushed the hair back from my face with wonder as he helped me mount Titan. Dancer and the wilfkin remained close to me, their presence almost as unsettling as what I had done.

Because the question was, truly, what *had* I done? And what consequences would follow?

CHAPTER 24

It felt like the edge of the world.

Behind us lay the desolate edge of Baldarskiel, long since abandoned by its people and guarded only by the vicious Hunters. The ground was smooth, laid bare by the wind for centuries. The only living things were grasses and small scrub bushes. Nothing else could live here, not without help. It was an empty place, a beautiful place, and a silent one.

Before us, lapping eagerly at our feet, was water. The ocean. Tali had told me that it was vast and ancient, wide and mostly uncharted, that water stretched from the edge of the horizon to the foot of the sky; sometimes, it was impossible to distinguish the two. All I saw, though, was a narrow band of water upon the sand, and a wall of darkness.

We had reached the void bridge that separated the mainland from the island of Ynysfawr, where the First Star was said to have fallen. We would have to cross it in order to reach the island. We would have to face the void before we could—before *I* could—even consider pushing it back at the source.

"How do we cross?" I asked, my voice a rasp.

Casimir dismounted his horse and stepped up to me, his hands on my waist to help me down. Ever since my display of power at the Hunters' camp, he had been deferential, almost reverent. It disconcerted me more than his secret keeping. Every awed look and revering touch had made my stomach squirm. This man, while devoted, was not who I had given my heart to, and I began to distance myself. Just another consequence of being the Chosen One.

It was better this way, I told myself. After all, once I faced the void, there wouldn't be anything left of me for Casimir to love. It was selfish of me, really, to try and hold on to him as I had been. To revel in his touches, his smiles, the casual attention. To see his eyes light up and shadow over when I looked at him. It would all be for nothing once I gave my power to push the void back.

I knew little of the deaths of the other Chosen Ones, but I knew this much: it required all they could give to fight the void. Only the First Star would survive its touch.

My throat tightened. Dancer leaned his weight against me, and the wilfkin, whom Tali had taken to calling Whisper, nuzzled me with her cold nose. Their attempts at comfort, I supposed. It was little help.

"There," Casimir said, pulling me from my thoughts. He was pointing to a tiny boat washed up on the beach. It looked ancient, hardly seaworthy, with barnacles and seaweed wrapped around the hull. There was a single oar, the shaft cracked.

"We won't all fit in there," Tali said. She was right. It looked barely big enough for two people and was probably only meant for one.

"I am sorry." That was all Casimir had to offer the poet, that and a shallow bow. She fisted her hands on her hips.

"You would abandon me here, after coming this far?" Her anger made me flinch. Still, I was glad that the boat was so small, that she wouldn't be there to see my end. I wasn't sure I wanted my pitiful death to be recorded by her and spread to all the other wandering poets. I wanted only to have the task done.

"He's right, Tali." I offered her my hand, which she took and squeezed gently. As if we had become friends over this journey. Yet another thing to add to my guilt when I left this world behind. "Ynys-fawr is a sacred place. I don't know what will happen there, and I don't know if I can protect you."

"I am more capable than you think," she protested.

"I don't doubt it. But I need you to go back, to tell the queen what happened to Devereux. Tell her…" I took a deep breath. I had no love for the queen, given her cruel scheming had left Devereux to abandoning us, but she deserved to know. "Tell her that I will try to find him, try to save him and bring him back."

I would try, but I also had a feeling I would not get the chance to do even that much. My stomach clenched, and I knew one thing: I was afraid. My destiny was come, and I was afraid. I didn't need witnesses to that.

"I came to see you face the void!"

"Please," I murmured. "Please."

Tali squeezed her eyes shut and took a deep breath. Then, still holding my hand, she nodded. "I will wait here for exactly one day. I will see what changes appear in the void, and if you do not return, I will go and tell the queen what has happened."

I wasn't going to return.

Turning to Whisper, I said, "Go with her. Keep her safe."

The wilfkin ducked her head in a nod, moving to stand beside the *dharangui*. Dancer pressed his muzzle to my hand. He took two steps forwards, his paws now in the water. His tail lashed once. He would be coming with us, whether he had to swim the whole way or not.

I nodded.

"Come, Astraea," Casimir said, a quiet caress, "we must cross the void bridge by nightfall."

Tali surprised me by giving me a swift, sure hug. Whispering in my ear, she said, "You can do this, Astraea. I know you can."

I hugged her back and said nothing.

Casimir helped me into the boat, the wood creaking ominously beneath my feet. I sat in the front and he pushed it out into the water, scrambling in at the last minute. The broken oar was a poor tool to propel us through the water, but it seemed to work well enough. Within moments, we were slipping past the edge of the void and were consumed by darkness.

"Do we need light?" I asked. I still hadn't felt the stirrings of my light and shadow magic, though every now and again I thought the barest hint of flame was reappearing. The earth magic, though, remained the strongest. Constant, almost, its presence a drum that mirrored my heart.

"Wait," Casimir said. He sounded like he was smiling. "Just wait."

I did, unable to see anything and feeling compressed by the blackness. My breath hitched, my skin crawled, and I was certain that I would start panicking at any moment. Then, impossibly, the world lightened. A mote of light, so faint that I could swear it was a dream, flickered into existence just above my head. Another followed, then another, and more, until there were thousands upon thousands of tiny lights illuminating the shadows.

The colours felt washed out, like seeing the world on a cloudy day, and the void still fell upon the water like a bank of fog, softening any sound and concealing the way behind and the way before. Yet there was light.

"They're like stars," I breathed. Casimir chuckled behind me, saying nothing more, the only sound the dip of the oar into the water, and Dancer's sleek passage as he swam beside us.

The passage through the void was like nothing I could have imagined. It was beautiful, the lights magnificent and subtle, brushing against my skin and reflecting off the water. I gasped as something beneath the waves moved, then there was light there, too. A creature of water, with fins and a long, sinuous neck. It had spots and stripes along its back, glowing faintly. A second creature, larger, joined the first, taking a mirroring point across the bow of the boat, leading us forth. In the distance, I saw more fish and sea creatures, all with luminescent designs and whorls patterned on their bodies.

They lit the water from below while the motes lit the sky above.

The void, this thing I had been fighting and fearing for months, was *alive*, was thrumming with life and light.

"I don't understand. How can this be?"

"It's the secret of the void," Casimir said. "Known only to those foolish enough to step into it without light to guide their way."

"But..." I gaped as the stripes along Dancer's back began to glow softly as well, down to the tips of his paws as he swam. "Why? Why do they attack? Why does no one know? Why—"

"Think about it, my love. Humans are greedy, grasping for any beautiful thing they can. Wasn't Queen Raya like this? Beatrice? Even Devereux, though his desire for beauty was more in goodness than gleam."

The oar cut through the water with a whisper. I couldn't bring myself to look at Casimir, instead staring out at the sea of stars, my eyes full of tears. "The voidlings?" My voice was a croak.

"They sought out any light which wanted to destroy their own," Casimir answered. "Those that were driven insane by the harsh light of the outside, they were the ones who attacked."

The unicorn, wanting to know our strengths and weaknesses, to see which of us would be most a threat. The twisted, terrible creatures, the ones that I had been told consumed their own kind in desperation for life, for sustenance. They were driven insane by the world beyond. Had Devereux known, in the midst of the void calling to him? Was that why he went? Words dried up in my mouth. My knuckles were white as I gripped the boat.

Casimir continued, as if my distress were invisible, or understandable and would soon pass. "Now, I will grant you that some of the voidlings, the ones who hold their reason when they cross the void, seek out our world for their own desires. For a different light, a different beauty. For colour, for the things they lack."

"How many more secrets aren't you telling me?" I rasped. The steady paddling ceased for a moment, then started again.

"Telling the wider world of this would have been disastrous, surely you can see that. People would have invaded this place, and destroyed it as surely as they destroy each other for what they want."

Perhaps he was right. Perhaps people were more prone to destruction than otherwise. I had seen how the Temple of the Fallen Star had all but wiped the worship of other gods away. I had seen how people rioted at the mere thought of being close to me, something they saw as above them, better, no matter that I was far from it. I had seen the opulence of the people in the palace, showing off their wealth and wares. People were wanting, desperate for more, but that didn't make us bad.

Tali was desperate. She wanted stories and tales to pass on to her people, to preserve for all time. Was that so terrible?

Devereux, too, had wanted. He sought a fair world, where all were cared for and cherished, even when he was so often cast aside or used as a pawn in some political game. He had abandoned us for that want, and with the impossible world before me, I understood why, even if I could not quite forgive him.

And me? What did I want? The answer was simple: I wanted to push back the void, to fulfil my destiny.

"Why didn't you tell *me*?" I asked. "You had plenty of opportunity."

Casimir was silent. The boat slid onto rocky ground, and I realised we had crossed the narrow channel of the void. The stars here were not so numerous, the creatures in the water were already fading away. Dancer's stripes dulled, and as he stepped from the water and shook droplets from his pelt, they faded entirely.

Ynysfawr. We were here. The place where the First Star fell.

It was time for me to do what I was meant to.

"Let's go to the temple," Casimir said, jumping

from the boat and holding his hand out for me. I reached to take it and hesitated. He didn't comment as I rose from the boat of my own capability, but I could see the hurt in his eyes. That I wouldn't trust him.

Why should I, after all he'd kept from me?

Wrapping my arms around myself beneath my cloak, I trudged up the rocky beach, trying not to slip on the slick rocks. The void slipped farther away as I went, until, when I looked back, it was nothing more than a wall of blackness. An intimidating front for a world of wonder hidden beneath.

It changed everything, this new understanding.

It changed nothing just as much.

I barely glanced at the island as we went, noting only that it was craggy, with mosses and lichens barely clinging to life on the rocks. The earth beneath my feet pulsed deeply with life, though, as if the mere promise of it could overwhelm what actually was. There were a few wildflowers tucked away in nooks and some beginnings of twisted, wind-torn trees on the sheltered side of boulders. A single path led from the beach onwards, and I followed it blindly, barely aware of Dancer beside me, Casimir behind.

Cresting a hill, I saw the destination of the path before me, and I quavered. I knew, then, why this place was sacred. There was indeed a temple there, long since fallen to ruin, the square structure open to the sky with one of its four walls fallen to dust and others on the way. But beyond the temple, illuminating the sky with an impenetrable glow that was keeping back the void, was a crater in the ground. And it burned.

The flames sprang from the crater like living spirits, grasping for air and freedom. They licked the sky and the edges of the crater, then receded, only for others to take their place. The closer to the centre of the crater, the brighter and more fierce the flames. It was alive, this fire, in a way that many others weren't. What little fire magic remained to me surged at the sight of the flames, invigorated. I shivered, even as my hands grew warm and my skin flushed.

"Let's have a look at the temple," Casimir said, a coaxing suggestion. I followed him, only because I did not know what else to do, and I was unable to think properly, my body warring between earth and fire. The light and shadow were gone, burned away.

The temple had obviously once been grand and beautiful, a true place of worship rather than a place of ostentatious display. The walls and floor were a vast mosaic, telling tales of things long since forgotten. Tali would have loved it here, I thought, and would have known the stories that were told.

I tried to piece them together, holding her in my mind as I did so. She would have started with the floor, right at the entrance. The beginning.

Two beings, impossible and vast, were laid out on the floor, reaching for each other. One was female, her form wrapped in ivy and trees, blending into the very earth. The other, male, had the sun and moon written upon his skin, with clouds and sky stretching in between. Mother Earth and Father Sky, then.

The left wall had more figures, and I turned my attention to them. The two gods frolicked with several others, all joyous and free. Then, the stars were born, springing forth from flame and sky. They joined the gods, dancing and leaping, much to the awe of the humans—poor, huddled, naked figures upon the ground. The stars and the gods came together, and from them seemed to pour hundreds of creatures. The unicorn, a malgrwm, a tiger like Dancer. Voidlings.

The voidlings were born of the stars and the gods.

I traced my fingers along the mosaic, now at the centre wall, where the humans were rising up, killing the voidlings and the stars, capturing the gods and warring upon one another. Mother Earth and Father Sky took their divine children in their arms and turned their backs on the humans, leaving only a single door to the realm of the gods.

Through which a single star stepped, a creature of black following after her.

The star and her lover went through the world of humans, adored and worshipped by them. Until the humans grew preoccupied with their own strife. The star, forgotten, went back to the door. Here, the mosaic was damaged, though it looked like she was performing an arcane spell. Then, there was a vast piece missing. I stepped over rubble and went to the final wall.

The void was now in existence, populated by voidlings. The doorway to the realm of the gods was in pieces, blocking off the way forever. The gods were forgotten, the void spread, and the star stood at its centre, her light pushing it back. Much to the adulation of the humans.

"What is this?" I demanded, rounding on Casimir. He stood in the centre of the room, his hands spread in supplication.

"The truth," he said. "You wanted it. You wanted to know what I've been keeping from you all this time. This is it, Astraea."

"The star did this. She brought forth the void and drove the voidlings insane as they tried to search for a way home." I jabbed a finger at the wall and parts of it crumbled away under my touch. "Every story I've heard about the star, about the Chosen Ones, it's all a lie!"

"No," Casimir insisted. "No! It's—"

"I have to undo this." I was breathing heavily, now. "I have to push back the void, separate the realms again. I have to undo what the star did."

If it were even possible, that is. No. It had to be. I *would* fix this. I would save the people, and the voidlings, and right that wrong. That lie.

I turned to face the glow of the crater, its flames calling to me louder, their song joyous and eager, as if they had been waiting for me. I took two steps when Casimir's hand wrapped around my arm, holding me in place with a strength that was unshakeable.

"No, Astraea," he said. "You don't."

I tried to pull back, tried to escape, tried to reach that fire, but his grip was so firm, his eyes so sure. "What she did is *wrong*! She wanted the humans to worship her, so she cut off the gods and separated our realms with the voidlings."

"Yes," Casimir said simply.

"Don't you understand?! I have to undo it! I have to make it right!" I grew frantic, trying to pull away, but Casimir held me firm.

"You don't understand. Your choices have consequences, Astraea," he snarled, more anger in his eyes than I'd ever seen. "They will come to call, and then what?"

"By then, I'll have faced the void! I'll have righted this wrong." I was fully aware of my consequences, of what truth I now faced, yet he continued to treat me as though I was blind.

Casimir took a step closer, the sound echoing on the stone floor. The drafts that ran through this vast, empty place set goosebumps upon my skin, yet my anger heated me, burning with my inner flames.

"And then what?" he asked in a low voice.

I faltered.

"After the void, after you 'right this wrong', what will you do, when the consequences of your actions come to bear, when the gods emerge again, what will you do? Accept them?"

"You assume there is an after," I said darkly. "That the void won't swallow all my power until I am nothing more than a husk to be buried in state. Isn't that what's happened to all the other Chosen Ones? When they tried to do what I must?"

He was standing so close to me. Close enough that I could see his throat bob as he took in my words. I saw the secret that he still kept from me in his eyes. He let out a long, slow breath. "What if..." Casimir broke off and paced away, turning his back to me. "What if you aren't emptied by the void?"

I scoffed. "Unlike every Chosen One all the way back to the First Star herself? She died because of the void! Because of her own hubris!"

Casimir hung his head. "The stars have burned in the sky for aeons. Do you honestly think that the void could douse one?"

"What are you saying? Speak plainly for once, Casimir!"

He turned to look at me, and his expression was

sad and ancient and weary. "What if I told you that the First Star never died? That she only...appeared that way. That the Chosen Ones since then—all female, all young—were merely her as she chose to be."

I recoiled. My heart beat in my chest like a hollow drum, loud and echoing. My voice, when I found it, was a whisper. "Are you saying that I'm a star?"

Casimir nodded. He did not meet my gaze. "Beautiful, immortal, effervescent. Yes, Astraea, you are a star, and I am your guardian, born of the blackness between."

My stomach fell. "No."

"Yes."

"It is impossible. That would mean you...that I..." There were too many thoughts to consider.

Casimir held out a hand. "I have loved you, Astraea, since before you fell from the sky and brought the void to bear. Stay here, with me. Please!"

I hesitated, then did the only thing I knew to do.

I fled.

CHAPTER 25

I ran as swiftly as my legs would go, and with panic and confusion driving me, the wind was beneath my feet. I ran from the ruined temple towards the beach, not knowing where else to go. I stumbled onto the path towards the beach and ran into a figure, still dripping wet from her journey through the strait.

Tali.

"Wha—Lady Astr—"

I grabbed her arm and pulled her along behind me, leaving the path and forging my way through the barren crags of the island. Casimir, if he followed, was far enough behind that I didn't see him as I looked over my shoulder. I saw only rocks and lichens and stunted plants. After a few more minutes, I tugged Tali into a hollow formed by two boulders that had fallen, perhaps centuries ago. Dancer ran behind us, crouching in the entrance, keeping guard.

I collapsed on the ground, the earth surging up between my fingers to try and comfort me. It sprouted wildflowers from stone, an impossible feat, and yet one that I seemed to accomplish with ease. Because I was a *star*.

"Stars above," Tali panted. I flinched. "What's going on?"

I didn't ask what she was doing here, how she came to be on Ynysfawr. Obviously, she had disobeyed Casimir and swam along behind us. Which means she had seen the void as it was. Perhaps I should have been upset with her for disregarding our request that she stay put, that she return to Altier and tell the queen of her son, but I couldn't bring myself to care.

I plucked a blue flower from the ground, my fingers trembling. It withered away into dust with the slightest thought, and I pulled back as far as I could go, wrapping my arms around my knees.

"Astraea?" Tali asked, reaching out and resting a hand on my shoulder. I squeezed my eyes shut.

"He lied to me," I murmured. "Over and over again."

"About the void?" Tali sounded awed, and when I opened my eyes to look at her, I could have sworn she had some residual starlight in her expression.

Certainly there was wonderment. "I saw it. It was beautiful, more beautiful than anything I've ever seen. The night sky come to life."

"It's the antechamber to the realm of the gods," I said. She sucked in a breath. As swiftly and precisely as I could, I explained the story in the mosaic. With each detail, Tali became still, her breath shallow. I could see her thinking, running through the stories she'd held, seeing how that fit, how it changed *everything*.

"If that's true," Tali said, "then the First Star...she banished the gods and tried to replace them. She trapped the voidlings here. The voidlings! Children of the gods and stars!"

She stared at Dancer, obvious awe in her eyes, and for a moment, I longed to wonder at that truth with her. I longed to be awed, to be so amazed by the hidden light of the void and the truth of the creatures that lived there, that I could barely speak. Instead, I had glass in my lungs and horror in my throat.

"It gets worse," I croaked. I hugged my knees tighter. "Casimir said..." I shuddered and took a breath. "He said that the star never died. That she just played at being Chosen One, over and over again, so that she could have the gratitude for saving the humans again and again and again and again. He said that he...he has loved the star from the very beginning, that he was her guardian, born of the black between, and that he would follow her to the ends of the world."

Tali was silent. I was too cowardly to look at her.

"That means..."

I nodded. A sob cracked open my chest. "He said I'm that star."

"My gods." A breath, a curse, and a statement of disbelief all in one.

It was a relief to have someone else know the truth. Someone who hadn't lied to me since the moment I opened my eyes and knew nothing of who I was. Of what I'd done.

"I have to fix it." I didn't know if I could. "I have to push the void back into its own realm. I have to seal it up again, or open the way to the realm of the gods. I have to...I don't know, create a door that separates this realm from the void. I have to do *something*."

"How?" Tali's word was a knife to the back, a sudden jolt and realisation that I had no idea what I was doing. I had no memories of how I had broken the world to begin with; how could I possibly undo it?

I shook my head, words lodged in my throat. Tali wrapped her arms around me. The touch was tentative at first, then more sure. I sank into the embrace, my whole body trembling and tears falling freely.

Dancer made a low sound in his throat, looking back at us, tail twitching, but he stayed where he was as if guarding me was more important than comforting me.

"Do you have any poems?" I asked, though I knew there could be none, not if what I had done was such a secret.

"I wish I did. How am I going to tell everyone that what they knew was a lie? That the void isn't darkness determined to snuff out the light, but a place of beauty? They'll think I've gone mad."

I chuckled, the sound dry. "I think we've all gone mad at this point. Devereux was right. My gods, was he right."

"Maybe, when all this is over, we can find him and say so," Tali said.

"I think he left to try and find a way to fix things. I think that's why the void called him." I sat up straighter, my thoughts whirling. "I think the void and the voidlings knew that they couldn't seal the breach, or open up a way to the gods, by themselves. Think about it! All the stories have *humans* as the ones who are able to reach the gods. Able to commune with them, able to traverse realms without losing themselves."

"Those are just stories," Tali said, but she was a *dharangui* and surely knew better than I the power that stories had. That some of them were true.

I was about to suggest we travel back into the void bridge, take the boat and see if we could summon Devereux, when the earth shuddered beneath me. Something was coming, something ancient and furious and with the strength to shatter the world. Dancer snarled.

"Casimir is coming," I breathed. And by the feel of the steps that echoed through the ground, he had shed all pretence of being human.

I wanted to run, wanted to be free of the terrible burden he'd given me, but I also loved him. It was, in all of this, the only thing I knew to be true with any certainty. I loved Casimir. I loved his strength, and his silence when no words were needed. I loved his goodness, his determination to do right, even when it meant someone might be hurt. He had been so over-joyed when I wasn't who I was, when I had wanted to make amends for things that I had done. Now, I knew the full extent of those wrongs, and I couldn't baulk now, even if he might.

"You can squeeze through there," Tali said, shoving me towards a gap in the boulders. "I'll hold him off. I'll talk to him. I'll take Dancer and we'll hold him back. Go to the beach. Go find Devereux."

"Tell him..." I hesitated only a moment. "Tell him that I love him. That I forgive him for keeping my past from me. Tell him I'm not the same star that fell."

Tali nodded, fiercely, and turned to face the path. I crawled through the boulders, the earth sealing itself behind me. As I moved through the gap, the path seemed to smooth itself before me. The ground levelled and cleared, the rocks shifted to let me through. It wasn't conscious magic on my part, the connection I had with the earth moved long past direct thought and intention.

I followed the path before me without question, even when it turned away from the beach and towards the centre of the island, where that crater burned. The earth knew what needed to be done, perhaps some guidance from the Earth Mother herself. I followed it willingly, descending down, down, to the place where the star fell. Where *I* fell.

When I reached it, I could see that the temple was now little more than rubble, only a few chunks of mosaic remaining. The most prominent was the star and the shadow that followed her, close by and ever watchful. My chest tightened; what must Casimir think of me, running away from him after all we had been through? I had to repair the damage I'd caused, even if it meant taking all my power, even if it meant taking me away from him.

The fires in the crater seemed to grow as I approached, that spark of fire in me rising in kind. I stepped to the edge, and the earth shifted once again, steps forming in the edge of the crater, descending into flame. I took that first step without hesitation. The second was harder.

The heat of the fire swelled upwards, wrapping around me like a miasma, making it hard to breathe. My own fire leaped joyously forth, forcing the flames higher. Ever since awakening my fire magic, I had not thought I could burn, but the more I moved downwards, the less I believed it. My skin grew feverish, flushed. I could feel blisters forming on my palms, then my arms. My clothes caught fire, disappearing into ash within moments. I panted, my breath catching in my throat.

The burns already healed grew warm, the first true sensation I'd had in those nerve-dead areas for months. The rest of my skin was hot, and I saw steam rising from me when I chanced a look at my feet. My hair swirled around me like a storm, caught in the terrible wind that roared through the fires. By the time I was at the bottom of the steps, I was in agony.

I fell to my knees, my hands sinking into the obsidian sand that coated the bottom of the crater. I pulled on every drop of fire in my blood to try and stem the tide, to try and keep from disappearing into a wisp of smoke. The earth beneath me shuddered as I tried to ground myself there.

Then, in the space between heartbeats, the flames grew still. The wind ceased its roar. My pain vanished.

I looked up and saw a woman striding towards me, beautiful and impossible, her features so perfect that no human could ever hope to replicate them in art. Her skin was the colour of fresh earth, her hair the shade of a dying fire. She was clothed in green and grey and purple and brown, the colours of earth. Her feet were bare, and where she stepped, flowers bloomed.

Everything was still but for her.

You have come, she said, her voice the coming of spring. *I have been waiting for you.*

Not knowing how to answer, or what else to do, I bowed, my head touching the ground, curling over my knees. The woman—the goddess, for she could be no other—chuckled.

You need not bow before me, she said. *I need no obeisance from you.*

"I—" My voice caught, the taste of ash on my tongue. "I have come to heal the wrong that was done."

I know. It is I who sent you to do so. She looked a little sad. Reaching for me, she touched a strand of my hair then brushed her fingers over my burns, and looked sadder still.

"You did?" Was this part of my memories that I had lost? Was this why I had been so incapable at Starfall Meadow? When seven Runners died, and my magic was so weak that I couldn't even keep myself from burning, let alone fight of voidlings. "When? How?"

When the earth was born again and the star fell, the goddess said. I waited for clearer answers, but she said nothing, keeping silent and just watching me as if I consumed her world.

"How do I fix the void?" I asked. The goddess closed her eyes and took a breath.

You must use the star's powers. The light, blinding and cold. The dark, empty and deep. Together, with the powers of a god, you must open a breach into the Beyond and call the void to you.

"I don't understand," I pleaded. "Tell me more! Do you know who I am? Do you know what I was before?"

I am sorry, she said, a single tear falling down her cheek. A flower grew where it fell. *I am sorry I could not see you become what you are. I am sorry I could not give you more.*

"Please," I begged, reaching up to try and touch her. "Just tell me!"

I am naught but a memory, the goddess murmured, just out of reach. *Bound here in this place for you to awaken. The last of what I am is yours to discover. I am sorry.*

She took a step back, the edges of her form fading slightly.

"Wait! No! I...I can't feel the light and the dark

anymore, not since I pushed back that void pool and bound myself to Dancer and—"

You know what must be done, the goddess said. She smiled at me, a look of tenderness and affection, one that set my heart to aching and tears to my eyes. *Goodbye, my child.*

"No!" I screamed, even as the flames started burning again, the wind started roaring, the world began moving once again. My skin was hot, my eyes dry and my lungs thick and full of smoke. "Come back!"

No amount of screaming would return the goddess to me, and my voice gave out before I could even try to call to her again. If I stayed here, in this crater of fire and lost memories, for much longer, I would burn alive, star or no. From somewhere beyond the walls of the crater, I could feel the earth trembling. Casimir was approaching, and I knew that he would try to stop me.

Part of me wanted him to succeed.

I stood, my legs weak beneath me. Taking a deep breath, I seized onto the fire magic in my blood and *pulled*. The fires around me flared, then went out in a sudden huff. I could feel the darkness descending on the island almost immediately, the void filling the gaps where the light had been moments before.

Casimir let out a cry, but he was still far enough away that I forced myself to ignore him.

My skin cooled almost immediately, then began heating again, only this time it was from the inside. All that flame, pulled inside, its heat strong enough to consume, strong enough to break through the world. I was shaking, now, the power taking every drop of my concentration to contain.

Squeezing my eyes shut, sweat dripping down my temple, I shoved the fire down as far as I could, then called for the light and the shadow. They appeared at the corner of my mind, two wayward spirits that did not want to be bound, did not want to be contained.

You will not command us, the light said, the shadow twining around it like a cat.

You are not capable of it, the shadow agreed.

I ignored their taunts and reached out with my thoughts, snaring them with earth and fire. Bending them to my will. The light flared, shattering my concentration for one brief moment. The fire nearly escaped, pouring through me like a flood. I screamed and doubled over, forcing my eyes shut, forcing the fire back. Back. Back.

As I reached for the light and shadow again, only distant motes compared to the power I had once claimed, a memory came to me unbidden.

It felt like a dream, an echo of reality, and I wondered if I had experienced it, or if I had made it up entirely.

I was in a room. Stark, formed entirely of stone.

The details were a blur, but the figure in the room was not. A woman, skin of earth and hair of fire—the goddess I had just seen—bent over me. Her touch was cool, soothing. Her words sent shivers into my soul. They were the words I had heard before blacking out at the battle of the wall, when my magic was drained, when I was nothing but an empty shell, waiting to be poured into.

✦

One part earth, one part the fire beneath, one part stolen light, one part shadow complete. With this touch, life I give, and where once was I, now you remain. The voice who spoke was soft, female, and ageless. In each syllable was an ache and a tremble, but I sensed no pain. Though I could not see, I knew I was safe, cocooned there in that warm space between moments. Then, there was a brush of a hand on my forehead. I gasped as air filled my lungs. Suddenly, I could feel my fingers, my toes, my face, my entire body. It was coarse and worn, yet smooth where the faceless hand had touched me.

Daughter mine, awaken.

✦

S tabbing pain flared in my mind where the magics I held warred with each other, earth and fire against shadow and light. Releasing a breath, I could not even scream, frozen in the grip of that pain.

A strangled sound at the edge of my hearing had my eyes flying open. I saw Casimir standing at the edge of the crater, ready to leap down. He was exactly as he had been, only more. Solid, yet with an ephemeral look. Steady, yet with the power to shake the world to its core. The features of his face had been honed, sharpened, until he was just beyond human. The shadows in his eyes, though, shone through.

The guardian, born of the darkness between stars, come to rescue the one he had fallen for. The star who fell.

The star whose light I held.

I met his gaze for a terrible instant, then the world became too much and I released my hold on the magic. It surged from me in a tidal wave of power, a pillar of fire and light burning through the sky, a mirror of shadow and earth burrowing into the ground. These twin points delved so deep and high that the world itself began to splinter. I could feel reality fraying, shattering, until a single crack rent the air.

I stood in three places at once: the crater of fires

now extinguished; the void of starlight; a place of stunning beauty where beings of staggering power walked and waited. My breath caught, my heart stopped, and I could feel the eyes of the entire world, all the realms therein, branding me.

Casimir stared at me, full of fear, his breath like fog in the air that now held frost rather than fire. "Astraea, no."

A single tear snaked its way down my cheek, freezing as it went. I wanted to say something, anything, but the truth weighing down my chest kept me silent. So I stood at the rend in the world, unable to tell him what I felt, what I knew. All I could do was what I had been born—made—to do.

I tilted my head back and called forth the void.

CHAPTER 26

"Hello."

I spun around and found Devereux standing behind me. He was dressed simply for him, a tunic and breeches, only a faint glimmer of starlight at his wrists and throat to signify any sort of wealth. A crown of mist lay on his head. The black of his clothes was darker than the grey of the world around us, and I realised a moment later that we were far from the crater where I'd split the world. We were in the void.

I wore the dress of starlight that I had donned the day of the ball, only the stars were red and orange and yellow and white, rising from a base of green and brown and grey. Fire, and earth. None of the light and shadow.

"You did it," Devereux said, holding out his hands

to me. He was still that shadowy creature that had been pulled into the void, but this time I saw hints of the man I had known. The smile, slightly crooked. The kindness in his eyes.

I slapped him.

Devereux recoiled, pressing a hand to his jaw, but he didn't look at all surprised.

"You bastard," I hissed through my teeth. "Do you know what you have done?"

"In what? Stepping into the void as its king, or in lying to you?" He smiled, but there was little joy in it. "You know as well as I that even though you've opened up the realm of the gods once again, that the void cannot be contained as it was. It has been its own realm for too long. It now exists as a place between, a veil if you will, between the realms. We cannot be cut off from the human world, for we have been a part of it for too long. Nor can we be separate from the gods, for they are our kin."

"And, what, the malgrwm offered you the leadership of the void, and you accepted?" I scoffed. As I spoke the creature's name, it appeared, the unicorn at its side. Both creatures looked at me with the sort of intelligence that I thought had once only belonged to humans. To those with stories to their names.

"This realm was shapeless for so long, torn apart by the Star that Fell. We were left to founder, which is why so many of our kind went mad." The malgrwm clicked its beak together and ruffled its feathers.

The unicorn tossed its head in a nod. "So much of our power was drained off by your human light, even as it fuelled us. We could not be anything other than the shapeless place of starlight that you saw. Now, with the realms stable, bound, we can be more. To become greater, we need guidance. A human is the only one with the ability to provide that guidance, with their gifts for creation and destruction in equal measure."

Devereux shrugged, looking apologetic. "Do you deny that this is a better place for me than Altier? You know how I was languishing there, given power in name and denied it in truth. I tried to help, tried to make things better so many times, only to have my efforts undercut by my mother, by my sister, by the Council of Nobles. My whole life, I—"

"I know all that!" I snapped. I clenched my fists at my side, the gems of my dress cold against my arms. "Do you think I'm *blind*? I saw the way you were there. I know that you weren't suited for that life. I don't *care* that you are here, leading the void or the veil or whatever into its new incarnation. You and all your fay creatures may do what you like."

Devereux took a step back, uncertainty flickering in his gaze. I lifted my chin, letting my anger simmer to the surface. Then, Devereux trembled.

"What I want to know," I seethed, "is why you *lied* to me."

"It wasn't all a lie. Our friendship wasn't a lie."

"From the moment I awoke, no memories to my name, you lied to me. You deliberately misled me into thinking that I..." My throat caught and I swallowed. To my utter shame, tears filled my eyes. "That I was *capable* of doing this."

Devereux shook his head. "No! No. Even if you are not the Chosen One, I knew that you could push back the void. And you have done so much more than that, more than anyone could have ever imagined."

Because I was touched by the gods, I wanted to say, but couldn't.

"Why did you say I was the Chosen One, if you knew I wasn't?" My voice was small. The lights of this realm seemed to dim slightly with my despair. The malgrwm flared its wings, but I wasn't afraid of it any longer. "What *happened* at Starfall Meadow?"

Devereux shook his head. "I don't know. I only know that the Chosen One I knew left with seven Void Runners, to test herself against the void pool. Only you were found in the wreckage, a circle of scorched earth around you, flowers growing over your fingers. I knew that you were powerful, though I didn't know how powerful. I knew that we needed a

Chosen One, in name if nothing else. I knew that the world would despair if the Chosen One were dead. So—"

"So you lied to me and to everyone. Who else knew?" Had Casimir known? My ears rang at the thought, and the ground seemed to sway beneath me.

"Just me. And Eugenie, the healer. The Runners you—she—had trained with were dead. Casimir was just returning from an extended trip across the void into the neighbouring countries. No one else at the palace had seen you—her. We wanted to keep her secret until she could make a grand entrance. Word had spread that the Chosen One was there, yes, but no one knew her."

Devereux stepped forwards again, his arms slightly raised as if he expected me to collapse into them. And where I might have done before, when he was my friend and I his, when he was a safe space in the midst of a world that was weighed upon my shoulders, now I did not move. Now, I held my ground. After a moment, Devereux lowered his arms.

"We needed to keep people from panicking," he murmured. "It wasn't meant to go this far. It wasn't meant to last beyond the parading about the palace and Altier."

"And when the void spread?" My voice was caustic. "When the voidlings attacked and when there was nothing anyone could do but your precious Chosen One? When people realised I was a fraud, what then?"

A shrug, casual, sharp. "We would have sent you off to the void and grieved when you did not return."

I hissed through my teeth. I wanted to pace, to rage, to pull the ground up over my head and burrow into it until the urge to scream myself silent passed. Instead, I laughed, a cruel, broken sound. "I apologise for not fitting into your plans."

"See, that's the thing, Astraea, you did so much more than we could ever have imagined! You *stabilised* the realms!"

"My name is *not* Astraea!" Now I was screaming, the ground beneath my feet quaking. The malgrwm let out a terrible screech, and the unicorn pawed at the ground. I pointed at it, baring my teeth. "You! You knew that I wasn't the Chosen One. That I wasn't your precious star."

The voidling snorted and retreated. "I knew. That and more."

Devereux winced. "I wanted to tell you so many times. You became my friend, in a way I never could have imagined. You were the only person there who *saw* me, even when we weren't to be engaged, I cared about you."

"Then you walked away." My temper vanished,

smoke rising into the air where fire had once been. Suddenly, I was so tired, a bone deep exhaustion that had me sagging under the weight of the world. Everything I thought I knew about myself was wrong. I wasn't the Chosen One, I wasn't the star, I wasn't anyone but a vessel without memories.

Even if what I suspected was true, even if what the one vision I had proved to be reality, then it changed nothing. I had no past, no defining traits, I was a being newly crafted and used for everyone else's gain except my own.

"The void needed me. Needs me."

"I know," I sighed.

In the back of my mind, I could feel a prickling, a call of sorts that was telling me that this time I had salvaged, this space between realms, was running short. My magic was emptying, and I needed to do what had to be done. I was the only one who could. I raised a hand and called the void to me, pulling it from every corner of the world to this doorway between places.

"A warning, young one," the malgrwm said, even as the edges of this starlit place started to fade. "The gods and their children have been bound to the Beyond for many centuries. Now that there exists a door, do not expect them to be easily contained. They have long missed the devotion of lesser beings.

This veil, this *fay* threshold between the human lands and the lands of the gods, as you put it, will not keep them at bay for long."

I nodded and said nothing, not because I could deny the words and the warning, but because I feared he was right. Many things had changed since the gods wandered freely, and I was opening a door for them. No matter how good a lock, it would be opened again, and soon.

The light of the void faded almost entirely, only the three figures still retaining a sense of solidity. The unicorn and malgrwm turned and vanished, leaving Devereux standing there, watching me. "We'll see each other again," he said.

"I know." Maybe then I would have forgiven him.

"Fare well, Ast—" His expression softened. "Fare well, whoever you are. Whoever you choose to be."

I closed my eyes, swallowing back a lump in my throat. "You, too, Devereux."

Then he, too, disappeared.

The void that existed in the realms of humans started rushing faster, gathering momentum as it answered my summons. My own magic was holding the door open, earth and fire and shadow and light keeping that rift in the world from closing, but it was fading. The void moved faster still, and all at once, it slammed into me.

Crying out, I fell to my knees. Shadows tinged

with starlight flooded through me, filling my body until it was bursting. Just as swiftly, I was emptied, the pull on the void so strong that it filled the veil, the threshold between realms, in a matter of heartbeats. Heartbeats where I could not move, could not breathe, could do nothing more than grit my teeth and hold in a scream as I was torn to pieces and put together again and again and again.

The light and shadow that had been stolen and placed in me guttered, then vanished, fleeing along with the last of the void. My fire magic faded next, a single spark filling my vision as it gave out, blinding me to the shift in the world. The earth beneath me trembled and crumbled, and suddenly, I was falling.

There was no air, no light, nothing. Just a seam in the world, pressing against my senses, reaching through three realms and touching each one. Then, when the formation of the doorway was complete, and every last drop of magic I possessed was wrung from me, I slipped into a dreamless sleep. One from which I did not expect to wake.

A twinge of sadness shuddered through me; I did not want to die.

I became aware of sensation, sharp and rigid. The edge of a rock pressing into my face. There was grit in my hands and my knees stung. My whole body ached, muscles stiff and joints weak. My mouth was dry, and I was cold. Carefully, I opened my eyes.

I was laying prone in the bottom of the crater where once a thousand fires had burned. Now, there was nothing but obsidian rock, shining like glass. The sky was startlingly blue, a single wisp of cloud floating across it.

I wasn't dead.

Groaning, I managed to leverage myself into sitting upright. I realised a moment later that I was wearing that gown of jewels, shimmering like fire. It did nothing to protect me against the bite of the wind that cut across the bottom of the crater. I managed to stand, barely, and took a few wobbling steps forward, trying to regain my balance.

My body felt as it had when I first woke: unfamiliar, strange, and aching, as if it were new. Thankfully, there was no pain from burns this time. I was also grateful that I retained my memories. I knew who I was, even if I was not Astraea. Not who I thought I'd been.

Did I even have a name?

I stumbled forwards and nearly fell, catching myself on a larger rock that jutted from the ground. A tingle of magic—raw, powerful magic—jolted through my arm. I recoiled and staggered backwards. There wasn't just one rock spire emerging from the ground, there were nine. All arranged in a circle, evenly spaced, about waist height and crackling with power.

The doorway I'd created.

I ran as quickly as I could, wanting to be as far from that place as possible. I did not want to be present when something came through. There was no if, despite the fact that I knew instinctively the doorway was not active at the moment. There would only be when, and whatever came through would likely be dangerous beyond knowing. Beyond memory.

Tali! I wondered where the poet had escaped to, if she was safe. She would be the only one with answers as to what might face us when the doorway opened. Mostly, though, I wanted to know if she was alright, if she had survived. If she had seen what happened. If she and Dancer and Whisper were together, were still whole.

The ridges and rocks I had climbed over seemed barren, even the few lichens and wildflowers that managed to eke out an existence here gone. The whole island felt dead, no living thing but the rocks beneath my feet.

I started and stumbled again as I realised that I still had my earth magic. Closing my eyes, I reached deep into my mind and found the steady thrum of the earth beneath my feet. Then, a spark in the darkness. My fire. But no matter how I sought for the light of the star, and the shadows that followed along, they were gone.

I could not even feel my connection to Dancer, that thread in my side cut.

My eyes welled with tears. I told myself I was being silly, that everything was fine, that I had *survived* what should not have been, yet I still felt an ache there. The magic was only part of it, a piece of myself that I had lost.

Though, it wasn't really mine to begin with, was it?

I climbed from the crater, grabbing onto pieces of rock that cut into my hands and feet, tearing into the dress between the myriad of gems. When I reached the top, I paused.

I could not see the whole ocean from where I was, given the depression in the ground and the hill that led to the beach, but I could see the horizon. It was not shrouded in black any longer. No, where there had once been a wall of darkness, now there was open sky, birds wheeling through the air as if they had been there all along, instead of fled and afraid.

The void was truly gone from this realm, locked behind the door that I had made.

I had done it.

My destiny. No. I shook my head. Not *my* destiny. The star's. And even then, it wasn't destiny to battle the void, but a game to win the affection of the people.

Victory tasted like ash in my mouth.

Still bleeding, I dragged my ragged feet over the ground. It did not smooth my way, did not move when I asked, only remained as solid as ever. My magic was still there, yes, but it was depleted. I was, for the moment, ordinary. No magic, no destiny, nothing marking me as special.

My fingers traced the lines of the burns on my cheek. A mark, perhaps.

The walk to the ruined temple was faster than I thought, its rubble looking more sad than ominous now. I was about to pass it by and head to the beach, where Tali surely waited, when I saw a figure moving inside.

Casimir.

I still loved him. For all that he had done, I wept. Yet I loved him. But when he knew the truth, would he still love me?

I walked in a blur, not quite sure how I managed to come to stand in the temple, smearing blood over the faces of the gods etched into the floor. Casimir had his back to me, looking out over the ruined crater. He rested his hands on the remains of a wall, and I knew he had seen me climb out, knew he had seen me move towards the temple. He knew I lived, yet he did not turn to look at me.

He slammed his fist onto the stone wall. A tiny chip of marble cracked from the edge and clattered to the floor. Almost without thinking, I moved to pick it up, the rough edge sharp on my skin.

"I am so tired of playing this game," he said. I expected anger and fury in his tone, given his fist and the set of his shoulders. Instead, he sounded merely sad. "Over and over, around and around. The star, fallen from the sky, meant to save these poor souls from themselves. Never telling me the truth, never letting me see your plans. Never letting me know whether I'm playing the hero or the villain in her story. Which am I this time?"

His words felt like more than metaphor, and I thought that just maybe I was beginning to understand. Casimir loved Astraea, desperately. Enough to follow her into exile when she broke the world. Enough to do her bidding, play his part in this charade of destiny and adulation. Did Astraea love him, or had it all been—as Casimir said—a game? Did it truly matter, when I held the truth in my hands?

I set the marble chip on the wall with a gentle click. He took it in his fingers. They were still dark, ink-stained, yet I could see now that the shadows made up a pattern so intricate and beautiful that it could hold a thousand stories in its twists and turns and dancing lines. All that humanity had been stripped away, and what was left was beautiful. Sad. Broken.

"What," Casimir sneered, the hurt apparent, "nothing to say?"

He did not look at me.

"I do not think..." I took a breath. It suddenly seemed impossible to get the words out. He finally turned and looked at me out of the corner of his eye, mouth twisted. Expecting disappointment. I licked my lips and tried again. "I do not think I am Astraea. I am someone else."

Silence. Shock, plain on his features. Casimir reached out a shadowed hand, skin soft and warm against my face. "Who?" he choked out.

I closed my eyes. "I wish I knew."

But I did. I had a hint, an idea. That I wasn't a star, but a goddess, made by the one who had appeared to me in the crater. That I had been made from the earth and the fires deep beneath the surface. That I had been made at the cost of Astraea's life, given her light and shadows, and set into the world to fix her mistakes.

I did not tell this to Casimir, though. Not now. No, instead I wrapped up this knowledge in stone and buried it deep inside, right beside the knowledge that the world I had fought to save was in fact not saved at all.

That I had made it possible for something far worse than the void to be released.

I kept silent, and instead smiled softly as Casimir's hand fell from my face and slipped into my hand.

"We will find out," he said.

"Yes," I breathed. "We will."

AUTHOR'S NOTE

Thank you for reading *Remembrance*! I hope you enjoyed the start of Astraea's story, which will continue in book two, *Resurgence*. Book two will be released in the autumn of 2023, but in the mean time, if you would like more updates, feel free to sign up for my newsletter here. You will get access to my free newsletter books, as well as cover reveals, book news, and pictures of my animals (the latter mostly because I can't stop myself from taking their pictures; they're just so cute).

Until next time, look to the stars!

ACKNOWLEDGMENTS

Thank you to all of those who helped to make this book a reality. A special thanks to my beta readers, Faith and J.R., who took a chance on this book and gave excellent feedback. Thank you also to Allegra Pescatore, who designed the original image for the case laminate copy of this book. Thanks to Krafigs Design who handled the redesign of the original cover. Thank you to all of the friends who helped critique the cover design for this book and made it what it is.

Thank you also to my family, who as always, seem to accept that I'm just going to be a weird writer lady for the rest of my life, and are somehow perfectly alright with that.

And, of course, a huge thank you to you lovely readers. You who wait patiently for my next books and always seem excited when I finally (*finally*) get around to releasing them. Who are eager to devour more. Who review, who send me messages, who are just amazing. I could not do this without you.

Evelyn Grimald "E.G." Stone is an independent author, editor, and linguist who has been writing, creating and causing vast amounts of trouble since a young age. When not writing, she is off musing about the workings of languages - both real and created - or drawing and sewing. E.G. reads voraciously, perhaps to the point of slight-insanity. Weird, nerdy, perhaps a little crazy, she is having a grand old time writing, reading, editing, musing on language, and, naturally, continuing her endeavours in causing trouble.

ALSO BY
EVELYN GRIMALD STONE

<u>The Wing Cycle:</u>

The One Who Could Not Fly

To Never Hear the Song

The Forsaking of the Blind

<u>On Behalf of Death:</u>

The Innocence of Death

Knowledge Aforethought

A Party of Certainties

When Death's Away

Mischief, Mayhem, and Shakespeare

The Long Way Home

Miss You When You're Gone

Me, Myself, and I

The Order of the Owl

The Crow and the King

Speaker of Words